A

VIOLET

SEASON

a novel

"In this stunning debut, Kathy Leonard Czepiel illuminates the sometimes heartbreaking choices women can face as they struggle to preserve their families, their marriages, their very sense of self."

—LAUREN BELFER, bestselling author of
City of Light and *A Fierce Radiance*

༄♣༄

"[*A Violet Season*] is a wonderful and well-earned debut for a brand-new writer, and I so look forward to her next book."

—ROBERT OLMSTEAD, author of *The Coldest Night*

༄♣༄

"The best historical fiction doesn't bring the past to the reader but carries the reader into the past, to see it, touch it, smell it, live it. In *A Violet Season* Kathy Leonard Czepiel transplants her readers among the blooms at a turn-of-the-century violet farm in New York State, a captivatingly unique time and place, and teaches them how hardy a plant—and a woman—can be. Smell the violets with Joe Jacobs, and with Joe you will 'hardly imagine anything wrong with the world.' See Ida Fletcher's pain—'a great room with a cold floor and a light so bright it hurt to look,' and you won't be able to leave Ida's side, through mistakes and accomplishments large and small."

—SALLY GUNNING, author of *The Rebellion of Jane Clarke*

༄♣༄

"*A Violet Season* by Kathy Leonard Czepiel is a moving and detailed look at the hopes and hardships women faced at the turn of the last century . . . fascinating . . . rich in historical detail."

—TAYLOR POLITES, author of *The Rebel Wife*

A

VIOLET SEASON

KATHY LEONARD CZEPIEL

Simon & Schuster Paperbacks
New York   London   Toronto   Sydney   New Delhi

Simon & Schuster Paperbacks
1230 Avenue of the Americas
New York, NY 10020

First Simon & Schuster trade paperback edition July 2012

SIMON & SCHUSTER PAPERBACKS and colophon are registered trademarks of Simon & Schuster, Inc.

For information about special discounts for bulk purchases, please contact Simon & Schuster Special Sales at 1-866-506-1949 or business@simonandschuster.com.

The Simon & Schuster Speakers Bureau can bring authors to your live event. For more information or to book an event contact the Simon & Schuster Speakers Bureau at 1-866-248-3049 or visit our website at www.simonspeakers.com.

Designed by Jill Putorti

Manufactured in the United States of America

10   9   8   7   6   5   4   3   2   1

Library of Congress Cataloging-in-Publication Data
Czepiel, Kathy Leonard.
    A violet season / Kathy Leonard Czepiel.—1st Simon & Schuster trade paperback ed.
        p.   cm.
    1. Wet nurses—Fiction. 2. Farmers—Fiction. 3. Married people—Fiction. 4. Hudson River Valley (N.Y. and N.J.)—History—19th century—Fiction. I. Title.
PS3603.Z825V56 2012
813'.6—dc22

                                                                    2011031733

ISBN 978-1-4516-5506-3
ISBN 978-1-4516-5508-7 (ebook)

For my parents,
who told me I could write

My mother? Oh, dear. What do you want to know about my mother?

We're interested in what life was like for women in Albany County dating as far back as memory takes us. You don't mind if I tape this, do you?

No, that would be fine.

So, tell me a little bit about your mother.

I'm an old woman, and I still don't know what to think of my mother.

—excerpt from an interview with Mrs. Alice Vreeland for
The Women of Albany County, July 6, 1972

WHITEWASH

THE POUGHKEEPSIE DAILY EAGLE NEWS

April 22, 1898

WET NURSE—By a respectable woman with plenty of nourishment; a healthy baby to nurse at her own home. Mrs. Fletcher. Violet Ridge, Underwood, New York.

1

The *Mary Powell* was due to leave Rondout Creek at half past five. From the barnyard, Ida watched the wagon carrying Alice and her cousins as it wobbled down the rain-rutted driveway on its way to the dock. Of the four girls, Alice was the tallest, but she wasn't looking up like the others, who were straining to hear their aunt calling to them from the big porch. Instead, she slouched, her eyes on the wagon floor.

Ida raised her hand to wave, and milk pulsed into her corset pads. Grief lapped again at her feet.

Clinging heavily to her skirt, Jasper asked, "Susie?"

Ida set down her empty laundry basket and lifted him to her hip, though her breasts were firm and soaking, and she didn't wish to hold him close. "Our Susie has gone home," she told him, still watching as the team pulled the wagon left onto Dutch Lane, then tilted over the ridge toward the river.

"Susie," Jasper said, gripping Ida's shoulder, then squirming to get away. She set his feet on the ground.

"We're going for a ride on a steamship!" she told him as he toddled away in search of the baby.

Susie was home with her own mother now, as Ida had always hoped she would be. Yet it was terrible to think they would never see her again—never see her wispy hair grow into thick curls, nor hear her babbling turn into language, nor discover what kind of a girl she would become. She had been Ida's first nursling, a boarder of sorts. But Ida had surprised herself by falling in love with this one as hard as with her own babies. It was impossible, she knew now, to be responsible for the life of a child—for whether it might thrive or perish—and not to love it. Impossible for her, at least.

Frank would rail at her for this softness if she showed it. Wet nursing was a business, a way for her to help him keep up. Always, always, he was struggling to keep up, and she must do her part. Today that meant finishing the chores in time for his nephew Norris's twenty-first birthday party and behaving at that party as if nothing were wrong, as if she were as confident of her position on this farm as her sisters-in-law. As if she, like Alice, weren't always tense with watching and waiting.

Ida carried her basket to the line where Susie's sheets and Jasper's bibs and her own cotton nursing pads had dried in the sun. As she pulled the wooden pins from the stiff laundry, she could see her sister-in-law Frances up on her porch in a feathered hat, directing the loading of another wagon with crates of party supplies: satin streamers and paper lanterns and floral centerpieces made from Frances's cutting garden, for the violets were out of season. From down here, only the staccato delivery of her words could be heard, but Ida knew just how she was speaking to the poor driver, just as she herself would be spoken to later, no doubt.

Within the hour, Ida was dressed in her striped shirtwaist and Sunday skirt, with clean padding in her corset, and Jasper on her lap in his coverall suit. The older children had all gone ahead, and now the women followed: Ida with her other sister-in-law, Harriet, in the back of the phaeton, and Frances in front with the driver, fussing with her gloves. In the small pasture, the milk cow and her pregnant daughter stood with their haunches to them, heads in the dewy grass.

"The steamship should be *lovely*," Harriet said.

"Yes, indeed," Ida said, and was surprised to feel a rush of anticipation, for unlike Frances and Harriet, who frequently took a steamer down the Hudson River to the city, she had not ridden a steamship since her girlhood up in Albany.

In fact, all of Ida's recriminations were forgotten, at least momentarily, when the cross-river ferry landed at Rondout and she saw the steamship up close. It was massive; she reckoned the upper deck alone covered the area of two greenhouses, maybe more, and the paddlewheels were taller than her house. She was received on the main deck by the captain himself, who took her hand and bowed his head to her just as he did to Frances and Harriet. Jasper broke free and ran to the rail, shouting, "Mama! Water!"

They were indeed on the water. It was nothing like being on the train; with no track to restrict the boat's movement, Ida imagined it could take her anywhere. It was different even from the ferry, which had a prescribed back-and-forth route, never out of sight of the Underwood shore. On this ship, everything felt possible. Ida turned her back to the breeze and gazed up the river, to where its broad shoulders bowed slightly east. That way was home. Funny she would think of Albany as home after nearly twenty-three years away. No one was left there to receive her. But just imagining that this boat could turn north as easily as south at the breakwater made Ida feel light. She closed her eyes and breathed in the weedy green smell of the creek before a whiff of smoke from the coal-fired engine broke her reverie.

Jasper lifted his arms, and she picked him up for a view over the railing. The whistle shrieked, and the passengers covered their ears, all but Frances, who raised her shoulders and half closed her eyes, as if the steamer's whistle were a personal affront. From the promenade deck, Norris let out a shriek nearly as high as the whistle and attempted to celebrate the start of his party by climbing on the railing, though one of the crew pulled him back by the scruff of his jacket before he could stand.

The whistle blew again, and the boat drifted from the dock and pushed into forward motion. The wheels were concealed in brightly colored paddle boxes, painted red and gold like the canopy on a carousel, but despite that protection, spray from the great wheels clung in droplets to the wisps of hair at Ida's forehead. Jasper pressed his face into her shoulder and rubbed it on her sleeve, and she laughed. "It's only water, my boy."

Ida turned to see Frank leaning against the wall of the stairwell, arms crossed, slouch hat low on his forehead, responding when necessary to passersby with a smile that more resembled a grimace. He and the boys, Reuben and Oliver, had been whitewashing the empty greenhouse beds all day in preparation for a new load of soil and the next crop of violets. A streak of whitewash remained under his jaw. He was clearly unimpressed by the party, and for a moment she slipped there with him, feeling its ugly underside, the showy excess meant to put the rest of them in their place. Then, determining not to let him ruin her evening, she pointed Jasper to the bow, where Alice stood with her girlfriend Claudie. "Let's go," she said, and they hurried to watch the boat's entry into the Hudson, past the Rondout Light.

There was the ferry, already moored at Coburg Landing. There was Halfway Hill, its lone old oak tree standing like a rooftop chimney. There were so many more trees from this vantage point than Ida had imagined, all of them yellow-green with the quickening of spring. The steamship shared the river with a few smaller craft, but mostly it had the run of the water, flags snapping, smokestacks chuffing, spray suspended in its wake as it raced the receding tide.

"It's splendid," Claudie called out to Alice, lifting her chin to the sky, and Alice reached over the rail as if to catch the droplets of river mist in her hands.

Reuben and two of his friends raced up the stairs to the hurricane deck, and Frank followed them. When the girls decided they, too, needed to explore, Ida and Jasper trailed them to the uppermost deck, where a dozen guests were gathered around the pilothouse. Captain Anderson's bull terrier stood on a deck chair, paws on the backrest, head bowed like a serious old monk. "Amen," the captain said, and the dog jumped down to laughter and applause, wagging his tail and trotting from one child to another in search of their approval. Jasper held out his hand, and the dog ran to him with his owner not far behind.

"Good evening, little one," Captain Anderson said to Jasper. "This is my friend Buster."

"Dog!" Jasper announced with delight.

"Can you tell him to sit?"

"Dog!" Jasper repeated, stomping his feet in excitement, and the partygoers, their attention now on him, laughed again. The only other dog Jasper knew was the hound that lived on the Mortons' farm next door. It impressed Ida that he recognized this stubby pup as a dog just like the wiry, floppy-eared kind.

Ida bent low to Jasper's ear and directed, "Tell him to sit. 'Sit.'"

Jasper lifted his face to her, his eyes glistening. "Dog, Mama!"

Alice looked at Buster and said firmly, "Sit," and the dog dropped his hind end to the deck.

"There you go." Captain Anderson laughed, touching the brim of his hat as he winked at Alice, and then said, clapping his hands, "Come, Buster." The dog scurried to his side and followed his master into the pilothouse.

Behind them, Reuben and his friends were more enthralled with the machinery set high in the center of the deck. They stood much too close for Ida's liking to the massive up-and-down motion of the towering pistons pumping on their A-shaped frame. But Alice and Claudie barely noticed the engine. "Where is the ladies' saloon?" Claudie wanted to know.

"When you're a lady, they'll show you," Ida answered.

"Just joking, Mrs. Fletcher," Claudie said, but Ida caught the glance that passed between the girls as they headed down the stairs to the promenade deck.

There was plenty of room to stroll the decks as the *Mary Powell* pushed south toward the Highlands. William and Frances had invited the families of all of Norris's classmates, a good part of their church, and a number of prominent businessmen and their families from the valley. The guest list totaled well over a hundred, but by the size of her, it appeared the *Mary Powell* could carry ten times that number. Ida allowed Jasper to roam among the guests, following him closely to prevent him from wandering too close to the edge. When he tired, she pulled up a wooden deck chair and sat with him on her lap, watching the backlit curves of the west bank unfurl.

She felt heavy with milk again. The new baby was coming on Sunday, two weeks old with a mother whose milk had never come in. Surely Ida had plenty this evening, but her body would be quick to recognize that Susie was gone and taper her supply if she didn't take care. She had ordered an English breast pump from Sears, Roebuck several weeks ago, but it hadn't worked as well as she'd hoped, and it wasn't practical to carry out of the house. She needed Jasper to nurse again, if he would.

She had noticed one woman among the Negro stewards on the boat, so she went in search of her, hoping for a small, enclosed space in which to sit for twenty minutes. She found the woman leaving the empty dining room with a stack of table linens in her arms. She led Ida to a private parlor with a solid door against which she could position a chair so no one would enter and interrupt.

Ida let her boy wander the room while she untucked her shirtwaist from her skirt and unfastened the lowest few buttons. She had given up dresses, for the most part, finding the shirtwaist more convenient for nursing; it was easier to be discreet. From the top, she unbuttoned her corset cover and unfastened the left flap of her nursing corset. She called to Jasper, and he toddled obediently to her. With her feet raised on an ottoman, her lap was deep and snug, and she didn't have to hold him tightly to keep him in place. He tucked one tiny arm under hers at her waist. The other hung limp at his side as he matched his mouth to her breast and closed his eyes and drank himself to sleep.

It was simple now, no effort at all to nurse an infant or her little boy, except for the monumental amount of time it required from her already busy day. But without a mother or a sister to show her what to do, Ida had struggled to learn how to nurse her first baby, fussy Oliver. She had never watched a woman nurse up close, and though Frances had already had Norris, she wasn't the type to nurse in front of other women or help Ida on her way. So Ida had been left to figure out how to hold the baby properly to prevent the agonizing pull of sore nipples, and whether to keep him on one breast or to switch, and how often to nurse him. She had learned by trial and error how best to bring up the air when he was finished and later found this was different with every baby. Those first several months of weighing Oliver on the grain scale and fretting about whether he was getting enough nourishment had left Ida exhausted and fragile. Finally she had confessed her fears to the one woman she felt she could approach, a woman from church named Mrs. Schreiber, who had seven grown children and never seemed surprised by anything.

Mrs. Schreiber had come to call and shown Ida how to hold the baby's head in the cup of her hand so she could guide it securely to the opposite breast, and how to break the baby's suction with her fingertip rather than pulling him off. She had placed a footstool under Ida's feet to raise her lap and plumped a pillow there to support the baby until he grew bigger, so Ida's arm wouldn't tire from holding him. She had shown Ida how the muscles of his tongue moved under his chin and the way his throat shifted under his creamy skin as he swallowed. Of course he was getting milk—look at him drinking! And she could see, couldn't she, the rolls of milky fat on those chubby arms and legs? Her baby was going to be just fine, and so was she. That one visit had done more good than all the visits of the village doctor, and it had set Ida on her way to such confidence that it was hard to remember now, twenty years later, being that woman who had cried at the sight of her hungry baby.

Jasper slept heavily on Ida's shoulder even as dinner was called and they were all escorted to the dining room on the main deck aft. Ida transferred him carefully to Alice, who took him out to the deck so Ida could eat with Frank and another couple. In the beautifully appointed dining room, tables of four were covered with white linen tablecloths and set with heavy flatware and sharply folded napkins. The room was trimmed in mahogany complemented by two lighter woods, and the entire space was flooded with orange sunlight from the deep plate-glass windows, which offered a spectacular view of the river on both sides. Between the windows, patterned sheets of hammered brass and silver reflected the light, as did large mirrors on either side of the wide main doorway. The room was radiant.

There were two seatings for dinner, followed by the music of a Hyde Park string quartet on the promenade deck. At Cornwall the *Mary Powell* turned and pushed back up the river, and a two-tiered cake with white frosting and sparklers was rolled out. As Norris stood with his parents in the center of the crowd, singing "For He's a Jolly Good Fellow" to him, he seemed to lose his cockiness. William, looking polished in the new Prince Albert suit and silk scarf Frances had purchased for the occasion, made a brief, heartfelt speech in Norris's honor that charmed his guests. At one point he alluded to the four babies he and Frances had lost, and Ida, who had suffered such a loss herself, felt the tender press of that pain as she watched her sister-in-law turn her face away. Then William announced the news that Ida and Frank had feared.

"Now that this young man," he said, shaking Norris's shoulder, "has reached a certain age, it is time for him to take on more responsibility. Tonight we celebrate the entry of Mr. Norris Fletcher into the family business as a junior partner."

Norris's eyes widened as his father hugged him quickly with a slap on the back. Frances stepped up to kiss his cheek. Around them, William's friends cheered, and someone handed both Norris and William cigars. Beside Ida, Frank stood so still that she couldn't be sure he was breathing.

The quartet began again with some familiar Brahms and Schubert, but by the time the boat was passing Poughkeepsie's lights on the eastern shore, the mood had loosened, and the ensemble had launched into popular favorites like "After the Ball" and "The Band Played On." The youths and some of the adults sang and danced on the deck beneath the shimmering blue satin streamers and the delicate paper lanterns that hung under the electric lights. Some of the younger boys, Reuben included, stood at the rail shooting imagined Spanish warships in the dark. Jasper, fortified by his nap, bounced and tottered at the edges of the dancing, and Ida let him enjoy being part of the party. She stood in the swinging shadows, holding the portside railing behind her back, wondering at what point Frank would break.

"What did you think of the party?" Ida asked Frank that night when they were safely home. What she really meant was, What will you do next, now that Norris has been pushed ahead of you? But she couldn't be so direct without aggravating him into silence.

Though Jasper had fallen asleep on the rocking ferry, Ida had roused him long enough to nurse again. Her other breast was firm and hard, and she stood in her nightgown before the washbasin to relieve it. Shirtless, with his suspenders hanging over his trousers, Frank stepped behind her and cupped his hand under her breast, ignoring her question. She pushed him away, saying, "It's tender." He stood close behind her instead, his hands on her hips, watching over her shoulder as she held the new breast pump awkwardly against her and squeezed the bulb. She worked it over and over until her hand ached, emptying her breast as best she could and leaving a milky puddle in the basin. Prissy mewed at her feet, and Ida laughed, then set the basin on the floor, tilting it so the cat could put her paws on the edge of the bowl. Prissy sniffed and lapped at the milk, her pink tongue flashing in and out of her mouth.

"At least someone will benefit," Ida teased, waiting for her to drink her fill.

"Cat belongs in the barn," Frank said, as he always did when Ida and Alice indulged her. Ida buttoned her nightgown, then carried Prissy out the back door and dumped the remaining milk at the edge of the garden. Frank was in bed, waiting with his face to the wall. She slipped in behind him, covering herself with the sheet and one wool blanket. Already the nights were warming.

"Are you all right?" she whispered to his back, and he rolled to face her. He slid his hands up under her nightgown and kissed her mouth once, then burrowed his face in the curve between her shoulder and neck, not unlike Jasper when he was tired or frightened. She understood: he was worried, always worried, and he didn't know what he would do.

2

On the farm, Sunday was never a day of rest. Frank and the boys were up early to feed the animals, milk the cow and turn out the horses. Alice fed the chickens and collected the eggs while Ida stoked the range and cooked breakfast. This Sunday morning, as was often the case, Frank had a reason for not going to church; he needed to finish building the new beds in greenhouse 21, and in any case, the first-calf heifer was so close to calving that he didn't want to leave her. The barn was far from the greenhouse where he would be working, and the heifer could calve without him, but Ida let this go. Lately Oliver and Reuben had been managing excuses to miss church, too, and this morning they volunteered to run an errand put off all week, picking up empty boxes left at the train station after the last shipping day. Sometimes Ida protested and won the company of Reuben, at least, but this morning she was satisfied to take only Jasper, who would pay Ida and Alice no mind as they talked.

They set off at the usual pace in the old chaise pulled by Trip, the stronger of their two horses, but as soon as they had rounded the bend, Ida slowed Trip to a walk. "If it weren't for church, your father would have us working round the clock," she said, easing into the seat and stretching her limbs. The new nursling was due in the afternoon, and she was keenly aware of these last hours of relative freedom.

"It's not so bad," Alice said, looking across Mr. Aiken's freshly plowed field to his irrigation pond, where a mallard duck and his mate dipped and paddled in the sun. Mr. Aiken's barn was close to the road, and Alice fanned away the flies and the odor of manure with a postcard she used as a bookmark in her Bible. With every puff of air from the postcard, her wavy bangs lifted from her forehead. She had pulled up her thick hair this morning in an oddly mature topknot, forgoing her usual girlish braid, and Ida saw she was wearing her grandmother's heart-shaped locket, a treasure Ida had given her as a feeble consolation prize when Frank had declared her schooling at an end.

Jasper, sitting between them, reached for the postcard, and Alice gave it to him.

"Your father worries so," Ida continued.

"About what?"

"Money, mostly," Ida said.

"I don't believe I know anyone who doesn't worry about money," Alice said. "It seems no matter how much folks have, they don't feel it's enough. Even Aunt Frances. She always has to have the next new thing."

"That's true," Ida said. "She's never satisfied."

Alice sighed and she, too, leaned back in her seat and hitched her skirts up to catch the breeze. It was the first truly warm day of spring, as if summer were ambling just behind them on the tamped dirt road.

"I could work with the boys again," Alice said. "Papa knows I'm strong enough." In addition to pulling Alice out of school, Frank had told her she was a woman now, and there would be no more boys' work for her, the kind of work she preferred to do. She would do some of the picking and the packing—seasonal women's work—but there would be no more loading the wagon and driving the team to the train at Coburg, no more tagging along to stoke the fires. She was to find consistent work befitting a young woman and contribute to the family's income.

"It's not just Papa," Ida said. "Uncle William and Uncle Harold aren't willing to give you steady paid work."

"Why shouldn't they if I can do my fair share?"

"They should. But they don't always do the right thing."

"That doesn't make sense," Alice said. "What puts them in charge? Papa works harder than both of them, and he knows more about the violets."

"I would have to agree."

"How could they be so unfair?"

This wasn't the direction Ida had hoped their conversation would take. She and Frank had never explained their position to the children. Clearly Alice, at least, had seen for herself the way things were. It was hard not to, when their family lived in the three-room tenant house and William's family fancied themselves one step below the Vanderbilts.

"Papa did something to make them angry a long time ago, and they've never forgotten it."

"What did he do?"

"Oh, Alice." Ida sighed. "Never mind what he did. It was a youthful mistake, but they haven't forgiven him. As a result, they own the farm, and he merely works on it." They were nearing the Four Corners already, and in a quarter of a mile they would enter the village and pass their neighbors walking to church. So Ida told Alice outright: "Your father is going to want you to marry soon."

"Has he said so?"

"No. But I know what he's thinking. He's worried about us all, and when he thinks of you, he's going to think it would be best if he could find another man to take care of you. Do you have your heart set on anyone?"

"Mama, I'm only sixteen!"

"I was sixteen when I met your father," Ida said, and when Alice shook her head, Ida said again, "I know what he's thinking."

Jasper stood to reach for a white moth flying in front of him, and Alice caught him before he toppled off the seat.

"Claudie's brother, maybe," Alice said, sitting back.

"Why Claudie's brother? Because that would make her your sister, or because you actually like him?"

Alice shrugged. "He tried to steal a kiss once."

Ida looked into Alice's brown eyes. "I'm asking what *you* want. Not which boy wants you."

"I would rather work than get married. For now, at least."

"It's hard to find work off the farm right now. You know that." Ida would have liked Alice to become a teacher. She was a good reader and writer, and she was patient and gentle with the younger children. But Frank wouldn't budge on the question of her finishing school in order to teach. Every day she spent at school, as he saw it, was a day of income lost. "I'll do my best to find you something," Ida said. "Let's not be late to church."

They drove into the village past neatly arranged blocks of houses, nearly every one flying an American flag in support of the war against Spain. Mr. and Mrs. Schreiber were closing the front gate of their boardinghouse, and the two women greeted each other. Mrs. Schreiber's climbing rose canes were covered with tight new buds, and her irises, wrapped in their translucent green casings, were about to make a purple show. Mrs. Schreiber wasn't much for the violets, however. As the nation had begun to emerge from its five-year depression, many of their neighbors had noted the fortune of the Fletchers and the other violet growers and had constructed greenhouses in their backyards, sending their small harvests to the city for a reasonable profit. But Mrs. Schreiber, though she was one of the most accomplished gardeners in the town of Underwood, had shown no interest in building a greenhouse. Instead, her backyard was full of herbs, which she reached via narrow mowed paths winding through unmarked beds. On breezy, moist summer days when one walked the village sidewalk, a startling aroma sometimes rose from her lot, and passing her house felt like walking through a fragrant curtain. Ida had seen Mrs. Schreiber's rear garden just once, when Dr. Van de Klerk's prescription of bed rest and a shot of liquor had not eased Frank's back trouble. Mrs. Schreiber's cayenne poultice had mended him well enough to return to work in a week, and with the continued use of her remedy, his back had pained him less since.

Up the street, they passed Dr. Van de Klerk himself. Though he was respected in town—and needed—he was not particularly friendly, and as usual, he was walking with his head bowed. Ida and Alice did not say good morning. As they pulled the chaise up to the horse shed, their neighbor Mr. Morton was helping his young wife, Jennie, several months pregnant, to step from his carriage onto the horse block in front of the church, and the seamstress Anna Brinckerhoff and her lawyer husband wished Alice and Ida a good morning.

The Dutch Reformed Church's dominie, Horace Jacobs, was back from New York City, where he had attended a meeting of missionaries to China. Ida expected he might preach on that this morning. The Scripture—read by his son, Joe, recently returned from seminary at Princeton—was from Matthew's account of the Last Supper. Ida tried to listen, but the passage was too familiar, and her attention wandered to Dominie Jacobs's son himself, whom she hadn't seen in over a year, since he left for his studies in New Jersey. He had grown more poised in that time and now conducted himself with authority in the pulpit. Joe Jacobs had always taken after his mother, thin and energetic; but her features, which Ida had once seen in the boy, were hard to discern in the man with the trim mustache and the reading glasses. Ida thought about the life this young man could expect, following his father's calling as a scholar and a minister. Though it was not a financially promising life, it was secure. No one would let the dominie's family starve, and the profession came with the sort of respect Ida could only dream of for her sons.

Joe Jacobs was followed in the pulpit by his father. As the sermon began, it became clear that Dominie Jacobs would not speak about his recent experience in the city at all. Instead, he gestured to the communion table, where the bread and grape juice, serving for wine in deference to the Temperance Society, lay waiting under a white linen cloth. He read again the words of Jesus as told by Matthew: "O my Father, if this cup may not pass away from me, except I drink it, thy will be done." Then he began his sermon on the war with Spain.

In February, a devastating explosion on the U.S.S. *Maine* in Havana Harbor had created a furor. Many Americans had long felt the Cuban people should be independent, but Spain had refused to let its colony go. Now the big newspapers were insisting the *Maine* had been sunk by Spanish forces, and war had been declared. Women who had lost their fathers and uncles to an earlier war stood by helpless as their sons took up the call: "Remember the *Maine*, to hell with Spain!" Just days ago, Commodore Dewey's forces had sunk Spain's entire squadron in Manila Bay.

This war, Dominie Jacobs told his congregation, was not one the nation had asked for. But it had become unavoidable and therefore must be fought. "Christ sounds no call to arms," he said. "The trumpet of war is not in His hand. But when war comes, Christ sounds the call to the Cross, that the men who must fight, and the women who must weep, may learn from Him to accept their bitter cup because it is inevitable, and to endure their sacrifice because it is for the sake of others."

Ida looked around the church at some of her neighbors—the Pruitts, the Ellerbys, Nora Hoskins, the Harrises, and a few of the Negro families—all of whom had sons the same age as Oliver, boys eager for a chance to fight. The men nodded at Dominie Jacobs's message, or tilted their heads in thoughtful agreement. But old Mrs. Walker stared out an open window with a defiant scowl. Her son—a decorated member of the U.S. Colored Infantry—had been buried in the churchyard thirty-five years ago. She and most of the other women already knew too much about sacrifice.

Unlike his son, whose voice took its calming undertones from Mrs. Jacobs, the dominie spoke with a forceful bass. He was much more imposing in the pulpit—a broad, double-chinned figure in black who lowered his head to regard his congregation over his glasses as if skeptical of their intentions—than he was in person. The few times he had visited their family, Ida recalled being surprised by the tenderness of his private prayers. He had sat at her sickbed when she lost her second baby and placed his large, cool hand over hers, and before he had spoken a word, the resonance of his voice had hummed in his chest, as if he'd been about to sing rather than to pray. Ida had felt some force of life in that visceral sound—something untapped, unspoken, so that the words of his prayer had seemed inadequate afterthoughts to what had been conveyed in that first private moment.

Despite her reservations about the war in Cuba, Ida found herself drawn in the same way to his earnest appeal this morning. Yet she could not abide the thought of her own boy answering the call to war. By the end of the thirty-minute sermon, which lasted far longer than Jasper could sit still, Ida was spent. Communion was served, and at last the congregation rose to sing the closing hymn. It was one of Ida's favorites, "He Leadeth Me, O Blessed Thought," which she remembered her mother playing. On the Sundays of Ida's girlhood, after dinner they had stood around her mother's piano and sung hymns in four parts: her father's wavering voice on bass, her mother on tenor, her sister Grace on soprano because she had trouble carrying the harmony, and Ida on the alto part. She slipped into the alto line now, and Alice glanced at her in irritation, then picked up the soprano more forcefully. Ida's mother's locket gleamed in the hollow of Alice's throat. As they sang in harmony, Ida felt the weight of homesickness for her own parents, long dead. She pressed on, singing the low A's deep in her chest, and as the congregation bowed their heads for the benediction, she wiped her eyes.

On their way out, Ida and Alice greeted the dominie at the door, then wished young Mr. Jacobs good morning.

"Are you home for the summer?" Ida asked him as Alice hurried off in pursuit of Jasper.

"Actually, I'm home for good," he said. "I'll be doing odd jobs here at the church, and I'll be working on your farm."

"My goodness! You're not returning to seminary, then?"

"I'm not," he said. "I had a fine year, but my calling is elsewhere." He must have sensed what she was thinking, for he added, "Folks think my father must be disappointed, but he knows you can't enter the ministry without hearing the call."

"I'm sure your parents will be very proud of you no matter what route you take," Ida said. "Even if it turns out to be farming," she added, and he laughed.

"My mother thinks I need the fresh air," Mr. Jacobs said. "But I'm afraid I wasn't studious enough to have ruined my health in the library."

"Well, they'll do their best to ruin your back up on the farm," Ida said, and though he smiled at her, she heard the unintended bitterness in her voice. Frank's back had been ruined, both literally and figuratively. But her brothers-in-law had a reputation of being generous with their workers and the community. In fact, if anyone were known for being harsh, it was Frank. Ida made an excuse about the laboring cow and said a quick goodbye to avoid further embarrassing herself.

*   *   *

When Ida and Alice arrived home from church, Frank reported that the heifer was restless. But Ida had dinner to cook, and the cow might labor for many hours. They had their Sunday dinner, as usual, at two o'clock—today a loin of pork from the Mortons' farm with last year's potatoes, from which Ida had cut many eyes, and some new asparagus, a sure sign that summer was coming. By three o'clock Ida and Alice were back at work, cleaning the kitchen and collecting the week's dirty clothing to soak in a tub of soapy water in preparation for Monday's laundering. The new nursling arrived at four, as Ida was scrubbing the last soiled trousers for soaking. She had just enough time to dry her hands on her apron, hang it behind the back door, and smooth her hair before greeting her guests.

The nursling's aunt and uncle stood on the stoop with the infant wrapped in a white knitted blanket. He came with a basket containing two sheets and another blanket, some diapers and dresses, a soft little hairbrush with a cherrywood handle, though he hardly had a hair on his head, and four glass feeding bottles with removable nipples made of India rubber. The aunt later took great care to explain how to clean these properly. This laborious process included sterilizing the bottles in the oven for a quarter of an hour and then, once they were filled with cow's milk, steaming them for thirty minutes to kill any germs. Ida couldn't imagine ever using them.

Alice served them a cup of tea and some cake, and they sat at the kitchen table, the baby in the aunt's lap, and talked pleasantly for the better part of an hour. The baby's name was longer than he: George Ashley Higgins King III. The family called him Ashley, a fitting name, for his skin was gray as ash. They spoke of his mother at some length, as if they felt it important for Ida to know he was loved and missed and must be given superior care.

She assured them she would write Mrs. King often regarding his progress. Then the conversation shifted to other topics; they had questions about the farm and Ida's children and Underwood itself, for they had never traveled north of West Point. Finally the baby began to fuss, and after his aunt jostled him on her lap for some time, his wails became more insistent. The aunt looked directly at Ida and said, "May I watch you?"

"Of course," Ida said, standing. "Alice, would you clean up, please? Perhaps Mr. King would like to read the newspaper." Then she ushered the aunt into the rear bedroom.

When they had closed the door behind them, the aunt handed Ida the baby for the first time. He weighed barely more than a bowl of bread dough. Ida tried not to show her surprise. She laid the bundle on the bed and unwrapped the infant from his blanket. Indeed, there was almost nothing to him. Though he was two weeks old, he looked like a newborn, without a pinch of plump on his arms or his legs. He had too much skin, which wrinkled at his forehead in generous folds. Only his mouth seemed big; she could see clear back into his red throat as he screamed.

"Please, you may sit here," Ida said to the aunt, gesturing to the edge of the bed, and the woman sat primly, fingering her skirt as she watched Ida carry the baby to the rocker in the corner.

"There, there, love," Ida said as she loosened her undergarments to release her breasts, already dripping at the sound of the baby's cry. Ida cupped his head in her right hand and, holding his body the length of her right forearm, guided him to her left breast. He choked and fussed and flailed his arms. He sputtered and pulled his face away and wailed some more. Ida dared not look up at the aunt. "There, there," she said, and tried again. Her milk fell in large drops on his cheeks and his bare head, and she slowly rocked and stroked the fragile top of his head with two fingers. He smacked his lips then and rooted about, searching for her nipple. When she guided it again into his mouth, he sucked and gurgled before pulling off and gasping, then sucked again and pulled off again, on and off, choking and wailing until she managed to settle him in for as much as two minutes before he arched his neck again and sneezed. Ida laughed then and looked at the aunt.

"Is he getting anything?" the aunt asked.

"He is, just a bit," Ida said. "Did he take the bottles?"

"Not well," the aunt said in a timid voice. "The doctor recommended them, but he never took to them."

"We'll give him a rest and then try the other side," Ida said. "I think he's going to do fine." And it was true. When she shifted the baby to her other breast, after a fussy moment, he latched on and nursed himself to sleep in a few minutes' time.

"That's more than he's had to eat in all his life," the aunt said with a nervous smile, and Ida, still rocking, gave her a reassuring nod.

The woman and her husband didn't know what to do after that, with the baby full and asleep. It was getting on to suppertime, and though Ida's family had had their large meal, she invited the pair to stay. They asked instead where they could find a hotel. They would stay the night and call again in the morning.

The baby lay beside her that night, and Ida slept lightly, waking often to see that he was breathing. What had seemed a manageable challenge that afternoon haunted her in the night hours, when worries lay their ceiling low over her. He must nurse some more, he must gain weight at once. What if he were to perish in her care? At the slightest whimper, she pulled him close, and he suckled briefly before falling again into his own fitful sleep.

So when the heifer began her frightful lowing—an extended moan, leaping high at the end—Ida was already awake. Frank got up and pulled his overalls over his nightshirt and stepped into his boots without any socks and trudged out to the barn. The baby and Jasper didn't stir, but Ida couldn't bear it, imagining how the poor heifer felt. Finally she, too, put on her wrap and pulled on Oliver's old boots to join Frank in the barn.

This heifer, the daughter of their milk cow, had never calved before, and she was clearly anxious. Whereas she usually greeted Ida with a nuzzle, tonight her eyes bulged fearfully and seemed to see nothing. She had lain on her side, and from time to time she lashed her legs so hard against the stall that Ida thought she would knock it down. But Frank knelt at the young cow's side, his head close to hers, and mumbled nonsense in her ear as he stroked her tawny neck. When he saw Ida in the lantern light, he glanced up but made no move to leave the heifer's side. He simply said in a quiet voice, "You can see the hooves. She's coming along."

Ida peered over the stall's edge, and the astringent smell of amniotic fluid rose up. The heifer strained her neck and lowed again, and Ida could see the two pointy black hooves of the calf poking through the tender, fleshy opening of her birth canal.

"Poor girl," Ida said, coming around to her head again, though she didn't reach in to touch her. Frank continued his stroking and his low murmur, words meant only for the heifer.

"Are you going to help her out?" Ida asked, wondering if he would rope the baby's legs and pull it into the world.

"Give her some time," he said, and ducked his head to the heifer's again.

Much as she felt for the cow and wanted to see her through, Ida knew Frank would call if he needed help. It was more important to stay with the baby. Reluctantly, she left the heifer to her labor. In the house, Ashley was sleeping soundly, a tiny bean of a baby in the middle of a great mattress.

Not long after, as the room lightened before dawn, Ida heard a final squawk from the barn, then quiet. Her heart quickened, waiting for word. Twenty minutes later, Frank returned with the news that a female calf had been born. He sat on the edge of the bed and mussed his short-cropped hair with wet hands; he had already buried the placenta in the woods, to keep predators at bay, and washed at the outside pump. He might have caught a few minutes of sleep before his day began, but as he dropped his hands to the mattress, the baby yapped in disapproval, then latched on to Ida's breast ferociously and suckled for several minutes. Frank stared at Ida and the baby, his face slack with exhaustion. Then he stood and padded barefoot into the kitchen.

Not half an hour later, Ida rose to join him, and by the time Ashley's aunt and uncle came to call, the household was awake and at work. They said they imagined the baby looked a mite better than he had the afternoon before, and though Ida felt considerably worse, she was relieved at the suggestion. After the aunt kissed Ashley a tearful goodbye and they took their leave, Alice watched them depart from the kitchen window.

"What will you do when you get one that won't nurse, Ma?" she asked.

"I hope I never shall," Ida said.

"But what if he hadn't nursed last night?"

"Eventually he would have died," Ida said. "But he's going to be all right now, aren't you?" she cooed to the baby in her arms, knowing that her words were really a prayer.

3

Shortly after Ashley's arrival, Frank brought home a few burlap sacks of new violet cuttings. That evening Ida and Alice got to work, pulling or slicing off all but the top two or three leaves, pinching off early roots, and discarding damaged runners. The work was important, for the cuttings they prepared would grow the next year's violet crop. While the cuttings took root in raised beds outside, the men spent the month of June plowing up new soil and harrowing in manure. The resulting mixture was shoveled into the freshly whitewashed greenhouse beds.

In a few of the greenhouses, the plants had been allowed to set their own runners, but the job of planting eight thousand cuttings in each of the remaining twenty greenhouses was monumental. It called for the help of most members of the family, as well as a good number of hired workers from the village, mostly older children who were out of school and women who would set aside their housework to earn a dollar a day. Even with extra hired hands, planting was a two-week job.

They began the first week with the greenhouses behind Harold's house in the old wheat field. It was an expansive level spot where they had constructed eighteen of their twenty-nine houses in three neat rows running north and south, a lesson they'd learned after building the first three houses east-west on the hillside. These newer houses were pitched sixteen inches higher at the south end to allow the hot water from the stokehouse on the north end to rise and the cool water to flow downhill to the furnace. The heat would keep the cool-weather violets just warm enough to make it through the winter.

This time of year, of course, no heat was needed, and to allow the air to circulate while the workers were planting, several glass roof panels were raised on a pulley system, the ropes tied off on large nails in the adjoining packing house. Each greenhouse had a single aisle down the center with deep beds full of fresh soil, which should be free of harmful nematodes that could stunt the plants. The beds began at thigh height and stretched back to the walls farther than any man's reach; planting the rear half of the beds required the assembly of narrow boards on which the workers would lie in order to access them.

This first morning Harold instructed the boys and the men to climb up on the boards and plant the rear of the beds. The women and the girls would stand in the pathways and plant what they could reach from there, a job that, despite the stooping, was easier on the body and could be interrupted to tend to the children and the meals.

Experienced planters were assigned to help the inexperienced; Ida was paired with Joe Jacobs, the minister's son. He had never been out on the boards, so Ida showed him how to hook his board on the heating pipe that ran along the wall and secure it to the bed frame at the lower end, then inch himself sideways up the slanting plank to the rear of the bed. There, he must balance on elbow and hip and reach down into the bed to set the plants in the fresh soil. He wobbled precariously on his way up the board, and Ida assured him, "It feels impossible at first, but you'll soon feel stable. No one ever falls."

Joe waved his upper arm in the air for balance as he shifted his weight. "Most find it easiest to bend the lower leg—that's right," she said.

"They didn't tell me this would be a circus act," he said.

"It's a business," Ida told him as one of the boys set the first bucket of cuttings at her feet. "We can't waste the space for lots of walkways. Every foot of it needs to be planted."

"Mowing the church grounds is looking pretty good right now," Joe said. "What do I do next?"

The men came along to set the planting grid with a spiked wooden bar that left holes in the soil ten inches apart, ten wide and four deep. Then Ida showed Joe how to set his trowel in each hole and make room for the cuttings. She set to work on her own planting, reaching her arm's length into the beds to the point where Joe's plants would have to meet her own. Next to them, Oliver helped the Hoskins boy through his first day; Joe and Oliver exchanged some talk about the war. Two of Oliver's friends— Claudie's brother Avery and Alan Harris—had already enlisted and were headed to Tampa.

While Ida worked, Jasper amused himself with a pile of dirt and a wooden spoon outside the greenhouse door for a good long time, but by nine-thirty Ashley was beginning to squirm and fuss in his basket. Ida set her work aside and took him to the house for his nursing. While she was gone, Alice took her place at the beds with Joe. Later Ida nursed the baby again while she ate her lunch of bread and cheese and strawberries from her garden; then he slept soundly until two o'clock and amused himself by contemplating the light and shadow above him for a half hour before he began to fuss again.

By midafternoon, Ida could see that Joe's arms were tiring. His sleeves were rolled above the elbow, and under his gritty skin, his tendons rolled and stretched like straining ropes on a pulley. He frequently paused to dangle his arm and then shake it before reaching for the next cutting.

"You're tiring," she said. "It's a long day."

"I never realized how hard you had to work to grow these little flowers," he said. "I don't imagine any boy who gives them to his sweetheart has any idea."

"When you get home tonight, allow yourself a steaming-hot bath," she said. "And rub some liniment on that arm."

"Thank you. I surely will."

"You're a good worker," Ida said, gazing up the row at some of her neighbors, whose pace had slowed considerably since morning. The Hoskins boy had gone home at noon for lunch and hadn't returned.

"I'd be happy for steady work here this season," Joe confided. "The caretaking job at the church isn't much."

A few minutes later, Norris wandered up the aisle to ask Ida how Joe was doing. His shirt was nearly as fresh and ironed as it had been this morning, and his vest was buttoned snugly. Like William, who kept to the books and avoided the workers, Norris had taken on an air of superiority. William, at least, knew the business.

Ida saw Frank enter the greenhouse at the far end, his hat low on his forehead. He had a habit of pulling on the brim when he was angry or frustrated, and she worried over what had happened this time. She prayed he would not walk up their way.

"Mr. Jacobs is doing quite well," Ida told her nephew, playing her subservient role for the sake of keeping the peace. "He's picked up the rhythm. Be sure to have him again."

"The rest of this week and next," Norris said, nodding at Joe, who thanked him.

"Norris!" Frank called out, and taking larger than usual steps, he strode toward them. Frank was almost a head shorter than Norris, and Ida was embarrassed for him, making a show in front of the workers.

"We're missing a dozen buckets. Where've you put them?" Frank demanded. "I've got four workers waiting and no cuttings!"

"Why don't we talk about this outside," Norris said in a voice that mimicked William's. It might have been funny if not for the threat to Frank's livelihood underlying everything Norris said or did.

"Why don't you just get your goddamned job done," Frank said. As he turned away, Norris caught his upper arm. Frank shook him off and drew back as if to throw a punch, and as Norris flinched, Ida blurted, "Frank!" With a swift backswing, Frank pounded his fist on the side of the wooden bed, and Ida felt the vibration in her own hand. Then he yanked his hat low and pushed past Norris.

It had always been like this with William and Harold, though the indignity of taking orders from Norris was worse still. Frank knew the plants better than either of his brothers and certainly more than his nephew. William and Harold were better with the accounts and sales and shipments, but it was Frank who was always the first to catch the start of the rot and eradicate it before it took a whole bed. It was Frank who experimented to find the best mixture of manure and soil, and Frank who regulated the amount of water and sun and shade and the temperature the plants needed. Frank grew a perfect crop nearly every season, and without a beautiful, hardy crop, there would be no accounts to figure, no sales to make, and nothing to ship. But Frank was the youngest brother, the one who could be bullied, the one who owed them and who didn't have to be taken seriously. He seemed to believe that one day he would prove himself to his brothers, but Ida was certain that no matter what he did, he would never be granted their respect.

Ida felt done for the day, but she and Joe, who had lain quietly on the board throughout Frank and Norris's drama, had another bed to plant. Ashley was about to wail. Outside the greenhouse windows, Reuben and Jasper were running back and forth in a game that Jasper found hilarious. He kept toppling over, which appeared to be the part Reuben enjoyed most, but Jasper would be tired soon. When Ida left, Joe would be obliged to finish the front of the bed for her.

"I'm sorry," she said to Joe. "I'll see if I can find Alice to help you finish up. You've been very understanding today."

"It's a pleasure to work with you, Mrs. Fletcher. What say tomorrow you take this job and I take care of the children?" he joked. "My joints sure would thank you."

"Ah, but you'll bicycle home in an hour or so, and I'll be tending the children all evening," Ida said. As if he had been cued, Ashley opened his mouth and let out a full-lunged cry of hunger.

"I see your point," Joe said.

Ida washed her hands at the pump, then sent Alice to finish her job and watch Jasper. Ida carried Ashley up to Frances's veranda. Cook was sitting there peeling a kettle of potatoes. The only live-in help at William and Frances's house, she could always be counted on for a refreshing dose of irreverence.

"She's been out there all day," Cook said, nodding toward Frances, who was wandering her cutting garden in a calico apron and an expensive straw hat, deadheading the spent roses, then stepping back to admire her work. Like Ida, Harriet had been working in the greenhouse all morning. But not Frances.

Ida shifted the weight of Ashley's head up her arm and settled herself deeper into Frances's lawn chair. Despite her annoyance, she was grateful to be sitting in the shade of the arbor, which was covered with grapevines and wisteria. Frances had designed the veranda after the one at her parents' summer home in Newport. The flat stones, which had been pulled from the woods or hauled from the earth when the house's foundation was dug, had been placed by a skilled stonemason from across the river. Their odd facets fit together like the markings on a tortoiseshell. The stone stayed cool until late in the day, when the low sun from the west ducked under the arbor and gave it a warm soaking. Frances had arranged groupings of wicker chairs and tables for garden parties and informal gatherings, and it was here that Cook sat paring and Ida sat nursing.

It wasn't long before Frances noticed Ida's presence. Picking up her basket, she strolled over to the veranda. "He's a hungry one, isn't he," she said, stepping into the shade and removing her apron, which she draped over the back of an empty chair.

"He's doing fine," Ida said. "His mama is quite satisfied."

"Have you heard from her?"

"She answers my letters faithfully. She misses him terribly, but she can't nurse him herself. He'll be staying awhile longer, I reckon."

"How many times have you nursed him today?" Frances asked as she sat down. She took off her hat to fan her face, then replaced it with its long pin. She asked the question casually, but she was unable to mask its real intent. Cook glanced up at Ida, her paring knife never pausing.

Ida took a deep breath to calm the undertow of anger. She mustn't let it pull her in deep with her sister-in-law. Let the men do battle; she would remain civil. "I nursed him at six this morning, at nine-thirty, and at noontime while I ate my lunch, which brings us to this, his fourth nursing," Ida reported. "He'll nurse again before supper and before going to sleep, then again late in the evening. If I'm lucky, he'll wake just once in the night."

"It's been so long since Norris was a baby," Frances said. "I can hardly remember."

"It's a gift that we forget," Ida said. "I sometimes think God makes us forget so we'll go on populating the world."

Frances drew her chin back at this and then looked away. Ashley opened his mouth to yawn, and Ida took the opportunity to switch him to her other breast.

"Each time you nurse him, it takes you how long? Half an hour?" Frances asked.

"Twenty minutes or so," Ida said.

Frances nodded. She was looking down the hill toward Frank and Ida's shabby tenant house, its roof shingles curled up at the edges like a little girl's hair. Beside it, the chicken coop hunched among the wandering hens, pick-picking all day in the grassless yard.

"Discounting your earliest nursing, then, you're taking nearly an hour out of your workday to nurse the baby," Frances said.

"I nursed him over my own lunch break," Ida said. "And generally I would say forty minutes total for the day is the most I've lost. Perhaps you should log my hours like a factory timekeeper."

Frances focused her gaze directly on Ida, though Ida had noticed she was reluctant to do so when the baby was latched on.

"You can't possibly believe I'm not doing my fair share of the work," Ida said, and in the swell of this thought, she added, "when you yourself have been out here fussing in your garden all day."

Later she thought if it hadn't been for this last snap at Frances, she might have escaped with a scathing glare. But as soon as she said it, she knew she had crossed some invisible boundary. There were always boundaries with Frances. Knowing where they were was the trick. In hindsight, Ida speculated that she might have known where this boundary was and crossed it with intent, simply for the satisfaction of holding Frances's hypocrisy up before her. Perhaps if Cook hadn't been there to hear it, that would have made a difference. In any case, the next day at lunch, Frank took Ida aside and told her that William and Harold had decided she would have to make up for her nursing time by working an extra hour after supper each night until the planting was done. That evening Norris knocked on their door before the dishes were washed and said two final beds needed to be finished in greenhouse 7. He looked directly at Ida as he said it, but Frank stepped forward and took his hat from the peg by the door and said, "Oliver and I will be right down." Norris turned to go, and Frank muttered a curse, which Ida couldn't be sure wasn't directed at her.

4

Mostly to keep her mother quiet, Alice had begun stitching some linens that she would bring to her marriage to some unknown man. In the meantime, her mother had said it would be good practice in case she found Alice intermittent work as a seamstress. Ida had already attempted, without success, to find her a position as a clerk in one of the village shops—the cobbler's, the tailor's, the pharmacy, the mercantile—but with the economy creeping along, those jobs were more likely to go to young men or to older women with families to support.

Alice worked slowly, not because sewing was difficult for her; she'd been doing the household mending with her mother since she was seven, and she had already sewn some of her own clothing and some of Jasper's. But she did not want finished linens to suggest to her parents that she was ready to wed. She did not want to draw her father's attention away from the planting and toward her in any way. So to keep herself bent to her needlework, she had chosen an elaborate design for the scalloped edging on a set of pillowcases. The floss for the edging was the color of peaches, and when she was through with that, she would embroider tiny clusters of leaves on every scallop in two different shades of green.

She brought her sewing to Claudie's house one July afternoon, hitching a ride into town with Uncle William, who would pick her up when he'd finished his business. Alice and Claudie sat on the screened porch at the back of the Pruitts' house, half in sun and half in shade. Claudie's mother made them a pitcher of sweet lemonade and brought them two glasses with frosted P's etched on them.

Avery had sent a letter home from Tampa, Claudie said, reporting that he and Alan Harris and hundreds of other young men were waiting to be shipped out to the fighting in Cuba any day. He'd mentioned a huge bottleneck at the docks. "He'll probably run anyway once he hears a gunshot," Claudie said, pulling a sapphire thread as long as her arm through the fabric of her sampler. She couldn't be bothered to rethread her needle too often, preferring to deal with the unruliness of a long strand. "Bet you he'll be home soon without having seen a lick of fighting, and then he'll spend the rest of his life acting like a war hero."

Alice wasn't especially fond of Avery herself. He was boastful and paid no attention to what those around him said and did. Still, she always felt Claudie was too hard on him. She would never speak of Oliver that way.

"My father says it's not the same as the Civil War," Claudie continued. "He really is a hero. You can tell because he hardly talks about it."

"I reckon it's different when the war is fought at home."

"I'll say. Had you even heard of Hawaii or Guam before this?"

"They were on the map at school," Alice said.

"Oh, school," said Claudie. "You're lucky you don't have to go back. It's silly I have to finish when all I'll end up doing the rest of my life is laundry and cooking and mending." She flipped over the muslin to pick at a tangle that had stopped the thread.

"You'll have a more interesting life than that," Alice said.

"Why on earth would I?"

"I just know you will."

"Well, then I'll have to marry a man like Mr. Brinckerhoff who'll let me run my own business and take me on trips to see the world. He's handsome, don't you think?"

"He's old!"

"I think he's handsome, for an old man. Don't you think men get handsomer as they age, as long as they don't get fat?"

"Claudie Pruitt, you're not going to marry an old man!" Alice cried, though she loved Claudie's outrageousness.

"Better than marrying someone like Norris," Claudie said. "No offense to your family, Alice, but he's a pest."

"Why? What's he done now?" Alice asked, her head bowed to her sewing. It was tricky to line up the graduated stitches around the scallops. Each time she paused to react to Claudie, the stitches lost their uniformity. She considered snipping them out and starting over.

"He's asked me twice to the church social this week alone. It was my impression that when a lady says no, that should be the final word on the subject."

"Persistence is flattering, isn't it?" Alice asked.

"Not in this case."

Alice paused to shrug the tension from her shoulders. A breeze rustled the leaves of the poplars in the Pruitts' backyard.

"I'm not getting married until my late twenties," Claudie announced, pulling her blue thread long again. She was making a sampler of a peacock that she had drawn herself with colored pencils on the muslin. It was completely impractical, Alice noted, and completely like Claudie, who could afford to be impractical. Her parents would happily support her for as long as she wished and would help her make the best possible match when the time came. Or even no match at all. Alice pinched her needle and hunched over her work again.

"Who will you marry, then? What kind of a man?" Alice asked.

"Maybe an older man *would* be nice," Claudie said. "Not much

older. But don't you think an older man might be more . . . solici-
tous?" She said this with a flicker in her eyes that suggested she
meant something more, and Alice laughed. Despite the difference
in their fates, Alice loved Claudie. She wished that she could stay
on this porch forever, talking with no care in the world except
keeping her stitches even and close.

"Well, who do *you* like?" Claudie asked.

"No one," said Alice. This wasn't entirely true. She had listened
attentively to Joe Jacobs's voice when he had read the Scripture a
few weeks ago. It was warm and calming, not cold and curt, like
her father's. Since then she had helped Mr. Jacobs at the farm, and
they'd exchanged some friendly words. But it was foolish to even
think of him; he was older and had been to college and would
never consider a farm girl like her.

"Honestly! Who could you possibly think of having come to
call?" Claudie said.

"All the young men think the world revolves around them,"
Alice agreed.

"Because it does!"

"That will never change."

"Mrs. Brinckerhoff thinks it will," Claudie said. "She and Mr.
Brinckerhoff were here to dinner last night. The men didn't leave
the table to have their own private conversation. They stayed
right there, and Mrs. Brinckerhoff joined in, and so did my
mother and I."

"I don't know," Alice said. "Someone has to stay home and run
the household, and you don't imagine men will ever do the laundry!"

"If a woman invents a machine to do it, they might."

"I can't wait for that," Alice said. "My parents are going to
marry me off if I can't get paying work soon." She was surprised to
feel a lump like clay in her throat, and she kept her head bowed to
her work so Claudie couldn't see her face.

Claudie dropped the needlework in her lap and began rocking her chair hard as if to work out a problem. "Maybe the war hero will marry you when he gets home, and then we can be sisters and sit here sewing together all the time."

"Maybe," Alice said, though she felt certain that having all the pretty things in this house and Claudie as a sister, too, would still not be worth marrying Avery or any other headstrong boy.

Ida was in her garden that afternoon when she heard the commotion and ran through the gate with Jasper behind her. William and Alice had just pulled in the driveway behind George Ellerby, on his sandy bay. The young man reined his horse in hard at the barn, shouting for Oliver, but already Ida could see the news was good, not the crisis she had feared.

When Oliver and Norris came out of the barn, they all heard George's shouted news: American forces had captured the hills outside the city of Santiago and destroyed the entire Spanish fleet as it attempted to leave Santiago Bay.

George turned his horse and galloped on to the next destination, leaving Oliver and Norris jumping and whooping in the barnyard. William gave Alice a hand out of the rig, and she scurried to the house to avoid the boys as they ran in circles, shouting and dancing and setting the chickens to frenzied clucking around the hen yard. Oliver banged two sticks overhead as he ran, and Norris seemed to have forgotten that he was a junior partner in the family business and a man of responsibility; he did a ridiculous dance in the bed of the wagon, then leaped in front of Oliver each time he passed, as if initiating a surprise attack. Perhaps if he thought war would be so much fun, he should enlist, Ida thought as she returned to her weeding.

Oliver was still fired up when, after dusk, she asked him to sit at the kitchen table, where she and Alice were sharing the newspaper.

"I can't sit, Ma," he protested. "Lemme go up and see what Norris is doing."

"You sit a minute and listen," Ida said. She slid the newspaper in front of him. "Have you read this yourself?"

Oliver dropped his head back in aggravation, then looked at her. "No, ma'am."

"Then I would like you to read it, just the headline story there, before you go off gallivanting. I don't care for the celebrating when two hundred men have lost their lives."

"That's what soldiers do, Ma! They die in battle."

Ida thought of Avery and Alan and wondered whether they were in danger. Or whether they were alive. "It's not such a glorious thing," she said.

Oliver glanced toward Frank, who was sitting in the rocking chair, but he was at least half asleep and paying no mind to their conversation.

"Ma," Oliver said. "A new century is coming, and the U.S. of A. is going to be the biggest power in it."

"Power," Ida began, intending to protest her son's view of the world. But the word stopped her short.

"The Philippines are going to be our gateway to Asia, and we're going to get Hawaii, too—"

"At least you're learning some geography." Ida leaned across the table and slipped the paper closer to him.

"—and I'm not going to sit around on this old farm growing weeds out my ears!"

At this, Frank gave a heavy grunt. Ida pulled back her ink-stained hands and regarded Oliver, her sweet boy almost grown, and saw that she was in danger of losing him if she didn't take care. "Go see what Norris is doing," she conceded. "But tomorrow I want you to read the newspaper."

Irritated, Alice yanked the paper from him and slid into better light to read it, while Oliver bent to kiss Ida's cheek on his way out.

Later that night, well after midnight, they were awakened by a pounding at their door. Ida stood fearfully in the shadows of the bedroom doorway in her nightgown and shawl, while Alice stood a few steps up from the bottom of the stairs. Frank opened the door to find Mr. Harris holding Norris and Oliver by their lapels, one in each wiry fist. Mr. Harris gave a push, and Oliver stumbled into the kitchen. The cloying smell of whiskey followed him.

"Should've been paying better attention to my barkeep," said Mr. Harris. "My apologies."

Oliver had groped his way into a kitchen chair, and Frank nodded at Mr. Harris. "Said they were celebrating the liberation of Cuba," Mr. Harris continued. "I got a boy sitting down in Tampa waiting to go off and fight. You," he said, staring at Frank, "got a boy looking for any excuse to drink." He waited a heartbeat or two, expecting Frank to say or do something, but Frank stood firm. "I'll take the other one up the hill, then," Mr. Harris said, and because Frank appeared to be about to close the door in his face, Ida called out, "Thank you kindly, Mr. Harris. It won't happen again."

Frank closed the door quietly—too quietly, Ida knew—and then said, "Ida, Alice, go back to bed." They did as they were told, and Ida covered her head with a pillow, attempting to block out the sounds of Frank in the yard, slamming Oliver against the side of the barn. Finally, astonished at the force of Frank's anger and unable to bear the noise any longer, Ida rose and called out from the doorstep to stop, please stop! Oliver had already staggered away from his father, who was kicking the barn door as if it didn't matter what he was fighting. Ida helped her boy into the house and washed the blood from his split lip and tended his back with a hot compress. Frank had whipped him on occasion with a strap, but never had he beaten him like this, like a man.

5

How the world had changed. The year Ida and Frank were married, 1875, there had been no electric lights or telephones. No one had ridden bicycles or taken their own photographs, and riding the train as newlyweds had been an exciting new adventure. President Grant had been nearing the end of his second term, and no one in politics had yet heard of William McKinley. Twenty-three years ago today, Ida and Frank had married in her father's parlor on Dove Street in Albany, with her father, her sister Grace, several neighbors, and a dozen friends from church in attendance. Ida had worn a lavender silk gown of her late mother's, remade for the occasion, and her mother's pearls, both of which she had left behind for Grace, knowing she herself was setting out for a life as a farmer's wife and would have no need of fine things. Though she had been in love with Frank, her wedding day had been among the saddest of her life. She would never forget watching her father and sister and closest friends wave goodbye from the street as she and Frank drove away in his buggy. Her departure had felt like a death. She had seen her father only once more, on a trip he had undertaken to meet the newborn Oliver two and a half years later. Grace had married shortly after Ida and moved to Ohio, and though they corresponded regularly, they had not seen each other again.

Ida and Frank didn't usually celebrate this date, but she always noted its passing. Today she thought she would bake his favorite dessert, blueberry pie. As she worked her hands through the flour and lard, adding cold water a few drops at a time to improve the consistency of the dough, she thought of that first year of marriage. Frank had been entirely devoted to Ida, always pointing out her virtues to others, sometimes to the point of embarrassment, buying her trinkets, delighted and proud to be with her. When she'd suffered an early miscarriage toward the end of their first year, he had nursed her faithfully himself.

He had been Ida's prize—the wanderer hired by her father to build a set of bookshelves who had so charmed Ida and Grace that he'd been invited to meals, then given more and more work in the following weeks. He was quiet, and onto that blank slate Ida and Grace had drawn what they'd imagined—Heathcliff, Rochester, Darcy. They had known a few young men from their neighborhood and from church, but this one was different. He was from somewhere else, he was handsome, he was a mystery. They found themselves competing for him, teasing each other as they lay in bed at night about which of them he would prefer, though not really teasing at all. And he had chosen Ida.

It wasn't until much later that she'd begun to understand the way things would be for them on the farm. Early in their marriage, she'd been oblivious to the negotiations among the men about the conditions under which she and Frank would be allowed to stay. Any rough patches in that first year, she'd chalked up to being a new bride in a new family. She and Frank had been allies with a bright future.

But once Oliver had arrived and her attentions had been diverted, Frank had become sullen with her, even angry at times, not understanding the demands of caring for an infant. It was as if he were competing with the baby, and for the first time she'd seen how childish he could be, always needing to be recognized, always needing to be in charge. The death of their second baby three short days after his birth had set them further apart. Frank had mourned that baby in his way, but he had never let Ida feel that her grief was permitted, not in front of him. She had found that hard to forgive.

After twenty-three years, she knew just how hard the shell of him was and where the tiniest cracks were. No one else, not even the children, had found those cracks. Sometimes they had fallen into one by accident when something they did struck him as funny, and he dropped what he was doing to scoop them up and toss them in the air, his finest display of affection. She had never seen him do this with Jasper. Sometimes it shamed her that Jasper hadn't come as the other children had—a hoped-for child in his own right, or a gift sent by God—but, rather, as a necessity born so she could nurse other women's babies. Still, he had been wanted, unlike some babies, and though Ida wouldn't dare allow the thought to surface for fear he would be taken from her, she loved him best of all, the one person who needed and loved her wholly and unequivocally.

But Frank. This evening, she promised herself, she would work on remembering the things about him that she had loved. They weren't so easy to see anymore. Lately it had been nearly impossible to get even a word out of him, and he'd spent several days in the city over the past few weeks. He said he was visiting the wholesalers, though she wasn't certain he'd been sent by Harold and William. Sometimes she worried he might not come home.

She poured her sweet blueberry filling into the waiting piecrust and rolled out a second plate of dough to cover it, then fluted the edges with her thumbs and pricked holes in the top with the tip of her knife. By the time the others arrived home for supper, the aroma of pie had filled the house. At the table, when Frank asked about it, she took the chance to tease him. "Do you recall what day it is?"

"Monday," he said gruffly.

"It's the anniversary of our wedding. Twenty-three years," Ida said, and Frank nodded. "After dinner, I thought you and I could take a walk." Frank didn't say yes or no, but after the dishes were cleared and the pie was set before him, his face softened, and he caught her arms and kissed her quickly in front of the children. She imagined she felt again that fierce devotion in the firmness of his grip.

"I'll clean up and watch the babies," Alice offered.

Ida changed into Oliver's old boots, and Frank put on his hat, and they set off on an evening walk. "Let's go up Halfway Hill," she suggested.

They climbed the lane toward the Mortons' farm, then continued to the low ridge, pausing to admire the river when it came in view, throwing thousands of sparks of light from its surface. One of the old sloops sailed languidly along the far shore, its sails barely catching a breeze.

A hundred yards over the ridge, the path up Halfway Hill cut off to the left, and they took it with long strides, Ida holding her skirts out of the dust as they pushed their way up the first fifty steep feet. Then they settled into the gentler curve of the path as it wound around the shaded east side of the hill, followed by another steep climb over some natural granite steps. After ten minutes of silent walking, they reached the majestic top of the hill, where a bold farmer had once planted a field of corn that now was a meadow of swishing timothy grass accented by Queen Anne's lace and chicory, buttercups and thistles, and that favorite old oak tree, which Frank said his father's father had remembered climbing as a boy.

From up here, the true breadth of the river could be seen. It commanded the landscape at this, its widest stretch. Despite the advent of the railroad, the river was a busy corridor of commerce, and they counted no fewer than half a dozen schooners, three barges, one with a tug, and a steamboat, though not the

Mary Powell, plowing its waters in both directions. Someone was also fighting his way across in a canoe, a crazy undertaking amid the north-and-south traffic.

To the south, the Rondout Lighthouse would soon be lit. Behind it lay the hills and farms and villages of Ulster County, and behind them the curved backbone of the Catskills, with the distinctive chin of Overlook Mountain turned to the evening sky. Frank stepped to the edge of the slope and smoothed some of the tall grass with his foot, then sat and raised his arm for Ida to sit beside him. She leaned against him and pressed her hand into the coarse, moist grass.

"I'd marry you again," she said after a time, and she felt a piercing tenderness for him. She brushed her nose in his hair. He smelled of a long day of work.

He stripped the seeds off a stalk of grass and threw them with some force over the hill. She waited, hoping he would say something in return, but he glared out at the landscape, as if it were to blame for something.

"Now that Norris is of age . . ." she started, but she dropped the rest of her sentence, unsure how to go on without provoking him.

"That boy is a fool," Frank said.

"All boys that age have a fool in them," Ida said. "They all need to learn the hard way, but they do learn, most of them."

"He's more of a fool than most."

"He's been indulged," Ida said.

Frank threw another pinch of grass seed. The steamboat on the river whistled in response to some danger they couldn't see.

"Perhaps it's time to talk about leaving the farm," she ventured. "I've had word from Ashley's mother that she wants him home again. She's planning to hand-feed him." This worried Ida—she knew what happened to babies whose mothers unwittingly fed them spoiled cows' milk—but his mother must make those choices herself. "I'd like to stop nursing," Ida continued. "It's tiring, with all the housework, and I could help you more without a baby to feed. We could find a place of our own and build our own green-houses. Or you could go back to carpentry—"

"I want Oliver to have more," Frank interrupted, pitching an-other handful of seeds. "He has just as much right to this farm as Norris. Reuben, too, when he's old enough."

"Do you think that's going to happen?"

Frank rocked to his feet and staggered straight down the hill, though it was too steep for Ida to follow. He stopped about twenty feet below and scrutinized the river again, his hands pulling at the brim of his hat. Then he veered to the left and made his way across the slope of the hill toward the path. She saw that she was meant to go with him, and she stood quickly to retrace their steps and meet him.

They walked down in silence, and for a few minutes he allowed her to take his hand, patterned with crosshatches pressed from the grass. When they reached the high ridge, he veered off the path and followed the spine of the hill. The way was rough; Ida's ankles began to chafe, but she hurried to keep pace with him. Eventually he slowed for her, and they walked on together as the light paled and the katydids sang and the church bell in the village tolled eight o'clock. Ida's milk was coming in heavily, and she longed to get home to Ashley and Jasper, but she and Frank plowed on together, cutting across the rear of the farm until they stood look-ing down on the south greenhouses looming in the near-dark like long, narrow warships lined up at dock in strict formation, ten feet apart. They wove around them, Frank pausing to check a few of the door latches.

"Alice needs to earn her keep," he said finally.

Ida took heart that he hadn't said she must marry. "I know a few women who need help with their fall sewing," she fibbed. "I'll get her some work as a seamstress soon."

"Very soon," Frank said.

As they descended to the house, Ida heard Ashley's hungry wail. A familiar stiffness rose in her breasts, a sharp tingling, climbing up hard, and then her milk let down.

Two days after Ashley's departure, Frank came home from the train station with a basket on the wagon floor. It was dusk, and Ida and the boys were helping unload a shipment of new cardboard flats when she heard a coo and looked behind her for Ashley. She knew he was gone, but perhaps in her longing for him, her ears were playing tricks. Another coo, and with recognition thickening in her gut, Ida walked around the wagon.

The basket was old and dirty, as if it had been used for years to pick vegetables and then forgotten in the corner of a shed until being unearthed that very afternoon. The baby inside was wrapped to its chin in a clean blanket from which it was struggling to free itself. It opened its mouth and uttered a hungry exclamation, and Ida raised her eyes to Frank, who stood on the other side of the wagon, watching for her response.

"It's your new baby," he said.

The baby's blackened umbilical cord was still sticking out from her belly like a tiny water snake when Dr. Van de Klerk came to call. When Ida unwrapped her, he raised his eyebrows but examined the baby in silence. Then he leaned back, hands clasped behind him, and gave Ida a long stare.

"She's a young one," Ida said, heading him off.

"Just a couple of days old," the doctor agreed. "Where did she come from?"

"She came in on the train. Someone brought her up from the city," Ida said. "That's all Frank told me. And that her mother died in childbirth."

The doctor nodded gravely, watching the baby. "She wasn't delivered by a doctor," he said. "Nor an experienced midwife. Nobody who knew a darned thing about it would cut a cord that way."

It was true, even Ida could see that. The shriveled cord was at least twice as long as the cords on any of her babies had been, screwed around itself, and sticking up sharply at the end so she had trouble changing the baby's diaper around it.

"Have you been paid in advance?" Dr. Van de Klerk asked.

Payment was none of the doctor's business, but Ida had to admit she hadn't considered it. Thus far she had nursed babies whose mothers missed them and were eager to pay promptly and well for their care. Both Susie and Ashley had arrived with the first month's pay, and their mothers had corresponded with Ida; this baby had arrived only with a blanket.

"What do you suggest I do?" she asked coolly.

The doctor shrugged. "Nurse her." He clipped his bag shut. "The cord should fall off within a few days. Keep it clean. Does she have a name?"

"I'm certain she does," Ida said. He cocked his head and scrutinized her, and she knew he was wondering what kind of a nurse wouldn't know a baby's name. She had never seen him fix his eyes on a person the way he was watching her this afternoon. She willed herself to meet his stare with her own, counting in her head with each breath: one, two, three, four . . . What did he want her to do? Send the baby back? Five, six . . . He nodded and turned to the door.

That evening as Ida sat in her rocker by the cold chimney nursing the baby, she asked Frank for the baby's name. He was pouring kerosene into the lamp and didn't look up, concentrating so as not to spill. Ida waited, watching the foul-smelling oil run into the chamber. Finally Frank set down the kerosene can and gave her a forced smile. "Her name is Mary," he said.

"May I have her father's address?" Ida asked. "I'd like to write to him, as I did to the mothers before."

"Fathers aren't so good at correspondence," Frank said.

"He'll have to correspond in order to pay us."

Frank nodded. "He will. But don't expect any of those chatty letters the ladies send."

"Whether he writes a reply or not, I'd like him to know how his Mary is getting on."

"Then I'll mail the letters for you," Frank said. "Just give them to me."

Ida wanted to object. Frank was busy and sometimes careless with his own correspondence. No doubt he was uncomfortable having her write to a man. Perhaps he wanted to read the letters over himself before they were mailed. Why was she feeling so suspicious? Simply because they hadn't placed an advertisement in the newspaper this time? Obviously Frank had come across this baby through his contacts in the city. He should have asked her; he should have honored her wish to stop nursing. But he was worried about money. He was determined to keep up with his brothers, and she must stand with him. She could nurse one more baby. She ran her palm over the baby's fuzzy, wrinkled head and whispered her name. Mary.

6

Summer was a long, humid crawl. It was difficult to keep the greenhouses cool this time of year. The violets couldn't stand the wilting heat, so the ventilation panels were cranked wide open, with a coat of slaked lime on the rest of the glass roof for shade. In addition, the plants were dampened frequently, so moisture clung to the air. The men often labored in and around the greenhouses in their shirtsleeves, and Ida would sometimes glance out her kitchen window to find them at the pump, their heads under a stream of water.

The men were most anxious during the summer, for the new plants were vulnerable to insects and black spot and other natural hazards. Until a good number were firmly established, the men kept a close watch. Though it wasn't yet time for picking, the boys and the men were up on the boards to weed in the heat, pulling out the unwanted sprouts of plants that had come in with the soil and the manure and snapping off early runners that shot out from the crowns and sapped the strength of the plants. They removed the faltering violets as well, to make space for the hardier plants to succeed.

With the planting done and picking not yet begun, the women had time again to do their household chores properly. When they could, Ida and Alice brought their work up to Frances's cool veranda, where they could shell peas or darn socks and Ida could nurse the baby while Jasper napped in the rear bedroom of Frances's house. Cook often sat out with them, and if Frances wasn't home, the three of them would enjoy some lively conversation about Cook's family across the river in Kingston or, more wickedly, the latest outrageous thing William and Frances had done. "Now Mrs. Fletcher wants to paper the parlor again! Says it's too dark, when she just covered up that pretty stenciling last year" or "They wanted me to give up my Sunday afternoon off again so they could have the Nathans to tea!" Some days Ida and Alice brought Cook the newspaper. They followed closely the news of the war in Cuba; not only Avery Pruitt and Alan Harris had enlisted, but also Cook's nephew.

On the days when Frances sat out on the veranda with them, reading one of her ladies' magazines or doing some needlework, there was no newspaper or lively conversation. When they sat quietly, they could hear the men's voices carrying over the ridge, the tone separated from the words. Ida could sometimes pick out four or five different birdsongs, a sprightly melody against the drone of summer locusts. Once in a while the crunch of a horse's shoes on the pebbly lane drew the women's attention, though from the height of the hill, it was hard to see who was passing. In this way, the lesser chores were completed with relative ease, and it almost felt to Ida that she had rested for an hour or two.

In the summer, Ida also tended the vegetables in her garden. She aimed to grow enough to feed her family into the fall, with potatoes and carrots and turnips to overwinter in the cellar. August was the time for canning: tomatoes, pickles, and the pears from a few trees that had survived the men's failed attempt at building an orchard. These trees stood behind the henhouse, and Ida had claimed them as her own when the men stopped caring for them. No one complained, for after she spent several hot, laborious days peeling and quartering the fruit and boiling jars eight at a time in the big canning pot, she always delivered several each to Harriet and to Frances.

August was also the time for Ida to plan the sewing she must do for the winter. When she had decided what she would need, she took a trip to Mrs. Brinckerhoff's fabric shop in town. Frank had just helped dig two new graves in the churchyard, and he'd passed some of the money to Ida to spend as she saw fit.

It was a rare treat for her to leave the little ones with Alice and ride into town with money in her reticule. Oliver dropped her off in front of the pharmacy, and she walked across the street to Anna Brinckerhoff's shop, where a bell on the door rang invitingly as she entered. Ida loved the smell of this shop, the polished wood floors worn around the edges of the old counter, and the clean, pressed fabric. Bolts of every imaginable pattern and color lined the walls on neat shelves from floor to ceiling, arranged by type—gingham and calico, cotton eyelet, wool, linen, silk, taffeta, chiffon, damask, cretonne, chintz—and within type, by color from dark to light. In the center of the room was the cutting counter and all around it notions: spools of thread stacked on wooden stakes, and buttons of every size and shape in miniature drawers, and glistening, sharp needles in crisp paper packets. There were pretty pincushion dolls with ceramic heads, handy snap-back tape measures, wooden darners, sewing birds, buttonhole scissors and lace scissors and a pair of fancy scissors from England with sterling silver handles.

Ida was quite fond of Anna Brinckerhoff, despite the shop owner's reputation of being somewhat odd. She had sewn herself two split skirts, the kind worn only by young women for bicycling. To add to the peculiarity, she had pushed the fashion so far that her split skirts looked more like trousers with very wide legs. She was often seen wearing them when she walked her pet dog—a silly, citified thing to do—and when she and her husband went sailing. The general conclusion of the men was that she caused no harm. They were sure their wives would not adopt her costume or her ways. But Ida and the other women who knew her were aware that she had been to suffragist conventions and had strong ideas about the future for women that went beyond split skirts.

As Ida wandered along the shop's aisles, she slid out bolts of cloth to finger the fabric for thickness and weave and to imagine what she would make of it. Today she was captivated by a blue flannel the color of the summer sky blown clear of clouds, and she was sorely tempted to spend some of the money to buy it for a shirt for Reuben, with his blue eyes.

But she had come for winter dresses. There was an elegant brown brocade too fancy for every day, though Ida could picture it setting off Alice's russet hair. Eventually she settled on a brown lightweight wool with a pretty thread of royal blue. She could sew Alice an everyday skirt with a separate jacket to fancy it up, a grown-up fashion that would please her. For herself, the decision was easier. She favored a maroon dress she'd been wearing for years that was too tight now that she was nursing again, and chose a broadcloth in a similar color with a pretty embroidered overlay for the collar. She would modify the pattern to create a flap with a hidden row of buttons behind the waistband so she could wear the dress while nursing.

"How are you this morning, Ida?" Anna Brinckerhoff asked warmly when she had finished with the other customers.

"Fine, thank you, and you?" Ida noted that Mrs. Ritter, whose husband ran the Post Road Hotel, had entered the shop, and nodded a polite good day to her as well.

"A new dress for yourself?" Anna asked, taking up her heavy tailor's scissors.

"For Alice," Ida said. "I'll need six yards."

As Anna cut the fabric, Mrs. Ritter injected herself into their conversation. "Now that your nephew is taking over, what will become of your place, Ida?" she asked.

"He's been made a junior partner," Ida replied. "I sincerely doubt he'll be taking over anytime soon."

"Oh! Henry says he heard your brother-in-law was asking about a piece of property in Florida. One of our regular patrons, a gentleman from Kinderhook, is selling it."

Anna laughed. "Florida, for heaven's sake!"

"They say it feels this warm all winter long," Mrs. Ritter said. "Quite a few of the men of means are buying property there."

"It's terribly hot in the summer, I would imagine," Anna added. "Six yards, Ida. And will you need any notions?"

"Some buttons for the jacket, and a hook and eye," Ida answered. "At any rate, Mr. Fletcher is a wise man," she said, addressing Mrs. Ritter. "He has no intention of turning over the operation to an inexperienced boy, his son or no."

"It's what I heard," Mrs. Ritter said with a twitch of her shoulder, and the old-fashioned leg-o'-mutton sleeves of her blouse shrugged stiffly with her.

Ida chose her notions carefully as Anna cut her maroon broadcloth and then some calico for Mrs. Ritter, who was sewing curtains for her kitchen. When the woman was gone, Ida brought her things to the counter and watched Anna tally them with a pencil on a piece of brown wrapping paper.

"Don't pay her any mind, Ida," she said. "You know she's full of gossip, and half of it is entirely made up."

"And the other half?" Ida asked.

"The other half is unkind."

"So it is," Ida agreed.

"Now, I'm glad you came in today. Before you go, I have something I've been wanting to give you," Anna said. From under the counter she drew out a red volume with the bold title *Women and Economics*. "Have you heard of it?" she asked. It had been some time since Ida and Alice had been to the lending library, and Ida admitted she had not.

"It's just been published by a brilliant woman named Charlotte Perkins Stetson. She's for women's suffrage and more. You must read it."

Anna was clearly anticipating some kind of response from Ida, who was trying to figure why she had been singled out to borrow the book. She raised her hand tentatively to take it. She wanted to be gracious, but the title alone could send Frank into a fit.

"I understand," Anna said. From the stack of brown wrapping paper, she drew one large sheet and folded it, first lengthwise at top and bottom and then around the book itself, fashioning a paper cover. "Keep it in a safe place and return it when you're through. I think you'll like what she has to say." Ida must have looked skeptical, for Anna added, "It's food for thought, anyway."

Ida was embarrassed then to mention her other reason for coming into the shop, but she mustn't be deterred. This was the most logical place to ask for work for Alice. "While we're on the subject of women and economics, Alice is seeking work as a seamstress, if you hear of anyone who needs help with sewing. She'll go to ladies' homes, provided they aren't too far and Oliver can take her. Or she'll take work in."

"Wonderful," Anna said, and Ida was relieved to be spared the shame of having to answer any further questions. "I'll keep her in mind."

They exchanged a few parting pleasantries, and Ida stepped out of the shop with her package of sewing goods and the borrowed book sandwiched inside. A dark storm cloud was blowing in from the south, and before she could reach the pharmacy, where Oliver was to meet her with the wagon, large drops of cold rain were landing in the street, shooting up dust. Ida had no umbrella, so for a time she stood beneath the faded canvas awning of the print shop, listening to the deep toll of thunder. It was only a summer cloudburst, and she found herself quieted by it. Rarely did she have an excuse to stand still and wait. She watched the rain spill in jeweled strands from the awning to the sidewalk, where it puddled and then ran downhill as if it were in a hurry. She observed her own stillness as she watched the townsfolk scurry from door to door, holding newspapers and boxes and bags over their heads. She felt impervious, not troubled by rain or snow or the heat of the August sun. She imagined what it would be like to stand still forever, needed by no one.

It would be death. Her heart beat once, hard against her bones, then lay back in her breast.

A farm wagon rolled by, its wheels spinning muddy spirals of rainwater. Ida stepped into the easing rain and made her way across the street to the pharmacy to wait for Oliver.

The sky was still gray as an army blanket when he finally pulled up. Another storm was steering up the valley, and Ida wished she had brought her wrap. "Maybe this one will pass us by," she said as she set her heavy package beside Oliver, then lifted herself to the wagon seat.

"Dunno, Ma," Oliver said, glancing south and then west.

"Fall is coming," she said as Oliver steered the team toward home. "I can feel it."

"It's going to be a good harvest!" he said.

"Oh?"

"Norris'll be taking over." Oliver grinned as if he'd just won five dollars at horseshoes. Did he imagine his cousin would do him any favors? Ida wanted to shake him.

"How soon do you suppose?" she asked. Apparently she was the only one to have missed the news. She should have treated her request for work for Alice with more urgency. She nearly asked Oliver to take her back to Anna Brinckerhoff's shop.

Oliver shrugged. "Soon as he's ready. He's a quick study."

"Oh, I don't think so," Ida said, and she gripped the edges of

her hat as the breeze taunted it. She looked up to check the progress of the next threatening cloud.

"Well, that's what he says. Maybe he's wrong," Oliver said.
Noticing, as she had, that the cloud was bearing down fast, he
slapped the reins and clicked his tongue at Trudy and Trip. "Slow
old devils, ain't you," he said, but Ida pointed out neither his crude
language nor his bad grammar.

"Did you hear Avery is home?" Oliver asked her.

"No!" Ida said. What else was she unaware of, stuck in her own
backyard every day with the children?

"He's sick in bed," Oliver said. "Yellow fever. He never even
made it to the battlefield; caught it on the docks."

"That's awful!"

"I'll go see him. Maybe tomorrow," Oliver said. "Wish I could
have gone."

"What, and caught yellow fever?"

"I don't know." He shrugged. "I feel like I missed something
big. Now it's over already."

"You'll have other opportunities," Ida said, praying one of them
wouldn't be war.

For a time they rode in silence, while the lower clouds roiled
like bluing in the laundry water and bulbous thumbs of iron gray
stirred them from above. Ida and Oliver held their peace through
the outskirts of the village. It wasn't until they were nearing home
that Oliver spoke again.

"George and I have been talking, Ma," he said. He had worked
himself up to making some kind of announcement.

"About what?" she asked.

"A business plan. When the season's over, next spring, we were
thinking . . ." Ida waited, expecting him to have yet another rash
idea like prospecting for gold in the Klondike. "We thought we'd
head out to Boston. George's uncle has a fishing business, and he
says he could use our help."

"That's a difficult life," Ida said. "And a dangerous one. Harder than what we do here."

"No, George's uncle wants us to run a market for him. He's opening his own, and he'd still go out and do the fishing with his crew. He needs us to run the business."

"What do you know about selling fish?" Ida laughed.

"I've caught a few nice bass and a lot of sunnies," Oliver replied with a self-deprecating smile. "Look, Ma, sometime I've got to strike out on my own. It's Boston or New York. I can't stay here all my life. The city is where things are happening!"

"I quite agree," Ida said. "You can't stay here. I hope you won't."

Oliver pulled inadvertently on the reins as he turned to her, and the team stopped in the middle of the road. "I thought you were going to argue with me all the way home," he said. "I was scared to say anything."

"Have you said anything to your father?"

"Not yet. I told you first." This news warmed her, and then she felt ashamed, competing with Frank for Oliver's affection.

"I think it's time I tell you more about the farm," she said.

Oliver clicked to set the team walking. Ida hesitated then. Frank wouldn't want some of this said. But something had shifted, she realized, as she sorted the words she could use. Her loyalties were with Oliver, not Frank. She didn't know what was happening to her husband, what he was thinking or why he was behaving as he was, but if it came to choosing between what Frank would want and what Oliver needed, she would choose her boy. Perhaps that had always been true, and she had simply never been tested before.

"Your father," she began, then thought better of opening there. "Your uncles have been holding a grudge against your father for nearly thirty years."

"I know that," Oliver said. "He doesn't own his share of the farm. Why not?"

"When he was about sixteen, your father took some money from the family safe. He'd met a man he wanted to invest it with. He thought he could make a profit and prove to everyone that he should be taken seriously."

"And he lost it all," Oliver said, guessing the end of her story.

"He lost it all."

Oliver whistled gravely, and Trip raised his head, thinking the whistle was for him.

Ida went on. "Some of it, I suspect, he may have spent on other things—things he didn't need, like the fancy buggy he had when I met him. Trips to the city. I've never asked him, and I'd rather not know." Oliver did not press her on this account, but he looked embarrassed, as if he understood his father's youthful tendencies.

"They needed that money," Ida continued. "Your grandparents struggled hard to save the farm after that, and they both died within a couple of years. I've heard Uncle William say they died of grief—your grandfather over the farm, and your grandmother over him."

"Do you believe that?" Oliver asked.

"I wasn't there," Ida said. "All I know is my father grieved my mother's death horribly, but it didn't kill him. I think some days he wished it would."

Oliver nodded, and she could see that he was piecing the story to make his own sense of things.

"In any case," she continued, "once your grandparents were gone, Uncle William and Uncle Harold decided to start fresh. The market for wheat was poor. They sold some land to the Mortons, and Uncle William went down to the city to work. He charmed his way into society and met Aunt Frances, and brought her and all her money up here. That's when they built their big house. They tried pear trees first, and when that didn't work, Aunt Frances's money let them take up the violets. Now, of course, they're doing very well."

"But what about Pa?"

"He ran off for a while. First to New York, then to Albany. He wasn't here when his parents died. When he came back to claim his share, we were newlyweds. Uncle William wanted nothing to do with him, but he knew it wouldn't look good if he turned us away. Uncle Harold said we should be allowed to stay but that Pa would have to earn his way back in."

"Why did Pa come back? He could do anything." Oliver looked pained, and she could see he was building up a head of steam that might be released in the wrong way if she didn't take care.

"I think your father felt he had something to prove. He's the youngest brother. Think about how hard Reuben works to keep up with you." Oliver bowed his head and ran his fingers through his damp hair.

"Pa wanted to show them he could succeed," Ida said. "He thought he could pay them back what he'd lost, and that would vindicate him. It hasn't happened quite that easily." She didn't add that at one time Frank had tried to move over to working for the Tenneys or the DuMonts, the other major violet growers, but his reputation for hotheadedness had preceded him.

They had reached their turn onto Dutch Lane, and Ida hastened to finish what she had to say, for the sky was curtained and she didn't want to slow their pace. "That's all," she said. "We never left. I wish we had, but I think for your father, leaving would mean conceding defeat. Uncle William and Uncle Harold let us live in the tenant house, and they pay your father like a hired hand. They expect the rest of us to pitch in, and they credit our work against his debt. They say if he repays them what he lost, they'll give him the house and let him in on the farm as a partner. But he'll never be able to do that on nine dollars a week."

"Why doesn't he sue them?" Oliver asked.

She saw how tightly he was gripping the reins. "Your uncles are respected members of the community. It wouldn't reflect well on your father. And he's a strong-willed man. Like you." She smiled, meaning this as a compliment, but Oliver was too angry, and he looked away.

"I'd like to take a shot at both of them," he said.

"Take care, Oliver. Know your place."

"My place ought to be the same as Norris's!"

"It ought to, but it's not. You've known that all along."

"And now I know why! I wish I could march right up there and set a match to that fancy old house."

"I used to feel that, too," Ida said. "But your best revenge is to refuse to play the part they've given you. Go to Boston."

Her son, her young man, held her gaze then. For the first time, they were adults in league, and she had reached the moment when she would willingly send him away.

"I'll finish this season," Oliver said. "Do you think that's all right, to wait until spring?"

"That will give you plenty of time to save up and make your plans," Ida said. She placed her hand firmly on his and added, "Don't tell your father."

Oliver breathed in as if to speak, then let out a labored sigh.

"I can't guess his reaction," Ida said. "He thinks he's working the farm for you, and you know . . ." She didn't need to say more. Oliver still had a splinter in his neck from the night Frank had beaten him in the barnyard. "Tell him when you're ready to go."

Oliver nodded and guided the team up the driveway. He made it into the barn and Ida reached the house before the dark-lidded sky dropped its next load of rain. It rained all night, and in the morning, when Ida stepped into her garden, the ground was cold.

HARVEST

So, tell me more about growing up on a violet farm. I didn't realize anyone grew violets for sale.

Oh, they were extremely popular when I was a girl, more popular than roses are now. Whenever a woman went out on the town, she would wear a big bunch of violets pinned to her waist or her shoulder.

What made them so popular?

People used to say they stood for love and loyalty. They were seen as modest, innocent flowers. You find them everywhere in literature. Keats called the violet "that queen of secrecy." I'm not sure which poem that's from.

That seems contradictory, doesn't it? Innocence and secrecy?

Life is contradictory.

I suppose. I always thought violet—purple—was supposed to be a color of royalty. . . . What do you think of it?

The color violet? I don't know. I never really thought about it. I suppose it seems a little bit dark to me. Shadowy. I don't really care for it.

—excerpt from an interview with Mrs. Alice Vreeland for
The Women of Albany County, July 6, 1972

7

The book that Anna Brinckerhoff had loaned Ida lay wrapped and unread in her cedar chest for two weeks. In that time, she found no steady work for Alice. Frank had said nothing more, but Ida began to watch the young men of Underwood, considering which of them might make an appropriate match if things came to that. She thought the clandestine book might give her some other ideas about Alice's future. So one Wednesday afternoon, while her dough was rising and the children were napping and a misty rain kept her from the garden, she began to read.

She was put off at first by Mrs. Stetson's comparison of working women to horses. Both, the author claimed, were used by men, their masters, to earn more money, though neither had the independence to choose that work. Ida had to admit that was true. It might even be humorous if it weren't so pointed an observation. Mrs. Stetson argued quite logically and convincingly that society had assigned women a single wage-earning occupation: getting a husband. For the good of society, Mrs. Stetson said, women should participate in the economic world of work—work of their own choosing. Ida's experience had already proven this argument idealistic and impractical.

The world was changing, about that there was no question. In the city young women were indeed becoming secretaries and shop clerks, jobs they would hold until they married later on. Was it possible that her daughter would live in a world in which women could easily make the choice not to marry?

"What are you reading, Ma?" Alice asked after seeing Ida with the book over the course of several afternoons.

"Just something Mrs. Brinckerhoff gave me. About women."

This seemed to satisfy Alice, who returned to her own romantic novel without further question.

In the passage Ida read that afternoon, Mrs. Stetson chastised the economic system for pressuring mothers to withhold from their daughters the truths about marriage and motherhood, including the fact that they would be absolutely dependent upon their husbands, with no freedom to control their own futures. Instead, Mrs. Stetson argued, society spoke of the "sanctity" of motherhood and home because the young woman must be prepared for marriage—her only means of financial support—and prospective husbands preferred their wives to enter marriage innocent of its realities. Ida felt this reproach like a slap to the face. She knew there were many things she should tell Alice, but how to say them delicately, so as not to frighten her? And how to convince her, in the face of society's claims to the contrary, that they were true at all? These were precisely the problems to which Mrs. Stetson alluded. There was no way to say them delicately and convincingly, so they were left unsaid, as they had been for Ida.

She had lost her own mother at fourteen, and her professorial father had been ill prepared to raise two daughters on his own. He could talk at length about medicine and politics, and he could sing hundreds of hymns from memory, but he had not had the words to tell a daughter what she should know about men and marriage, and he had surely known little himself about childbearing and raising small children. Ida had often wondered what her mother's judgment of Frank would have been, and whether her mother, had she been alive at the time of their courtship, might have changed the course of Ida's life.

There was no point in speculation. What mattered now was that Ida had a daughter whom she did not wish to send naive into the world. She resolved that they should talk. Laundry day, when they worked side by side, would be the best opportunity.

The laundry always began with a good Sunday-evening soaking. Ida filled galvanized tubs with soapy water and sank the week's clothing in them, hoping to loosen the dirt and grime overnight and make Monday's task easier. In the morning, before breakfast, she set a large pot of water on the back of the range. By the time breakfast was done and Frank and the boys had left, the water had come to a boil. Ida transferred the soaked laundry into a basket and, with Alice's help, carried the tubs outside to dump. Then the boiling water, tempered with some cold from the pump, went into the first tub along with some shavings of laundry soap, and they started in on the most delicate clothing and the whites: collars and undergarments, as well as Frank's and the boys' good shirts. The baby's diapers were washed separately each night.

Alice stood and churned the wash with the dolly while Ida refilled the large pot to boil for the rinse and then worked on the stained clothing, left out of the first wash. She used lemon juice to lighten stains and sometimes kerosene to remove them, if they were serious, like the grass stains Reuben was infamous for bringing home on the knees of his overalls. The delicate items were merely stirred in the washtub, but the heavier items and those that were soiled were scrubbed on the washboard. For this job, Ida and Alice each pulled a low stool up to the tub and scrubbed together, each on her own board.

Sitting across the tub from each other, they sometimes spoke of ordinary plans or of the local and national news. Sometimes they were quiet. This was the moment Ida chose to bring up her sensitive subject.

"Alice, is there anything you would like to know about?" She realized the question was a lame one; she should be more direct if

she intended to succeed. Alice's head was bent over the tub as she
scrubbed the seat of Oliver's work pants.

"About what?"

"About . . . becoming a woman," Ida said.

Alice glanced suspiciously at her. "Do you mean about my time
of the month?"

Here Ida faltered. She had taught Alice the practical aspects of
dealing with her menses—how to sew her own belted pads, how
to remove the bloodstains, how to be discreet—but that was not
at all what she meant.

"I mean about becoming a wife and a mother."

"Mother!" Alice said, both echoing the word and censuring
Ida. She sat up and flicked the soapy water from her hands.

"Yes," Ida said, gaining courage. "Someday I imagine you, too,
will become a mother." She felt as if she were standing in a canoe
in the middle of the river, where it would be impossible to keep
her balance. The only question was whether she would fall into the
cold current to port or to starboard.

"Has Pa picked out a husband for me? I'm not getting married!"

"No, no," Ida said, seeing she'd begun the wrong way.

Alice struck her hands into the water and pulled out Oliver's
trousers, then tossed them into the empty rinse tub. "I have no
intention of becoming a mother anytime soon, I assure you," she
said in a haughty voice belying her lack of experience.

"We should talk about these things before it's necessary," Ida
said.

"Is it that book you're reading? The one with the brown paper
wrapper?" Alice's eyes sparked and narrowed, and a blush spread
across her forehead. Was she angry that Ida was bringing this up
when she had promised to help her find work instead? Or had something changed since their last conversation? Alice had once mentioned Claudie's brother. Ida wondered whether Alice had been to
see him in his sickroom on her visits to Claudie's house. Had some-

thing begun to develop between them? Ida doubted it, but she could see that Alice had secrets of her own, and true to her nature, she would keep them. Even as a little girl, she had squirreled her treasures in an old biscuit box under her bed, and if Ida happened to pull out that box in the process of dusting, it was an offense punishable by extended silence and sulking. Alice had matured and learned to be more gracious about her secrets, but they were secrets nonetheless.

Still, another opening for this conversation might not come for a while. So Ida tried once more. "Is there a young man on your mind?"

"Mother," Alice said firmly. Then she bowed her head to the tub.

"When there is a young man," Ida said, faltering, "I hope you will tell me. There are some important things we need to discuss."

"All right," Alice said, her cloth-covered fingers rasping along the washboard.

Seeing she was to make no further headway, Ida worked in silence. When she was satisfied that the clothes were clean enough and the water in the pot on the stove was hot enough, she and Alice poured rinse water over the clothing and left it to soak, then started on another tub of wash: their skirts and dresses and other heavier clothing that wasn't soiled from work on the farm. Ida prepared a cold rinse with bluing to brighten the whites in a third tub, and the first load of laundry made its final stop there. By this time, with three loads at three stages of wash, conversation would have been difficult anyway. In the midst of it all, Jasper and Mary needed attention.

When the first load had been rinsed twice, Alice helped Ida feed it through the wringer and into a basket that Alice carried to the line. It was not yet time for lunch, and both of them were too tired to speak. Washday, Ida thought as she worked, was one thing that had to improve in the new century. Mrs. Harris's friend in Pough-keepsie had bought a self-working washer a few years back from a company in Binghamton. The washer had a flywheel that hooked up to the faucet in her kitchen sink, and the water pressure drove a set of paddles in the washtub. But the bolts in the mechanism had left rust stains on her clothing, and once, the paddles had torn one of her husband's good shirts. That was the end of the so-called modern convenience, and the woman was back to doing laundry like the rest of them. Someone someday would make a fortune on laundry machines, Ida thought, if they could only figure out how to make them work without ruining the clothing. It would be the very first modern piece of equipment every housewife would desire.

Laundry was work that Alice could do to earn the income Frank seemed more and more desperate to have. Families more financially secure than theirs—Frances's and Harriet's included—sent their laundry out, and the women who washed and ironed for them earned two dollars for each family's load, a day's labor. But laundry was terrible work. The soap reddened one's hands, and hot-water burns were common. Lifting baskets of wet garments and pots of hot water broke down the back and shoulders. The laundresses Ida knew looked like old women, though they might not yet be forty. Ida prayed she would have better luck finding Alice work as a seamstress so that the thought of laundering would never cross Frank's mind. Marrying young and fairly, if not happily, would be a better fate.

Ida and Alice paused for lunch when the last load was soaking in its first rinse tub. Alice cleaned out the washtub and set it in the sun to dry while Ida sliced some bread and tomatoes and poured three glasses of milk. Then she sat to nurse Mary while she ate her own meal, the smell of soap on her hands.

It was always difficult to start again after lunch. The day had settled thickly around them, and after their rest, the women's arms and backs groaned heavy and stiff. But they rallied as they must, rinsing and wringing and ending their task outside at the clothes-lines, where a breeze blew the damp sheets and shirts against their bare arms with a cool slap.

The clotheslines ran parallel from the corner of the house to two large elm trees, with enough space between for Ida and Alice to pass back to back. The first line was already full, so Ida began at the tree with one basket and Alice at the house with another, and they worked their way toward each other. They saved the effort of bending by slinging several wet garments over their shoulders and standing to hang them with clothespins plucked from pouches at their waists. It was midafternoon when they met the end of laundry day at the middle of the clothesline—the end until evening, when everything must come down. Tomorrow much of it would need to be ironed in the hot kitchen.

As they stood at the center of the line, flanked by a sizable family of clothing gesturing nonsensically in the breeze, Ida put an arm around Alice's shoulders and gave her a squeeze. "It will work itself out," she said, trying to feel that optimism herself, but Alice seemed about to cry. What had Ida said or neglected to say? She raised her eyebrows, hoping for a hint, but Alice ducked beneath a wet skirt and disappeared behind the laundry.

Later that afternoon a letter arrived from Mary's father. It was addressed to Ida, and she opened it eagerly, for she'd written to the man for several weeks without a reply. But the letter struck her as strange. Handwritten in block letters and merely two lines long, it thanked Ida for her service. It was signed simply "Mr. Gordon," as if the man had no Christian name.

As Ida and Frank settled into bed that night, she mentioned the letter to him. Frank lay facing the wall as he always did; she spooned against his back, her crooked knees tucked into his. The nights had cooled, and she pressed her chilled feet against the soles of his warm ones. "The letter was very short," she told him. "He's not much of a writer."

"You make too much of things, Ida," Frank said. He squirmed

to find a comfortable spot, and the bed ropes creaked in their anchors. "He's lost his wife. Be grateful you heard from him at all."

Ida pressed her nose into his nightshirt and thought before speaking again. "He's been paying you, has he not?" she asked. She didn't want to doubt Frank, but she had seen no evidence of the money herself.

"Don't worry about that," Frank said.

"So he's paying you?"

"He's paying," Frank said. "Go to sleep, Ida. It's late."

But Ida couldn't sleep. In her wakefulness, she worried over Alice. Dark thoughts she had no time to entertain in the steady pulse of the workday slunk over her like nocturnal animals. Mary woke after midnight, and instead of nursing her in bed, Ida attempted to escape her fears by taking the baby out to the moonlit kitchen. They sat at the window, where Ida could see, past the empty clotheslines, past the driveway, the smudged shadows of trees and farmland. How peaceful the world was when everyone was at rest. Ida imagined the others who were awake this time of night: the women with infants, the newlyweds, the sick. In her cosmos, tonight, all was quiet. The barn door was latched, the chickens were asleep in their coop, the greenhouses were masked and still. It wasn't yet time for the stokehouses to be churning out their filthy coal smoke, keeping the violets warm for the winter. A movement on the driveway caught her attention: Prissy on the hunt.

Ida rocked, and Mary's body fell heavy in her lap. Though Ida rested her head and tried to find sleep herself, it eluded her, and she kept a vigil at the window until the first strokes of light sharpened the edges of the shadows and brought them into focus. Only then did she realize why she wasn't sleeping. It was the birthday of her lost baby, whose stubby slate stone in the family burial yard bore a crudely carved name and date because she and Frank couldn't afford a proper marker. She would visit him later in the day and bring him a sunflower, as she always did.

The September day he was born, there were sunflowers growing against the house, and two of them had turned their faces toward the window. The most vivid memory of her labor was the moment she'd noticed those flowers peering in like angels watching over her. She was sure the baby, in his three days of life, had seen them, too—all of the outside world that he'd known. Thinking of him was a relief, for the unnamed tugging that had kept her awake had a name then: Martin Francis, named for her father and for Frank. She bowed her head in sleep and didn't wake until Frank shook her shoulder, telling her to get up and get breakfast.

On her walk up to the family graveyard that evening, in addition to her cut sunflower, Ida brought a hoe and a pair of work gloves, for she imagined the place would need some upkeep. It was hidden at the top of the ridge among trees that had grown up around it, so the casual passerby couldn't see it. Frank occasionally went to visit the graves of his parents and grandparents; the old stone wall was a pleasant, cool place to sit in the heat of the summer and eat lunch. Frances's babies were all there, and Ida knew she visited frequently. Those small graves were always neatly trimmed, and Frances had set some hardy shade plants along the wall to discourage the weeds. But pulling up saplings and hoeing the bindweed was not Frances's priority, so Ida, when she went, took it upon herself. She didn't know whether anyone else bothered to go in. William was so worldly, and Harold so stoic and practical, that she couldn't imagine they had the sentiment to visit, and Harriet had no family there to mourn.

Daylight was slipping. From the top of the ridge, Ida paused to look west toward the river. She couldn't see it from this saddle, but pink and orange streaks of cloud whorled behind the old tree on Halfway Hill. She turned east and hiked to the edge of the woods, the hoe over her shoulder.

As she approached the trees, she heard the sound of low voices, and she paused, surprised. Who would be up here at this time of day? Sometimes the workers came into the shade for a break, but they had all gone home. Perhaps it was Norris with his friends—or a girl? She distinctly heard a girl's voice. She stepped into the woods and looped north a few yards, hoping the trees would conceal her movements. She thought how foolish this was, sneaking about. If she startled Norris and a girl, what of it? They shouldn't be up here alone anyway.

But it was Alice's low laugh she heard—a laugh so scarce of late that Ida's immediate response was joy. Then anger. She gripped the hoe tightly and maneuvered closer behind the cover of the trees. There they were, sitting on the wall with their backs to her. Not touching but sitting a foot apart, their heads leaned toward each other. Alice and Joe Jacobs.

Ida felt dizzy with anger, then worry. She thought of circling around and entering the graveyard as if innocent of their presence, but the humiliation that would cause Alice presented a risk Ida wasn't sure she wanted to take—the risk that she might interfere with the start of something. She wasn't certain she could trust them to maintain their good reputations. After all, they were hidden up here together, when Alice should be at home with her sewing or a book. However, under the present circumstances, it was not a development to be discouraged. Joe Jacobs was a respectable young man from an educated family with a secure future.

In the next moment Ida scolded herself; all the two young people were doing was sitting on a wall and talking. Still, she stood motionless behind the trees. She wanted to visit her baby, to touch the earth at the foot of his stone and say a few gentle words to him, but he would wait for her to come again. She laid his sunflower on the musty earth at the foot of the chestnut tree in front of her and took care to step silently, cutting directly north out of the woods and down the hill to home. Alice, she hoped, would follow shortly.

8

Despite her best intentions, Alice found herself smitten with Joe Jacobs. A few days after they planted together, he said hello to her in passing on the driveway, touching his hat and smiling; he seemed truly happy to see her. She nodded quietly, but her heart was galloping, and it took all her will not to look at him again as she walked toward the house. After that, she began to act foolish, watching for him to arrive in the morning and offering to run errands to the greenhouses in hopes of seeing him there. Once her mother caught her standing on the footstool at the window over the sink because she thought she had seen Mr. Jacobs. "What in heaven's name are you so eager to see?" her mother asked, and Alice lied so quickly and easily that it astonished even her: "A beautiful cardinal, but it's gone now." After that, she promised herself she would be more discreet.

It was a long while before she could get close enough to him again to speak, even at church, but one day when she carried lunch pails over the ridge for Oliver and Reuben, there he was, washing his hands at the pump. "Good morning, Miss Fletcher," he said. "You've caught me a mess." He shook the water off his hands and dried them on his trousers. "Heading down to twenty-five? That's where they are. Let me help you." He took one of the pails, and they walked on together.

"I understand things get busy around here in the fall," he said.

Alice feared her voice would crack when she spoke. "Yes, it does. Starting with the New York Horse Show. It's always a rush to supply it so early in the season."

"That would be something to see, the horse show," he said.

"It would," Alice agreed. "I've never been, but I hear it's grand. I imagine the horses are quite different from Trip and Trudy."

"Oh, probably not all that different. Just used to doing a different job," Mr. Jacobs said. "Have you ever been to New York?"

"No," Alice admitted, feeling childish and unsophisticated. She was sure he had been dozens of times, probably with the pretty girls from Princeton who knew where to shop and where to have lunch, like her lucky cousins across the lane.

"You should go sometime. It's something, I'll tell you. Huge and loud and crazy. You feel like you're at the center of the universe."

Alice was going to protest that she liked it here just fine, but before she spoke, she realized that wouldn't make a good impression. Mr. Jacobs would think she had no ambition, that she was only a simple farm girl who would be happy spending her life picking violets and stoking the range and wringing laundry. Then she couldn't think of anything else to say, so she kept quiet. They walked the last few steps to the door of greenhouse 25, where she could see Oliver and Reuben halfway down the aisle, watering the plants.

"Well, here we are," Mr. Jacobs said, and handed her the lunch pail he'd been carrying. "Nice to see you again."

"Nice to see you, too," she said, hardly knowing where she was finding the poise to speak to him, so struck was she by the fact that he was paying her any attention at all.

After that encounter, she became much worse, not only watching for him all day, every day, but unable to stop thinking of him. She looked forward to Sunday mornings, when she was certain she would see him again. Though he always greeted her in a friendly way, he greeted others, girls and boys, women and men, with the same friendly demeanor. He never read the Scripture again, so she didn't have the opportunity to sit and listen to his voice without having to think of what to say.

Then a miracle happened. She ran across him in town one day, and he walked with her all the way from the pharmacy to Claudie's house, a considerable distance. She'd been to visit Claudie and had offered to walk to the village to pick up a prescription of Avery's. It was Claudie's time of the month, and she wasn't up to the errand. Ordinarily it wouldn't have occurred to Alice to offer to do a personal favor for Avery. Certainly, before he had gone off to the war, she'd have avoided doing anything that might encourage his attentions. But this afternoon she had sat with Claudie on the coverlet at the foot of his bed and read to them both from their childhood copy of *Alice's Adventures in Wonderland*. They had all read it before, and they probably wouldn't have read it again, at least until they'd had children of their own, except that Avery had requested it. Alice remembered being teased by Oliver and Norris when she was younger for having the same name as this Alice; they would shove things at her—a can of oil, a mud ball—and demand, "Drink this!" or "Eat this!"

As she'd read aloud this afternoon from the book, so well loved that its binding was split, she'd found herself enjoying the story in an entirely new way. Alice the character was not unlike any of them. She had fallen into a world in which all the rules had changed, and she couldn't be sure who she was herself. In their world there were no talking caterpillars or rabbits in waistcoats, but there was work and war and all the unexpected worries of adulthood, and it was good to escape them in the pages of a book and to know that its heroine would eventually wake up and grow up happily.

Avery had sat in bed with a stack of four pillows supporting him, though as Alice read, he continually shifted from one hip to the other, trying to find a comfortable position. The yellow tint of his skin hinted at the jaundice he'd suffered; Claudie had said even his eyes were yellow when he first came home. Worst of all, he was a different young man. There was no sign of the boyish bravado that had spurred him to leave. Now he held himself like an old man who understood things of which he could not speak.

Alice had read for an hour; Claudie had refused to take a turn, saying Alice had a more pleasing voice, and Avery had agreed. Finally he had asked for some medicine, and when Mrs. Pruitt had come to administer it, she'd discovered it was nearly gone. Alice had offered to walk into the village to refill his order.

In the pharmacy, she ran into Joe Jacobs. The pharmacist had just filled her order and handed her the paper bag when she turned and nearly bumped into him, standing close behind her.

He said he was picking up something for his mother, but would she wait a moment, and he would accompany her to the Pruitts'? "Of course," she said calmly, though she felt like leaping in the aisles among the apothecary jars.

It was a late-summer day; the sun had lost some of its power, though it was still warm and inviting. Alice walked as slowly as she could without dallying, and Mr. Jacobs matched her pace. She had never had the true attentions of a young man. Avery had once caught her by surprise at the Pruitts' back door and said a few words—she couldn't remember what, she'd been so flustered—then pecked at her like a chicken, and she'd ducked and run, so his kiss had bumped on her shoulder. At a church picnic the year before, a younger boy in whom she wasn't at all interested had monopolized her conversation for half an hour before Oliver had rescued her. And for a few days at school once, a boy a year ahead of her had passed her some notes. She hadn't replied, and the notes had stopped.

Mr. Jacobs's attention was entirely different. He was not an awkward boy, but a man. He spoke easily with other men, though he was young, and he had left Underwood to go to college. Maybe he was merely being polite. But a polite young man would have asked how she and her family were. He would not have offered to accompany her all the way to the Pruitts', would he? What would Mrs. Pruitt say if she saw? Would she tell Alice's mother? Alice didn't care; for the first time she felt she was becoming a young woman herself. She had told her mother she didn't want to marry, but if Mr. Jacobs were a possibility . . .

They made small talk about the weather and news of the Trans-Mississippi Exposition, of the health of their families, of Avery, and of Alan Harris, who had returned from Tampa but was restless to leave again. Then she asked about Princeton, and he told her about the campus green, where two treasured cannons were nearly fully buried to keep them from being stolen by students from a neighboring college. They passed the hardware store, and in the edge of her vision, Alice saw her neighbor Mr. Aiken loading his wagon. He saw them, too, but she knew he wouldn't say anything to her father, with whom he wasn't friendly on account of an old dispute.

"There must be scads of smart young ladies in Princeton," Alice said as they passed the last of the village shops and headed into the open countryside. Mr. Jacobs looked at her in a funny way, his forehead creased, as if she had misunderstood everything about him. The way he looked at her made her feel so foolish that she would have liked to have bolted into the Ellerbys' field.

"There are a few," he said. "The daughters of professors. A bunch of snobs, if you'll excuse me. Some people don't appreciate the privileges they have, and they hold them over others."

Alice knew plenty about that, but she also knew better than to say so.

"If you're asking whether I socialized at college, the answer is no," he added, and Alice felt a sickening heat flash in her head.

"I'm terribly sorry," she said. "I never meant to pry."

"Not at all," he said quickly. "I didn't mean to say you were prying. Not at all!" He stopped walking and reached toward her, then drew back again. Two of the Ellerbys' cows stood at the fence, chewing their cuds and watching with disinterest. The flies that followed them buzzed in the quiet.

"I'm making a mess of this conversation," Mr. Jacobs said, and he turned toward the pasture and pressed one hand to the back of his neck. He wandered up to the fence. The cows watched him approach. One nudged her nose toward him, and he patted her gently. Alice tightened her grip on the brown paper bag, and it crinkled.

Mr. Jacobs faced her again. She waited for him to speak.

"The truth is, I'm not accustomed to walking with a young lady like you," Mr. Jacobs said, and Alice wondered what kind of a young lady he thought she was. "Any young lady, that is," he added. "I feel all nervous in your presence." He laughed then. She had never heard him laugh, but it may have been the most beautiful sound she'd ever heard, because his laughter had something to do with the fact that being with her made him happy.

It was her turn to say something. She was afraid if she tried, she might begin to laugh as well, uncontrollably, she was so excited to be standing here at the edge of the Ellerbys' cow pasture with a young man, with Joe Jacobs, and he liked her!

"I'm nervous, too, Mr. Jacobs," she said, and calling him that made her giggle. She didn't bother covering her mouth, just let the laugh spill out of her.

"You must call me Joe," he said, taking a step toward her. She wasn't sure she would be able to do that. "Maybe not in front of anyone quite yet," he added, and they laughed together. A wagon was cresting the hill in front of them, and instinctively they set their arms at their sides and began walking. Alice didn't recognize the driver when he passed, but Joe tipped his hat. Joe. There. That wasn't so difficult, at least, to think of him as Joe.

"Here we are," he said a few minutes later when they reached the turn for Aldus Road and the Pruitts' house.

"You needn't accompany me to the door," Alice said.

He seemed to understand that she didn't want the Pruitts to see he had walked with her all that way. "I hope to see you again soon, then," he said.

"I hope so, too," she said, and with a wave, she headed up the road. She couldn't wait to tell Claudie.

She found Claudie and her mother in the kitchen, shelling peas into a giant pot, where they dropped with a ping like BB shot. Mrs. Pruitt measured out the medicine in a glass and asked Alice to carry it up to Avery; she would be up in a few minutes, she said.

It hadn't been strange at all to sit at the foot of Avery's bed when Claudie was there, but now Alice hesitated at his door. It didn't seem proper, but Mrs. Pruitt had sent her. Alice wondered whether Claudie's mother had intentions of trying to strike a spark between them. After all, she could have sent Claudie up instead. But it didn't matter what Mrs. Pruitt's intentions were. Alice thought of Joe Jacobs and felt a thrilling spin. She rapped at Avery's door with one knuckle, announcing, "It's Alice, with your medicine."

"Come in," he said in a normal voice; the pain seemed to have subsided on its own. He was lying on his side, and Alice had to set the glass on the night table in order to help him up. He gripped her hand hard and instructed her to put her arm around him. She pressed her hand into his back, damp with sweat, and returned his grip and eased him to a seated position, then let go of his hand to reach for the glass. As soon as she could, she stepped away from the bed and averted her eyes to the lace valance over the window while he drank. She would not make a good nurse, she thought, for merely the hint of sourness in the room made her feel queasy.

"Thanks, Alice," he said, setting the glass on the night table and leaning on one elbow, then the other, then onto his pillow. "Thanks for getting that for me."

"You're welcome," she said. All the ease had gone out of their conversation now that they were alone. Now that she had touched his weakness. And now that her entire life had changed on the walk from the pharmacy.

"You know what's the worst of it?" he asked, and Alice felt a leap of fear that he was going to confide something personal to her.

"What?" she asked.

"I don't know if it's ever going to get better. If I knew that, I could wait. I think I could really be patient. But thinking the rest of my life is going to be like this is hell." Alice wasn't sure what to say.

"I don't know if I'll ever be able to follow in my father's business or have a girl." Avery's eyes were closed, but tears were rolling over his cheeks to the pillow. Alice pulled a wicker chair from the corner and sat beside the bed and took one of his hands in both of hers. It was the only thing she could think to do, since she had no idea what to say. She sat there with him awhile. He squeezed her hand once, but he didn't open his eyes, and as the medicine began to work, his hand went limp in hers and he slept. Only then did she set it on the bedcovers and get up, leaving the door ajar as it had been before.

She was grateful for the fresh air of the hallway, where windows were open at both ends. She paused at the mirror near the top of the stairs to collect herself and saw reflected at her a face that betrayed nothing of her earlier conversation with the minister's son. What Mrs. Pruitt and Claudie would want to know was what had transpired during her long visit to Avery's bedroom; all of that she could tell them truthfully.

9

The harvest began on a Tuesday early in October. Frank came home the night before, smelling rank from a load of manure, and announced the picking would begin tomorrow. Ida was permitted to stay in the packing room rather than picking because of the baby, but in the absence of other work, Alice was out on a board the first day in her oldest dress and her work shoes, her long hair pulled back in a braid, precut lengths of string around her neck for bundling the bunches as she picked. Ida was hopeful that Alice would be allowed to pick for the season, offsetting Frank's debt and buying Ida time to find her sewing work. Alice was one of the fastest pickers, gathering up to twenty bunches of fifty blooms in an hour. She knew just how long to pick the stems and how to hook each flower head to the others so the bouquet would resemble a single mass rather than a bunch of tiny individual blossoms. Even Harold, normally parsimonious with praise, complimented her work that morning, and Alice looked pleased.

Some of Alice's old classmates were out picking by the second or third day with her. Many of them, like Alice, were no longer allowed to continue their education because their families needed the income. Oliver picked with his friends Alan Harris and George

Ellerby. And there was Joe Jacobs, more steady on the board than he had been at planting time, though not nearly as adept as Alice.

The season always began with a rush to supply the New York Horse Show, held every fall at Madison Square Garden. The bandstand would be festooned with garlands of violets, and the Swanley White violets were always included in the winners' rosettes. Every bunch picked in the week or two leading up to the show was leafed and booted and set in a galvanized tank of water to keep it fresh; then a hundred thousand blooms were transferred into shipping boxes and sent to the Coburg station for the journey to the city.

William had obtained complimentary passes to this year's horse show, enough to take everyone to the city: Frances and Norris, Harriet and her girls, and four tickets for Ida's family. Ida would have enjoyed the trip, but Mary and Jasper were too young to go. Frank said he had business with a wholesaler in the city, so he would accompany Oliver, Alice, and Reuben. Harold would stay home to manage the pickers from town, and Ida would have a quiet Saturday to start sewing Alice's new winter suit after the baking was done.

On the first Saturday in November, Frank and the children rose before dawn to do their chores and catch the seven-thirty train. When Jasper realized they were going without him, he cried inconsolably and was placated only by the promise of a walk to the Mortons' farm to visit their hound.

The day was dark and spitting rain, and in the dim afternoon the little ones napped a good long while. Ida was eager then to sew on Harriet's machine, which had been carried up to her house on loan. She hated to borrow it, but owning one was out of the question. Harriet had paid fifty dollars for this one several years ago. Even a portable hand-crank model, not nearly as enjoyable to sew on, would cost fifteen or twenty dollars. Harriet's sewing machine had a rich walnut cabinet with three drawers on either side, though as Ida snooped through them in search of spare machine needles, she found Harriet had taken no care to organize the drawers. They contained long, leftover wisps of thread, loose buttons and needle tubes and even items that had nothing to do with sewing at all: a book of matches, a handful of pennies, an old church bulletin.

Ida began by winding a bobbin and threading the machine. Then she started with Alice's circular skirt, pinning the right sides of the fabric together with straight pins at the table before sitting at the machine. She was always surprised at how smoothly it ran. It took almost no effort to keep the belt running—just a rhythmic nudge of her foot on the treadle. In one minute she had raced a straight half-inch seam down the edge of the fabric, which would have taken fifteen minutes to sew by hand. Truth be told, the machine's stitches were nicer: perfectly even and straight and snug. Within a half hour or so, Ida had pieced the entire skirt and had only to ask Alice to try it on that evening in order to pin the hem to the proper length and finish off the waistband. She set her irons on the stovetop to heat and laid out the pressboard to press the seams.

The jacket was more complicated. She had taken Alice's measurements and penciled them on the edge of the pattern, and as with the skirt, the pieces were already cut. This pattern had a triangular panel in the back, as well as fashionable full sleeves, which had to be gathered carefully at the shoulder. On the front, there would be a smart square collar and five buttons. Buttonholes were tedious to hand-sew, but Harriet's machine had a special attachment for making them.

Ida pinned the back pieces of the jacket together and sewed those seams while she waited for the irons to heat. Jasper stirred in the other room. She wouldn't complete the jacket today, but Harriet would want her machine returned soon. With cold weather approaching, she had her own sewing projects waiting, and she had lined up the seamstress from Tivoli to work with her the following week. Unlike Alice, who had done a total of five days' sewing work for Mrs. Nathan and was promised a few days more in the next month for Mrs. DuMont, the Tivoli seamstress was well known for her skill and had an established clientele in several towns. She would bring her own portable machine and help a woman work through all her sewing projects for the season, new clothing as well as old. She was particularly known for having the creative flair to take an old dress, rip out the seams, and remake it into something new and fashionable.

Ida didn't mind sewing the way she minded some other household chores. If she could work uninterrupted, it was a calming task that didn't involve muscle or dirt, and at the end she always had a new garment, or a mended one, to hold up with pride. She loved the rhythmic click of the shuttle and the quiet whir of the flywheel, and sometimes she hummed along. Her fingers, tucking and pinning and feeding the fabric, and her feet, pressing the treadle, were in constant motion, but her mind was entirely distracted from the worries of the day.

As the machine galloped up the long seam of the first sleeve, Jasper stirred again, and his dreamy mumbling was followed by a wail from Mary, first low and exploratory, then rising to a full, hungry cry. Ida hurried to the end of the first sleeve seam and snipped the threads, then forged ahead to the other sleeve, wanting to finish at a logical place. Those tricky gathers would have to wait. She zipped along the other sleeve, snipped the threads, then piled the unfinished jacket pieces on the table and went to fetch the children.

Mr. Morton came late in the afternoon to take care of the essential chores—Frank had done the same for him the day his wife had delivered her baby—and Ida gathered the eggs and fed the chickens. A bold squirrel sat near the coop, late-afternoon sunlight casting a halo at the edges of its tail. Ida paused to admire the peculiar light before stamping her foot in the dirt, attempting to scare the squirrel away. The chicken feed was surprisingly cold when she thrust her hand into it, and the squirrel watched her scatter it across the yard before he darted under the fence and was gone.

Ida and the children had a quiet supper. Then, when Jasper and Mary were in bed and Ida had finished her evening chores, she sat at Harriet's machine a few minutes more and gathered up the jacket sleeves and sewed and pressed the collar, leaving only the fitting of the front panels, the hems, and the buttons for another day.

As expected, Frank and the children were home late. Ida had nodded off in the rocker awaiting their return. She heard the wagon on the driveway and rose to light the lamp for them. She expected Reuben, at least, to be full of stories of the day, but the boys came in looking tired. Behind them, Frank was awake enough but quiet, as always. And where was Alice? Ida stood clutching the matchbox and watched Frank. Surely Alice wasn't stabling the horse herself in the dark. Had she stopped at the outhouse? The boys solemnly walked past Ida and up the stairs without a word.

"Where is Alice?" she asked in as steady a voice as she could manage.

"She's in the city."

Ida's heart surged, and she heard the rush of blood through her ears. "What is she doing in the city?"

"Going to work."

Ida threw the box of matches on the table, wishing she'd held something that would make more sound as it hit, a sound loud enough to rouse Frank out of his infuriating calm. "Look at me," she said fiercely, and he stepped up to the table opposite her and looked her right in the eye. "How could you do such a thing, Frank Fletcher, without consulting me first? How could you do such a thing?"

"The money is my concern," Frank said, the corners of his mouth turned down as if speaking were sour to him.

"And Alice's future is my concern."

Frank nodded slightly at this and hung up his hat.

"What kind of work?" she asked.

"Factory work."

"Oh, no, Frank!" she said, slapping her palms on the table.

"Five dollars a week," he said, "and no charge for a room."

"Where is she living?"

"The sister of a man I know, a flower wholesaler."

"A stranger! Frank, how could you?"

"She's not a stranger, Ida. I've worked with the man for years."

"And have you met her? Have you seen her home? Where is it?"

He took a crumpled scrap of paper from his pocket and handed her the address. The woman's name was Miss Sligh. There was no telling whether this was a private home or one of those terrible boardinghouses where girls were subjected to coarse living among lower-class workers with no morals or scruples.

"She didn't even pack a bag," Ida said. "How could you do such a thing?"

Frank walked over to the counter, lifted the tea towel covering the day's leftover bread, tore off a piece, and chewed it, ignoring her.

Ida grabbed the lantern, opened the door, and slammed it behind her. She thought she heard Jasper cry out, but she resolved to keep going all the way up the drive to William and Frances's front porch steps, where she stood in the sudden quiet.

Only the beech trees clung stubbornly to their leaves as if winter might be avoided. Everything else was stiff and bare—the trees, the house, even the smoke plowing straight up from the chimney in the windless night. William and Frances had been there, too. They had allowed Frank to leave his daughter alone in the city. They must have questioned his judgment. But what was there to demand, to say, to do now? No one would do anything.

Ida had heard the stories of factory girls whose hair and skirts and fingers got caught up in the machinery, and of the kind of people who worked beside them, the kind of life Alice would be exposed to. Their daughter faced all sorts of dangers about which Frank was either unaware or unconcerned.

Ida backed away from William's porch. She could rely on no one. She would write to Alice tonight, in care of Miss Sligh. If only Alice would tell her what was happening, she would think what she could do about it.

10

In the wild, the violets were spring flowers, surprising one with their shy, folded blooms in unexpected places: the base of a stone wall, the corner of a water trough, the edge of a wooded hill. In the beginning Frances had lamented the men's plan to grow them over the winter. Despite her coolheaded, businesslike demeanor, she was actually quite sentimental, as Ida had discovered one day early in their violet-growing experiment, when only the first three greenhouses banked the hill and talk had begun of building more in the spring. The two of them had been sitting on the veranda, and Frances had spotted a clump of November violets in the browning grass. She had hurried into her shed, returning with a trowel, and Ida had watched in disbelief as she attacked the plant, clawing it out of the earth and carrying it like a pile of dung to the waste heap at the rear of her garden.

"It's bad luck if they bloom in the fall," Frances had said when she sat down again. She'd picked the wedges of dirt from under her fingernails and tossed them at her feet. At the time Ida had believed this display to be about the loss of Frances's baby a few months before, born just five months into her pregnancy. It would be the last baby she would have. However, since then Ida had heard the same superstition from Mrs. Tenney, whose husband also grew violets.

Shortly after Alice's disappearance to the city, Ida came across just such a row of November violets tufted at the base of her garden wall like the ruffle on a skirt. Her senses were suddenly keen as a cat's; she heard every clank and call from the greenhouses and felt the suggestion of the sun's warmth on her bare head. She smelled the bacon from breakfast on her hands and the heavy coal smoke from the first stokehouses lighting up over the hill. In her mouth was the taste of distress. Taking no chances, she fetched a shovel and worked quickly, slicing it under the base of the wall with a firm press of her foot and working it like a lever to uproot and destroy the intruders. At a penny apiece, they were worth nearly a day's wages for any of the pickers who toiled this moment in the greenhouses. But Ida wanted them gone.

"Ma!" Jasper called out from the back door, his little voice striking the same commanding tone as Reuben's and Oliver's when they called her.

"Be right there, love!" she called out, and assailed the wild violets again, tossing the uprooted plants in a mound that she would carry off to the weed pile later, so they couldn't take root again. There had been no reply from Alice in the nearly three weeks since Ida had sent her letter. As she stabbed the shovel under the last renegade flowers, she resolved it was time to make a trip to New York herself.

But that same week Frank came home with a letter. He tossed it, like ordinary mail from her sister, on the counter where Ida was chopping vegetables for supper. The single sheet of paper was folded in thirds and had already been removed from its envelope. The letter was addressed directly to Ida, and she was irritated that Frank had opened it, though of course he had the right to open her mail. He was probably concerned about Alice as well and glad to hear from her. Ida wiped her hands on her apron and read with greed the few short sentences penned in Alice's petite and precise hand. The letter didn't say much, but it said enough: Alice was working hard. She had a clean bed of her own and three meals a day. She missed Ida and the boys, and she wished to send Jasper especially a kiss.

Frank opened the door of the range to poke at the fire, which always annoyed Ida when she was cooking. "I'd like to go to the city and check on Alice," she said to his back. "I could travel with Frances the next time she goes."

"She's fine," Frank said. "Read the letter."

"I want to see that she's fine for myself. Harriet will take Jasper, and I can ask Mrs. Morton to take the baby for the day. She's nursing her own, and I think she'd be willing. I've thought it all through." Ida worried that she sounded too eager. If Frank heard a weakness in her, he would thwart her plans.

"If you're so concerned, I'll go down and check on her myself," he said, slamming the door of the range and scattering ash on the floor.

"When?" she pressed.

"Soon."

Ida held the letter up before her like a mirror, wishing she could see more than ink on the page. She read it again, lingering on each word, but it said no more to her than it had the first time. Alice had a bed and three meals. She had paper and pen and a stamp and an envelope. She would be all right.

A week or so later, Frank did take another trip to the city. Ida sent Alice's new winter skirt and jacket and a few other things with him, along with a newsy letter.

The lantern was lit, the children were in bed, the boys were in their attic room, and Ida was writing to her sister when she heard Frank's wagon return. She expected he would take Trip and Trudy in first, but he came directly in the house. She tossed him a cursory greeting, trying not to appear too eager for news of Alice.

When she looked up, he stood in the doorway, holding a bundle at his chest, and a gust of grief blew into her as she imagined what it might be: Prissy, run over in the lane or trampled by the horses. Then he stepped toward her and held it out and said, "This one's name is Anabel."

"What?" she asked, though she could see well enough now what it was. A sleeping baby. Another baby come up from the city. Frank stood before her, holding out the bundle, expecting her to take it.

"What in blazes do you think you're doing?" she asked.

"I'm bringing us some more income," he said.

"Have you gone and lost your senses, Frank Fletcher? I am already nursing a baby!"

He tried again to hand the baby to her, but she dropped her pen and put her hands in her lap. "I said, have you gone and lost your senses?"

"Watch your tongue," he said quietly. "Watch your tongue and take the baby."

"I shall not take the baby."

"Then I guess I'll just put her out for the night," he said, turning toward the door as if he would do it.

"And I guess her parents will be after you for murder in the morning," Ida said, though she was losing her resolve not to touch the bundle.

"You can suckle two at a time. It's why God gave a woman two," Frank said, nodding at her bosom.

"God gave me two breasts so one could have a rest each time," Ida said, though she had nursed two babies before. She had only just weaned Jasper. She stood, scraping her chair on the kitchen floor. "You're taking advantage," she said. "It's too much work. And thanks to you, Alice isn't here to help." She would nurse the baby. Of course she would nurse the baby. But Frank must hear her fury.

"You know nothing, Ida," Frank said. "You don't know what I put up with day in and day out."

"I know enough."

"No, you don't. There is nothing more important than getting out from under them now. Nothing."

"What about Alice? Did you see Alice?"

Still holding the baby like a bag of beans in the crook of his arm, Frank reached into his coat pocket and held out his other hand. In it was Ida's mother's locket, the one she'd given to Alice. "She asked me to give this to you for safekeeping," he said. "She broke it and she can't wear it anymore."

Ida saw as she took the locket from him that the chain had snapped two or three inches from the clasp. A jeweler would be needed to repair it. She wondered how the break had happened. She opened it to find that the lock of her father's honey-brown hair it had once held was missing. "Is she all right?" she asked, closing her fingers around the locket.

"She said to tell you she's well. She's happy to be earning some money. Take the baby," he said, holding the bundle toward her.

Ida dropped the locket in her apron pocket and took the baby. Like the others when they'd arrived, this baby weighed next to nothing. The sharp odor of a soiled diaper made Ida wonder how long it had been since someone had attended to her.

"Where is she from, Frank?" she asked, without even peeking into the bundle.

"The city," he said.

"Where in the city?"

"Someone a friend of mine knows."

"Her mama die in childbirth, too?" She wasn't sure why she was doubting him. The baby must have a family to pay him, otherwise why would he bring it home? But what he planned to do with this bit of extra money, how he imagined he would ever "get out from under" his brothers when he had never managed to in over twenty years, was a mystery.

"I don't know what happened to her mama," he said flatly.

Ida nodded slowly, her eyes pegged on him, though he wouldn't return her gaze. Part of her wanted nothing more to do with him.

"I'll be needing the whole bed, with two to nurse at night," she said. "You can sleep upstairs in Alice's bed."

Frank nodded as if to acknowledge she had won a point against him. Then he said, "For one week I'll sleep upstairs. I reckon by then you'll figure something else out."

An hour after she arrived, Anabel began to scream. After attempting unsuccessfully to get the baby to latch on and nurse, Ida slung her over her shoulder and began a bouncing walk round and round the kitchen. Upstairs, the boys slammed their door shut, and in the downstairs bedroom Mary picked up the cry, but Anabel's screaming went on, and Ida continued to walk and bounce, walk and bounce.

Finally Frank wrenched open the upstairs door and called from the top of the stairs, "Quiet that baby down!"

"You brought her home, Frank!" Ida shouted. "Well done!" Never had she spoken to her husband in such a way, but doing so in her anger and frustration gave her an unexpected thrill, and for a few steps she stomped her feet to emphasize that she was through with listening to him.

Anabel shrieked on. Finally Ida took her into the bedroom and laid her on the bed and unwrapped her to take a closer look. She was slightly older than Mary had been when she arrived, but not by much, and not much bigger. Her hands and feet had a bluish cast beneath her translucent skin, and she folded her skinny knees up to her chest as she screamed, a sign of colic. Ida tried placing her on her lap, rolling her on her tummy and rubbing her back, but the screaming went on for another half hour before the infant wore herself into a fitful sleep.

None of her own babies had been screamers, but Ida had heard of those who were—one of Harriet's girls had been—and she knew it was not a single occurrence. As she had expected, the baby was up three times in the night, waking Mary with her, and she nursed only fitfully, so in the morning, when the noise of breakfast awoke her, she was hungry and screaming again. Ida left her in the bedroom and closed the door, keeping Mary and Jasper in the kitchen with her while she sliced the bread and fried the eggs and brewed the coffee for the others. Frank glared several times at the bedroom door during breakfast but said nothing. As soon as he and the boys were gone, Ida left the dirty dishes on the table and went into the bedroom to try to nurse and soothe the new baby again.

However, any soothing Ida managed lasted only a short time before Anabel was twisting her body, throwing out her arms, and screaming again. There was no living with it. On the third morning, deprived of sleep and patience and exhausted by the new regimen of nursing, which had left little time for anything else, Ida walked across the lane to Harriet's, left Jasper and Mary with her, and drove with the baby into town.

Dr. Van de Klerk was out, so she left a note saying that she needed help. Because she was already in the village, she called at Mrs. Schreiber's house. By the time she rang the bell, Anabel was asleep in the basket.

Mrs. Schreiber answered the door in her apron, and Ida saw she was busy cooking for her boarders. She felt sorry to disturb this morning work, but Mrs. Schreiber took Ida by the hand and guided her through the front door. "She's a dear one, isn't she," Mrs. Schreiber said, leaning over to see the baby in the basket, which Ida had set down on the carpet. "Oh—it's a different baby, isn't it?"

"Yes, just up from the city this week. She cries and cries," and then Ida was crying, too. She made no move to wipe her face, and Mrs. Schreiber took her hand again, saying, "Leave the baby there," as if she understood that Ida secretly wished to do so and walk much farther away than through the French doors into the dining room. Mrs. Schreiber pulled out a dining chair and Ida sat. Through watery eyes, she saw the baskets of lush houseplants hung in the sunny front corners of the room and standing to the sides of the deep windows. Mrs. Schreiber's life, in which she had time to care for so many decorative plants, looked like heaven to Ida. She wiped her face with her gloved hands. Mrs. Schreiber sat opposite her, watching.

"It may be colic," Ida said. "The doctor is out. I thought you might have something for it."

"Oh, two of mine had the colic something terrible," said Mrs. Schreiber. "It's about as hard on the mother as it must be on the baby."

"What can I do?"

Mrs. Schreiber shook her head. "Not much, I'm afraid. The best is for you to eat as bland a diet as possible. Bread and milk, fruit if you can get it. Not much meat, and cook your vegetables until they're soft as can be."

For a second Ida thought she was in her mother's parlor, and recognizing it as the tag of a dream, she shook her head and straightened herself.

"You poor dear," Mrs. Schreiber said. "You're exhausted." Then she disappeared into the kitchen.

While Mrs. Schreiber was gone, one of the boarders wandered into the room. Ida was too tired to care who saw her sprawled in the straight-backed chair, but the man reared back as if he'd seen an apparition and hurried up the stairs. A few minutes later, Mrs. Schreiber returned with a small paper bag.

"Try brewing yourself a tea of this," she said. "If you can get the baby to take some cold, do that, too. See if it helps. I wish I could offer you more."

Ida reached out for the bag. "How much do I owe you?" she asked.

"Five cents, whenever you've a chance," said Mrs. Schreiber. "But only if it works."

"Thank you," Ida said, near tears again, for she had to stand and fetch that basket from the hall. This exhaustion wasn't the same as the exhaustion she felt at the end of a day of picking violets. She could always rub her muscles with liniment and sleep off that ache to work another day. This exhaustion was hung on desperation, dragging her down like a sinker through water until she felt help-less to ever reach the surface of normality.

"You could try one other thing," Mrs. Schreiber said. "With one of mine, a friend recommended a sling. It helped a bit. You can make it out of a scrap of fabric or an old sheet." She glanced around the dining room and picked up a cloth napkin to demonstrate. "Imagine this were large enough to tie around you. Fold a large piece of cloth in a triangle like so, and tie it across your front like a sash, with a knot on your back. Nice and tight, so the baby nestles in close to you. Carry her everywhere, while you're working—not by the stove, mind you, but everywhere else. That might help as well."

"Thank you," Ida said. "I shall." Her tears fell again, profuse as milk, but Mrs. Schreiber paid them no mind. She had likely seen many neighbors at their worst.

"The baby's still asleep," she said. "You lie down here a few minutes." She indicated a couch across the room near the fire-place. Ida needed no further invitation. "I'll take care of the baby," Mrs. Schreiber said, but Ida was already lying down, her head on a velvet-covered pillow. It seemed only an instant before Mrs. Schreiber was pressing her shoulder, and Ida could hear the screams of a large bird—no, the baby—and sat up to find that the light had shifted.

"There's one hour you've caught up," Mrs. Schreiber said. "I'm sorry I couldn't give you more. Would you like to nurse her here? There's a private room in the back."

Ida thought with sudden panic about Mary, who would be hungry and wailing at Harriet's house. But she didn't want to drive through town with these inhuman screams coming from her rig.

The private room was Mrs. Schreiber's office, with an open roll-top desk piled with papers and a bookcase holding an eclectic collection of volumes on ancient remedies, Chinese medicine, German history, poetry, gardening, philosophy, and a few romance novels all in a hodgepodge. When Mrs. Schreiber pulled out the desk chair, it nearly touched the wall behind it. "It's the old pantry," she apologized. "But it's a good place to escape. They never find me in here." Though she was speaking of her boarders, she had raised a houseful of children as well, and in her measured smile, Ida saw she was not alone.

At home, as soon as she had nursed Mary, Ida took an old sheet from one of the attic trunks, tore it to size, and bundled Anabel in it, tied firmly against her rib cage. It wasn't so convenient as it could have been if she weren't nursing another baby, but it did calm Anabel somewhat, and it allowed Ida to go about the rest of her day with her hands free to do the chores and mind the other children.

Before supper that evening, Dr. Van de Klerk pulled up in his wagon. The December wind was sharp, and night was gathering as the pickers dispersed for the day. From the kitchen window, Ida watched the doctor make his way through them as if they were dry leaves blown in his path. She was grateful he had arrived in time to see her without Frank present; it would take him another hour at least to check all the fires and come in.

The doctor raised his eyebrows at the sling and humphed when he realized it wasn't Mary she carried but another baby.

"How is the other one?" he asked, glancing around the room.

"She's right here," Ida said, pointing to the old cradle on the kitchen floor, where Mary slept soundly. "She's fine. Growing strong."

The doctor nodded. "And this one?"

Tears welled up, and Ida swallowed hard to contain them. "This one screams," she said. "She won't nurse well, and she doesn't sleep much. Evening is worst, but it happens on and off all day."

She leaned the sling on the kitchen table until it took the weight of the baby, then reached behind her neck to untie the knot and drop the ends of the sheet.

"You don't want me to wake her, then," he said.

"No, please."

He reached gently under the baby's dress to touch her belly and, noticing the blue of her hands and feet, he touched them as well. "Colic, probably," he said. "But there could be something wrong with her heart. I don't care for the look of her extremities. How much does she nurse?"

"A few minutes at a time, and then she wriggles away. I nurse her the same times as I nurse Mary, six or seven times a day, and more at night for this one."

The doctor stared at Ida. "And you, Mrs. Fletcher? How are you faring?"

Ida swallowed hard again. If she were able to step back and think, she could say it would pass. All babies grow up, quicker than expected, and Anabel would, too. Or she wouldn't—a thought Ida couldn't entertain. Dr. Van de Klerk took her by the elbow and guided her into a kitchen chair. Jasper dropped his wooden ship and came to the table's edge to watch her. The doctor sat across from her.

"You need a rest," he said. "What ever possessed you to take on another baby?"

Idiot! Ida thought. She had been prepared to confide in him, but to think she had chosen this for herself? She stood and grabbed a dishcloth from the sink on which to dry her eyes.

"One of these babies needs to go home," Dr. Van de Klerk said. "Or both of them. And then you mustn't take any more."

Ida turned to look at him. "You'll need to speak to my husband about that," she said.

On the table, Anabel was stirring, and Ida wrapped her up again, fearful she would roll off. The doctor made no move to help her as she gathered up the sling and fastened it behind her neck. Instead, he stood and collected his coat and hat. Then he reached into his bag and placed a brown bottle on the kitchen table.

"You can try this for the baby. Just a drop if she can't be quieted."

"What is it?"

"Laudanum. You could try it yourself, but it may pass into your milk, and the other baby will get some."

"Thank you," Ida said.

The doctor nodded. After he stepped out into the icy night, she placed the bottle high in a cupboard where Jasper couldn't reach it. She would not call the doctor again.

11

The Christmas season was always busy. Violets were part of festive decorations everywhere, and with so many parties, corsages were in demand. Ida hardly noticed the rush. Since Anabel had come, she'd slept no more than two hours at a stretch, with nary a rest in the daytime, for even if the baby was calmed and sleeping, neglected chores were waiting. Mrs. Schreiber's tea soothed Ida, at least, but whether it helped the baby was hard to say. Perhaps she was a bit easier to calm during the day, but her screaming fits still ran from suppertime through the evening hours. Once Ida tried the doctor's laudanum, and Anabel dropped into a deep, listless sleep. Exhausted, Ida slept, too, but later she awakened in a panic, for the baby hadn't cried. Fearful that Anabel would never wake up, Ida ran out into the snow, scooped a handful into a bowl, and rubbed it on the baby's arms and legs, raising a pathetic moan that eventually spread into the familiar scream. "Should have let her sleep," Frank muttered, and behind those words Ida heard his real thoughts: if the baby never awakened, it would be a blessing.

A screaming baby brought evil thoughts into the home, yet Ida's greatest fear was that a child might perish in her care. However, in the case of Anabel, no one but Ida seemed concerned. Frank had not bothered to answer her questions about the baby's family or to mail the letter she'd written to Anabel's unnamed parents.

Despite her exhaustion, Ida had continued to write to Alice several times each week in care of Miss Sligh, but the letters had all gone unanswered. This was unlike Alice, who had written long, literary epistles to her cousins in Ohio. Finally Ida asked Frank again about the address to which she'd been writing.

"You've transposed the numbers," he said, pointing with a grimy finger at the entry in her address book. "The four and the two are switched."

"Wouldn't my letters have been returned, then?" she asked, but Frank merely shrugged.

She tried again, mailing a letter with a package containing a scarf and a book of poetry for Christmas, gifts too dear for her budget.

On Christmas Eve, the temperature dropped into the teens, and a crooked wind knocked around the house. Ida stuffed rags along the windowsills and under the doors and hung a curtain between the front rooms to keep the kitchen warmer. The fire burned all day, but as soon as one stepped outside, no matter how bundled, the cold pried easily under layers of cotton and wool and numbed the fingers and toes. The boys and Frank wrapped scarves around their faces and went about their work. Ida was glad her work was in the kitchen.

After supper, she helped the boys bundle extra layers over their Sunday best so they could ride into town for the Sunday school Christmas exercises. Ida would have liked to join them. There would be singing and recitations and a visit from Saint Nicholas, who would bring something special for each of the children. Nora Hoskins had written a poem for the occasion, and Ida had hoped to hear her read it. But it was too cold a night for the babies, so Ida watched the sleigh bump down the driveway, lamps swinging wildly as it navigated the fresh, snowy drifts, then steady as

Frank and the children followed Harold's family down the lane into the dark.

Ida felt so forlorn, with the wind pushing at the house like a bully, that after the babies were asleep, she lit some fancy candles she'd kept for a special occasion. As she rocked in the kitchen with her needlework, she sang some favorite carols and breathed in the honeyed scent of the candles, trying to chase the darkness from the edges of things. The irregular orange candlelight flickered surprising patterns on the walls and the beamed ceiling, and everything in her own kitchen looked different. Maybe the places she counted as so familiar all had the possibility of being this way—completely changed and unexpected. The dark room with the jumping light seemed like a huge pot stirred by a mysterious, unseen hand, as if a spell were being cast, and though Ida couldn't say whether it would be a good spell or an evil one, she didn't feel afraid. The crazy shadows told her: if she could only see things differently, she might find her way.

Christmas morning fell on a Sunday, and though it was cold as the Arctic, sunlight skimmed the surface of the earth. Cold or no, Ida would not miss church. Again the family packed into the sleigh—the three boys in back with Mary in her basket and Anabel up front with Ida and Frank. "You're not wearing that thing to church," Frank said when he saw the sling tied under her wrap.

"I'll take it off when we get there," Ida said, and she did, for when they arrived, Anabel was asleep.

The white clapboard church was bright as the snow, its stained-glass windows tall and dark from the outside but casting jeweled light within. Evergreen garlands tied by the Ellerbys, whose farm included a hardy stand of Scotch pines, festooned the ends of the pews, and the dominie was wearing a new black broadcloth suit with a silk four-in-hand tie. Though Dominie Jacobs often preached in a resonant bass that made his parishioners fear the darkness, this Christmas service called for his quieter tone, the one

Ida recognized from his private prayers with her and one she had heard in Joe's morning greetings. She spotted him sitting beside his mother a few rows in front of her. When they stood to sing "It Came Upon the Midnight Clear," he turned to scan the congregation, and his gaze lit on her. In the instant it took him to nod politely, she saw a curious disappointment in his face, and then she realized—he was looking for Alice.

Toward the end of the sermon, Anabel began to fuss, and without waiting for an escalation, Ida slipped out the end of the pew and hurried to the lecture room to bind her into the sling. It was quiet and dark and cold there, in gloomy contrast to the sanctuary, and Ida's mind wandered into darker territory. What if she were to leave Anabel in the narthex, where a hundred people would see her shortly on their way out of the church? What if she were to drive off in the sleigh to New York? She would drive straight to this Miss Sligh's address—never mind how she would find it—and if Alice wasn't there, she would search until she found her. Together they would ride out of the city and find a place of their own. It wasn't even a good daydream because, aside from the impossibility of taking the horses and sleigh so far, it involved leaving Jasper behind. She and Alice would be hard pressed to earn a living on their own. And there were Oliver and Reuben, and Mary. She left Frank unaccounted for. This wasn't the solution. She thought again of the candlelight in her kitchen. How could she see things differently?

The organ sounded, and the floorboards creaked as the congregation stood. They were singing "Joy to the World," and soon they would be spilling out onto the snowy lawn with Christmas greetings for one another. Ida started up the hall with Anabel, who had quieted somewhat, and stood in the back of the church. The low notes of the organ beat heavily on the chorus—"Let-heav'n-and-na-ture-sing"—and she felt the music thrum through her body. Then her neighbors were patting shoulders and shaking hands and massing toward the church doors, and Ida stepped aside at the base of the balcony stairs to avoid the crush. Oliver worked his way to her and deposited Mary in the basket at Ida's feet. "A bunch of us are taking a sleigh ride," he announced, then wove through the crowd and out the front door.

Dominie and Mrs. Jacobs stood at the door to greet the departing congregation with Joe and their visiting daughters beside them, one modestly hiding her first pregnancy beneath an old woolen cape of her mother's that Ida recognized from their younger days.

"Mrs. Fletcher," a voice said from behind Ida. It was Claudie, alone and looking worried. "I haven't heard a thing from Alice. Have you?"

Ida had given Alice's address to Claudie the first time she saw her after Alice's move, but it was the address with the transposed numbers. Still, if Alice hadn't written Claudie on her own, something was amiss.

"I did get one short letter from her," Ida said, but fear fluttered in her throat. Claudie was toying nervously with the ties on her red cape. "I think the address I gave you was wrong. I'll write it down correctly and give it to you next time I see you."

"All right," Claudie said, but she made no move to leave.

"Her father saw her just a couple of weeks ago," Ida continued, as much to reassure herself as Claudie. "She's doing fine."

"I don't think she's fine," Claudie said. "Otherwise she'd write to me."

"She's probably working very hard," Ida said. "You keep writing to her, and I think you'll hear back."

Claudie seemed to sense that Ida's confidence was false, but she nodded and said, "Thank you, Mrs. Fletcher. Merry Christmas." She smiled politely and hurried to catch up to her family, who had already left the building. Feeling dizzy, Ida leaned against the cold plaster wall and took a deep breath. The weight of Anabel's sling pulled on her shoulder, and she wasn't certain she could pick up Mary's basket on her own. She was grateful to see Mrs. Schreiber moving toward her.

"How is the tea?" Mrs. Schreiber asked as she reached out her gloved hand to stroke the mottled top of Anabel's head.

"It helps," Ida said, swallowing hard, though what she meant was "not much."

"What helps the most is they grow up. They grow out of it," Mrs. Schreiber said. "You'll see. By spring it will be better."

"I hope it will," Ida said. "Thank you."

Without being asked, Mrs. Schreiber picked up Mary's basket and helped Ida toward the door.

Reuben had been granted the coveted job of ringing the bell this morning. He gripped the thick rope above his head, pulling hard in a squat and then nearly losing contact with the floor as the rope flew up into the belfry and the bell rang out once, then again on the rope's descent. Its sound was muffled from the narthex, but when Ida stepped out on the bluestone path, she heard the bell ring loud and true. She stared up at the steeple, standing bright against a cerulean sky, and held tight to that clear song, hoping it might guide her.

Christmas dinner was always held at William and Frances's house. For the holiday, the workers had strung swags of evergreen along the porch roof, and large stone planters of holly and English ivy flanked the door. The entry hall smelled of gravy and warm rolls. A small fir tree at the front door was decorated with paper ornaments in the shapes of Saint Nicholas, angels, girls in pretty fur-trimmed coats, and even a bulldog like Captain Anderson's with a red bow tied around his neck. Jasper was stopped short by this little tree, and in her holiday mood, Frances allowed him to finger the delicate treasures hung from its branches.

In the parlor, an eight-foot evergreen was more elaborately decked with colored paper and popcorn garlands, baskets of nuts and dried fruit, lead stars, angels with gold leaf wings, and German icicles made of glass. At the tips of half the branches were pinned slender red candles, which would be lit for only a short time while all the guests were nearby and a servant stood ready with a bucket of water. A fire played in the marble fireplace, and its light infused the glass ornaments with color. Christmas sheet music sat on the parlor organ, indicating they might have to listen to a concert later.

Frances's housemaid wore an Irish lace collar on her dress. She was stationed at the front door to take hats and wraps and capes and be sure no one tracked snow or mud on the Brussels carpet. Additional servants had been hired for the day, mostly friends and relations of Cook's, for after the family dinner, many guests would be dropping in for afternoon drinks and cigars, music, and charades. The children—Reuben and Jasper, Harriet's youngest girl, and even the babies—were taken into the sitting room, where they were to be served and entertained separately. Norris and Oliver and Harriet's two older girls were permitted to join the adults for Christmas dinner. All four of the young cousins began the meal sitting stiff and quiet, taking care to use the proper fork at the proper time. Oliver answered inquiries on his opinion of the current crop with the politeness of a gentleman, and Ida smiled as she watched him speak. Despite his sometimes misguided enthusiasm, he was becoming a fine young man. He knew what he was dealing with now, and he wasn't going to be brought low by them. She wanted to cheer for him as the girls cheered the boys on the sidelines of their baseball games.

Of the four cousins, Norris was the least impressed by the formality of the meal, and after an early pretense of politeness, he fell into his usual manner of eating too quickly and pushing out his chair, arms folded, waiting impatiently to be excused. Frances did not correct him. Ida was of a mind to do it for her, but she knew better than to antagonize on this occasion.

When talk turned to President McKinley and the Philippines, the boys perked up, though they held back from contributing to the conversation between William and Harold. Only Frank couldn't resist attempting to extinguish their glowing assessments of the president and his policies. "Waste of twenty million dollars, if you ask me," he said, referring to the agreed-upon purchase price of the Philippines as part of the peace treaty. "McKinley's advisers have been smoking too many Cuban cigars."

The others laughed at this, but Frank plunged on. "Mark my words, we'll be in the middle of a war against the Philippines before you know it." This last comment the other men ignored, but the boys took it up with excitement.

"Maybe Oliver and I will hop a ship this time, then," Norris said.

"You'll do nothing of the sort," said Frances.

"The new Rough Riders, huh?" Norris said, poking Oliver, who smiled politely through a mouthful of potatoes.

"Those men were unique to their commander," William said. "Now that Roosevelt's got himself a house in Albany, I'm afraid that glory is over." He cocked his head on the word "glory" to emphasize his questionable opinion of Governor Roosevelt.

"Who knows what kind of rowdy politics we'll be seeing?" Harold asked, and the men all laughed again.

"Roosevelt for president!" Norris shouted, his fork in the air, and the men roared. Frances looked as if she might tackle him. Ida caught Oliver's eye and was shocked to see him wink at her.

"Kindly save the rest of this conversation for the study," Frances said, but Ida was sorry to hear it end. She had her own opinions about what she'd been reading in the newspaper. For one, she feared William Jennings Bryan was right that the imperialistic

move to take over the Philippines was premature and required
more consideration, though she wouldn't say so in this mixed
company. Still, it was always fun to see the men get worked up at
Frances's expense.

With war and peace off limits, business talk was allowed, and
the conversation moved to the duller topics of the new variety
of violet the Tenneys were growing and whether it would prove
hardy enough; potential new wholesalers in Boston and Philadelphia; a planned trip to the Lord & Burnham greenhouse factory in
Irvington; and how a blizzard that had hit at Thanksgiving had af-
fected business. That same storm had caused the disastrous wreck
of a paddle steamer called the *Portland,* on which one of the families from the Episcopal Church had died, and they all debated the
safety of these vessels. Harriet reckoned she would be taking the
train to New York City from now on, but Harold countered that
the *Portland* had foolishly gone out in the storm and was in the
open sea when she sank.

"And how is Alice doing?" Frances asked. It was clear she
didn't want to speak of the *Portland* tragedy any further, for she
had known well the woman from her church who had perished.

Ida turned to Frank and waited for a response. It took him a
moment to realize she would not speak for him, and he looked
up to find them all watching him. He chewed and swallowed a
mouthful of food and took a drink of water from his crystal goblet.
Finally he said, "She's well."

"What is she doing?" Frances asked, her hand suspended over
the nearly empty gravy boat, which she'd been about to hand to
one of the serving girls. It seemed she had asked the first question
innocently enough but had been stopped by the sense that something was strange.

The turkey lay in tatters on its silver tray, the bowls of turnips
and Cook's special creamed onions sat nearly empty on their trivets,
and the white embroidered tablecloth was strewn with crumbs. Un-

daunted by either Frances's question or the fact that everyone else had finished eating, Frank cut another slice of turkey on his plate and mopped a forkful in a puddle of gravy. "Factory work," he said.

"What kind of factory work?" Frances asked. She had placed her hands in her lap and was staring at Frank, whose head was bowed to his plate. Harriet glanced at Ida, who kept her eyes set on Frank. *Yes,* she wanted to echo. *What kind of factory work?*

"Something a friend in the city got for her," Frank said.

"But you don't know what?"

"Really, Frances," William said, and Frances shot him a haughty expression that Ida had seen her use often on others but never on her husband.

"I should think, dear, that if you sent your daughter off to work in a factory, you would want to know what kind of work she would be doing. Wouldn't you?"

William raised his eyebrows noncommittally and returned to his glass of wine.

"A glove factory," Frank said. "Ladies' gloves."

Ida could see he had invented this answer, and Frances had taken no stock in his response, either. She nodded to the girl to take the dishes away, and the conversation moved on. Harriet tried to meet Ida's eyes again, but Ida watched out the window. The muted afternoon light had hushed the landscape. If she were to run out into the snow and scream for help, she thought, not a soul on this dead earth would hear her.

A young woman came in from the kitchen and touched Ida's shoulder, startling her back into the room, and whispered that she was needed to nurse the babies. By the time she returned, dessert had been eaten and the family had moved into the parlor, where the tree's candles had been lit and guests had begun to arrive.

"I saved you a piece of cake, Mrs. Fletcher," Cook said to Ida as she passed. "It's on the sideboard."

"Thank you," Ida said, and after greeting a few neighbors in the front hall, she retreated to the dining room, where she found the last piece of a white-frosted cake topped with sugared violet petals. She sat alone with her cake and a cup of coffee, but within a few minutes Harriet came looking. She closed the door behind her and pulled out a chair opposite Ida at the empty dining table. The cloth had been brushed clean, the only traces of the meal a few spots of red wine and gravy.

"It'll be quite a crowd today," Harriet said.

Cook brought Harriet a fresh cup of coffee, and for a while they sat together in silence, listening to the hum of conversation in the parlor, punctuated occasionally by the men's laughter.

"She's not in a glove factory, is she," Harriet said at last.

"I don't know where she is," Ida admitted. "I hope to hear from her when she gets her Christmas package."

Harriet pushed her coffee cup away and folded her hands on the soiled tablecloth. She stared over Ida's shoulder at the portrait of the colonel who had owned this land 150 years earlier, someone else's ancestor. William had bought the painting from one of the wealthy river families. Opposite Ida's seat at the table was the étagère that held Frances's collection of seashells, a reminder of her privileged childhood summers in Newport. On the center of the top shelf was a conch shell the size of a woman's hat. Ida had always had the childlike urge to hold that shell up to her ear. What might it whisper to her?

"Harold told me they've asked Frank to repay his debt in full by spring," Harriet said.

This news should have panicked Ida, but it felt more like a bullet grazing past her ear. "Go on," she said.

"He must pay by the first of June, or they'll take your house. To get Norris started."

"That's impossible, of course," Ida said. "They've been paying him as a farmhand all these years. We never get ahead enough to pay the debt."

"I know," Harriet said, and her cheeks flared red as the fire. She looked ready to fight the men.

"Well, then, what are their plans for us when he can't pay?"

"Mr. Tenney has agreed to take Frank up at his farm."

"The Tenneys already have a foreman."

"As a worker," Harriet said. "And they have a small house to rent."

Ida knew the house she meant—a two-room shack that was fit only for summer use. "We should go now," she said, "before they take away our horses and wagon, too."

"Frank has been paying them extra every month," Harriet said. "Maybe if he's paying them in good faith—"

"He's always paid them in good faith."

"I know, Ida," Harriet said, reaching out but not touching her. "And you're working so hard to keep up. It's not right. I know."

A thick lump was rising like dough in Ida's gut, just below her breastbone. A group of men coughed and choked with laughter in the parlor. She pressed her right hand to her abdomen, realizing she'd fastened her corset too tightly.

"I think," Harriet continued, "as long as he's paying them more than usual, they could be convinced to be more lenient."

"They want the house for Norris," Ida repeated. It was becoming more clear to her, Frank's growing desperation these past few months, sending Alice to the city, bringing more babies to nurse.

"Norris can continue to live up here," Harriet said. "Until he marries, which could be quite some time." She flashed a wicked smile.

"Quite," Ida agreed.

"I thought you should know," Harriet said. "I wasn't sure Frank ... He's so quiet, I wasn't sure ..."

"He hadn't told me," Ida said. "You were right to tell me. Thank you."

Harriet drew her cup of coffee to her. Ida watched her take a sip of the lukewarm drink and dab the corner of her mouth with her napkin.

"Harriet," Ida said. "About Alice . . ."

"Oh, Ida," Harriet said, and Ida was surprised to hear the compassion in her voice. Harriet had never been cruel to her in the way Frances had, but she had never been a confidante, either. That she had gone out of her way to deliver the news about Frank's debt made it seem, however, that she might be willing to do more.

"I can't go to the city to check on her myself," Ida said. "Whenever I ask Frank, he says he'll do it. But I want to see for myself that she's all right. And now, with two babies . . ."

"I can't feed the babies for you," Harriet said with a laugh, though Ida was in no mood for teasing.

"No, but I was wondering. Perhaps the next time you go to the city . . ."

"Oh, yes!" Harriet said. "Give me the address. I'll be taking Elizabeth to B. Altman in a few weeks for her birthday. Is it far from Sixth Avenue?"

"I don't know where it is," Ida said. "Do you think you'll be able to find her?"

"Give me the address," Harriet said. "We'll find her."

The doorknob turned, and a servant peeked into the room. "Your presence is requested in the parlor," she said to them, then withdrew.

"Shall we join the others?" Harriet said.

In the parlor, every seat was occupied. The men were standing about with unlit cigars, eager to be dismissed into William's study, where they could smoke and talk at leisure. Ida said hello to Mrs. Nathan and a few other women she knew from Underwood and then slipped into the corner, where Frank stood alone.

"May I have your attention, please," William called out from in front of the fireplace. Then, obviously feeling the heat on the seat of his trousers, he let out a comical whoop and took a large step forward, eliciting a laugh from his friends. He gestured to Norris, who walked across the room to join his father with a serious expression.

"My wife and I have been hearing about the attractions of the state of Florida recently," William began, "and we have decided to take a well-deserved vacation next month to spend several weeks soaking in the sun while the rest of you lot are in the belly of winter." He said this with a grin, and several men moaned or shouted at him before he continued. "While we are gone, my son, Norris, will take over my responsibilities on the farm as an equal partner with his uncle Harold." Ida felt as if she were on the steamship again, the floor rocking beneath her, but beside her, Frank stood steady. "It will be his opportunity to show me whether he is ready to take on those responsibilities on a more permanent basis. I hope you all will offer him the same professional respect you have always shown me."

Again, there was cheerful grumbling from the men, but with it a round of applause, and Norris flushed red as his father patted him on the back. In a few minutes' time, the men took him into the study, and Oliver confidently invited himself along. The ladies were left in the parlor to sample Christmas cookies with two different pots of Indian tea, and Ida distracted herself as best she could until a servant called her to nurse the babies again and oversee supper for Jasper and Reuben.

The letter, in a pale blue scented envelope, arrived the following day. Reuben brought in the mail, and it was sandwiched between two pieces of correspondence for Frank. But it was addressed to Ida, and after reading it, she decided not to show it to him. Not yet. She needed to think on it for a day or two. She slipped it under the tea towels in the kitchen cupboard and went about her day.

December 22, 1898

Dear Mrs. Frank Fletcher,

I believe you have my baby, Anastasia, and I want you to know I am so grateful for her to be healthy in your care. I dream of her every night and miss her terrible and hope she will go to a good family. I am not suppose to write you, but I am desperate to find out how she is, even if I may never see her again. You may write to me at this address:

c/o Mrs. Gertrude Gilhooley

157 White Street

Manhattan

Sincerely,

Miss Bridie Douglass

THE
STOKEHOUSE

You came to Albany County in what year?
   1899. May of 1899.

And before that you spent your whole life in Underwood?
   Yes, for the most part.

When you say "for the most part," what other places did you live?
   I went to New York City.

What can you tell me about New York at the turn of the century?
   Oh, I don't know. It was crowded, and frightening. I didn't really see much of the city.

Where did you go when you were there?
   I worked there for a short time, as a domestic. A housemaid.

For a wealthy family?
   No, it was just an ordinary boardinghouse. I changed the sheets, cleaned the glasses. That sort of thing. I'm happy to talk some more about Albany at that time. Isn't that what you really want to hear about?

   —excerpt from an interview with Mrs. Alice Vreeland for
   The Women of Albany County, July 6, 1972

12

November 25, 1898

Dear Joe,

This is just a quick note to tell you where I am. You may have heard that my father brought me to the city and left me here in a boardinghouse. I am working hard, but I have clean lodgings and three meals a day. I have not heard from my father or my mother since. I do not expect to hear from you either, but if I do, I shall be happy. It is your choice. You may write to me at the return address on this envelope. If I do not hear from you, I shall know that the time we had together is over.

Sincerely,

Alice Fletcher

December 2, 1898

Dearest Alice,

Your letter arrived today, and I was overjoyed. My mother was curious, but I have said nothing to her about it. I had not heard anything but that you had gone to the city. I wondered whether it was because of me, but now I know you didn't want to go. I wish I could do something to bring you home again. Where are you working? I am worried about you and pray for your safety.

I have been working steadily on the farm since you left. Things will be busy now into the winter, with the holidays coming. We had a rush to supply the Yale football games. They say the violet is the flower closest in color to the Yale blue, and I suppose it is. It is funny to imagine the flowers I have picked ending up pinned to the shoulder of a Yale man's sweetheart in Connecticut. I would bet they never give a thought to where those flowers came from. It makes me wonder about all the things I must take for granted every day.

I have gotten much better at picking, though I am sure I am still not as fast as you. I can pick a handful quickly, but I haven't perfected tying them, and often get tangled in my own string. You would laugh to see me. Your uncle Harold has asked me whether I would switch to nights soon in order to tend the stokehouses. I imagine I am a good choice for that work as I don't have a family and can sleep in peace during the day, so I will probably say yes and try it out. It could be a lonely job, but I don't mind working alone. It gives me plenty of time to think. I need to decide what I will do next, whether I will make the commitment to attend law school or maybe strike out on my own. I hate to think of leaving you, though, and if you were here, I would be tempted to work on the farm longer so I could be near you.

I will save my earnings and take the train down any Sunday to visit you. Please tell me how I may find you when I get there.

I remain yours,

Joe

December 16, 1898

Dear Joe,

I am so happy to hear from you, I think I may cry. I have read your letter over several times, until I nearly have it memorized. I hope you will write me again soon.

I am well enough here. I am working as a housemaid in a girls' boardinghouse. I sweep and dust and change the sheets—though I do not have to wash them!—and I wash the dishes, of which there are many. I have a cold little room of my own, but it is no worse than sharing the attic with my brothers, and I have not seen any mice yet, though the cook complains of rats in the garbage outside.

I do wish to see you, but I am not sure how. I cannot have visitors, and I do not have Sundays off, or any other day. However, I am earning extra money for my family, so for now that is all right. My father was here a couple of weeks ago. I don't know whether he will return, but I think he is collecting my pay. I have not heard a word from my mother. Since I cannot plan a visit with you right now, I hope you will keep writing to me and telling me all the news of home. I miss you and everyone there terribly, but especially you, and I hope it is not too forward of me to say that I dream often of the day when I may see you again.

Since it occurs to me that you might try to come down anyway, you should know that the address where you write to me is not where I am staying, but I am getting your letters. Please write again very soon.

Yours,
Alice

December 21, 1898
Dearest Alice,

Though you appear cheerful enough in your letter, which I just received this morning, I am worried about you nevertheless. What kind of place makes a young lady work seven days a week without even a break for the Sabbath? I suppose the work is not much different from what you were already doing at home, but I hope it will not go on much longer and your father will bring you home again. Will you come for a visit at Christmas? I will look for you in church.

You may be interested in news of your friend Claudie. She has a new beau, a young man she met at our church social last month. He is from Poughkeepsie and the son of a judge. I did not meet him, so I cannot offer any opinion on him. Her brother, Avery, has been in our prayers. He has been able to get out of bed some days, but is having difficulty with one numb limb that won't walk right. Other days he is laid up with headaches and back pain. My father has been to see him twice, but he is not hopeful when he returns. There are also rumors that your brother Oliver and his friend George Ellerby have plans to head out to Boston in the spring, but these may only be rumors. Do you know anything of this?

As for me, I am learning to tend the stokehouse fires, and other than that, I mostly sleep. Sometimes when I wake in the afternoon I do some odd jobs at the church—yesterday fixing a broken hinge on the chancel door—and I have been doing some reading in the law, still thinking about my decision of what to do next. I will admit it: I cannot make a decision without spending more time with you. I want to be near you, Dear, and I hope you feel the same. If ever it becomes possible for you to receive visitors, you must write me at once. In the meantime, I will hope to see you at Christmas, maybe even before this letter reaches your beautiful eyes.

I remain yours,

Joe

December 30, 1898
Dearest Alice,

I have been waiting every day for word from you, and none has come. I hope this letter will cross one from you in the mail. Every day that goes by, I am thinking of you constantly.

I saw your family at church on Christmas, and my heart was pounding, looking for you, but no use. Your mother smiled at me, but we have not spoken in some time. She seemed very tired. You say that she has not written you, but maybe she has and you haven't received her letters. Does she have Mrs. Gilhooley's address? I wonder why I cannot write to you at your boarding-house. Can you not trust your employer to deliver your mail?

I will write you more later when I know you are receiving my letters. For now, I will just tell you that work on the farm is going well, though I am on stokehouse duty, which is very tiring. I am up all night shoveling coal into one boiler, then stomping through the cold or the dark tunnels to shovel coal into the next, on up the hill, and then to the bottom to begin again. Sometimes if the stove at the bottom is still stoked, I can lie down on the cot there and catch a few winks, but then it's through the whole thing again. I find it hard to get a full night's sleep during the day, so I am worn out and, I am sorry to say, sometimes short on patience. I enjoy spending nights near your home. I like standing up on the ridge and watching your house. There is often a low light on even in the middle of the night. I imagine your mother is awake with her babies. I like to pretend that light is you, waiting for me. You will wait for me, won't you, Dear?

I remain yours,

Joe

January 7, 1899
Dear Alice,

I am afraid of two things: either my letters are not reaching you, or you have decided you don't wish to hear from me. As I have no way of knowing which it is, I will hope it is the former, but then there is no use in my continuing to write. If it is the latter, just a brief note from you will release me from my worry.

I will be sorry—I will even say heartbroken—if you refuse me, but then at least I will know. Please do me that kindness.

Yours,
Joe

January 15, 1899

Dearest Alice,

Again, I have not heard from you. Perhaps it is too soon to assume you did not get my last letter. In any case, I feel compelled to try to reach you again.

I am writing to you by the light of a candle as I sit in greenhouse 4, trying to warm up before I make my rounds again. I reckon the temperature to be close to zero. Just walking between the houses stings my face and the tips of my fingers. I am glad, in a way, that you cannot see me these days. This soft coal is a mess—all over my hands and face. My mother complains about the wash. She must use a separate tub of water for my work clothes.

Your cousin Norris is in charge for a month or so while your aunt and uncle are in Florida. He has a lot to learn about managing his employees. Reuben had the poor idea of complaining about how Norris was treating him, so he sent Reuben to shadow me on the overnight rounds without releasing him from the two days of work on either side. Your father didn't say a word. Imagine the state poor Reuben was in by the end of the second day. Of course, the result was he fell off his picking board and damaged several rows of violets and sprained his wrist beside. Now he cannot pick for several weeks. We are all looking forward to your uncle's return.

We have had very cold weather. The skating on Ellerbys' pond has been very good—the boys play hockey every afternoon, and the young people have been skating after church on Sundays. They have asked me to join them, but they are all younger (as you are!) and I do not care to socialize without you.

Is that foolish of me? It doesn't seem fair when I know you are spending your Sundays at labor.

I hope this letter finds you well. Please write me very soon, and when you are asleep at night, dream of me standing up on Violet Ridge watching over you.

Yours,
Joe

January 25, 1899

Dearest Alice,

As I have not heard from you, I am assuming you are not receiving my letters. Therefore, I should not be writing, but I cannot help myself, my dear. I am hopeful that one day a letter will get through again, and then you will write me immediately to tell me you are all right. Sometimes I cannot sleep for worrying over you.

Know that my love for you has not changed. Do you remember that September evening when we first walked up on the ridge and watched the sun set, and we confided our feelings for each other? I feel now just as I felt then, only more so. I hope I am not being too forward to say it in writing. I know you remember—please say you still love me, too.

There has been some snow here. Maybe you had it in the city as well. I had to shovel out all the greenhouse doors. Believe me when I say I was not happy about that job, and I was awfully sore the next few days. Now the snow around the houses is covered in black soot—very ugly—but inside, the perfume of the flowers is so sweet. Especially the white ones, I can't remember the name of them. When you smell them, you could hardly imagine anything wrong with the world. Then I think of you and I am worried again.

Please write me soon.

I remain yours,
Joe

February 1, 1899

Dear Joe,

I have received your letters. I am sorry I have worried you so, but I am afraid you would not love me anymore if you knew what had become of me. I am afraid to say I love you, too, but I am also afraid of losing you, so I am writing to you against my better judgment. I do remember, of course, all the things you mention, and more. I think most of all of the day I felt so desperate to see you that I invented an excuse to go up the hill, and I found you way up on the ridge. No one else was there, and we sat in the shady grass and you brushed my hair with your fingers. When I close my eyes at night, I often imagine that stolen half hour with you.

Now I must ask you to stop writing to me and stop thinking of me, for you do not know anymore who I am. I shall always love you.

Alice

February 12, 1899

Dear Alice,

I don't know what to think of your last letter, though I have read it again and again over the past several days. I am fearful for your safety. Also, I cannot decide whether you mean for me to listen to your advice, for in the same letter you remember me so tenderly. I have decided to ignore your instruction and hope for a time when I will see you again.

Things here are very busy for the Valentine's Day rush. I wonder if you have heard that some time ago your father brought home a second baby for your mother to care for. She looks to be overworked and tired out. I saw her just yesterday as I was leaving, early in the morning, for home. She was out in the barn, walking with the new baby, who was screaming. The big door was open, so I stopped and called out to her, but we could not converse over the baby's screams.

There has been plenty of snow of late. When I shovel the paths, in places it is as high as my waist, and near the stoke-houses it tells a story of the winter, with bands of black soot layered between every snowfall so you can tell how much there has been—eight inches here, ten there, and so on, and a top coat of six inches, already covered again with soot. It is ugly on top, but interesting when you slice into the layers.

I am told that after Valentine's Day things slow down, so I may try to do some extra work cutting ice on the river. I get a little sleep nights even though I am stoking the furnaces, and I don't sleep much during the day, so I may as well go there with some of the farmers and earn some extra cash.

I anxiously await word from you and I remain yours,

Joe

March 1, 1899
Dear Joe,

I realize I told you not to write me again, but I confess I live for your letters. Don't stop.

I am sorry to hear that my mother seems so tired. I have not heard from her nor from anyone else but you. Your letters are my only reminder of home.

I miss you terribly. I hope you are taking care out on the ice. Write again soon, please.

Alice

March 8, 1899
Dear Alice,

All you need to do is tell me where I may find you, and I will get on the train as soon as your word arrives and be there to take you away.

The nights are warming, and some nights I am no longer stoking the boilers. We will soon be picking for the Easter rush, and then I will be searching for a new, steady job. I could even come to the city and look for work near you. I am confident that I could support us both. I am asking you to be my wife. No matter what has happened to you, I love you.

I remain yours,
Joe

April 1, 1899

Dear Joe,

If you can think of the very worst thing that could happen to a young lady in the city, then you can think of my situation. Gert Gilhooley knows where to find me. You must understand that I am exposing myself to you to write such a thing, and I trust that if you decide not to come, as I expect you will not, that you will at least be gentleman enough to keep this dangerous news to yourself. Surely you understand what would happen to me if others knew. Perhaps it is too late already, but in my heart, I still hope that there is some way out of my situation, though I confess I cannot imagine what it is. I am sorry for any pain I have caused you.

Alice

13

The winter days between Christmas and Harriet's trip to New York were the longest and darkest Ida had known. The sun set before Frank and Oliver and Reuben came in to supper. For several frigid January evenings, Frank went out to the barn and built a crude pine cradle for Anabel. Jasper slept in the trundle bed and Mary in Jasper's old cradle. With a second cradle for Anabel, Ida could no longer keep Frank from his bed. They hardly spoke to each other in the cold mornings and evenings, but they again slept side by side. Between nighttime feedings, Ida often lay awake, watchful of the space between his body and her own.

Then Harriet returned from her shopping excursion to New York with terrible news. "We hired a cab and drove back and forth looking for the address you gave me," she said. "Ida, it doesn't exist."

Ida would have to go to the city herself, though where she would go once she got there was a mystery. She thought of the strange letter tucked away among her tea towels and wondered whether it had anything to do with Alice's whereabouts.

One day when the cold eased and Ida had use of the wagon, she called on Jennie Morton and asked the great favor of leaving Anabel with her to nurse for a day, with a promise to return the favor whenever Jennie needed it. She couldn't ask her neighbor to feed two babies, however. Mary was older and heartier, and this time of year there was less worry about babies coming down with diarrhea. She would leave Jasper and Mary with Harriet, who could hand-feed the baby cow's milk. Ida had no hand-feeding equipment, but from Ashley's brief stay, she knew what to ask for in the pharmacy. With money borrowed from her monthly allowance, she purchased a glass bottle and a rubber nipple. This set her back from purchasing her train ticket, but everything must be in place, and without Frank's knowledge.

The train schedule and fares were posted on the packing room wall. For four more weeks Ida saved her pennies and nickels, forgoing sugar and coffee and meat until Frank complained and grew suspicious. She imagined every coin put her a mile closer to Alice; she hoarded them like ducats in the toe of an old pair of stockings, taking satisfaction in their growing weight each time she added to her collection.

Finally, on the last day of February, Ida borrowed the wagon again. She stopped to see Mrs. Morton, then went to the station and purchased a ticket, praying the clerk wouldn't recognize her and mention it to Frank. Late in the afternoon she visited Harriet and instructed her on the use of the glass feeding bottle. In two days, she would make the trip.

On the morning of the first of March, a misty rain fell, so light that the slightest updraft would abort its fall. Those drops that made their destination froze crystalline in the cracks of the stone path and silvered the sky-facing branches of the spruce trees. In the barnyard, mud from a late February thaw firmed to flakes. Frank's and the boys' feet stirred it into a manure-like paste that they brought in the back entry and kicked off against the wood box. That night, before packing for the following day's trip, Ida scrubbed the floor from the mudroom to the sink to the kitchen table. She went to bed with a dull ache in her back and a throbbing in her head and woke twice in the night, thirsting for water.

When she woke in the morning, she couldn't move. She attempted to lift her head, but it felt heavy as a melon, and every joint—shoulders, elbows, hips—resisted with a leaden ache. Mary stirred and rooted for breakfast, but when she took Ida's nipple in her mouth, a sharp pain shot through Ida's breast and a film of sweat bloomed on her forehead. Gathering what energy she could, Ida rolled the baby over her rib cage and settled her on the other side to try the other breast. This Mary drained in ten minutes, while Ida cupped her sore right breast in her hand, wondering what she would do when Anabel awoke. Her skin was inflamed, as if a burning coal were beneath the surface, and her nipple throbbed with each beat of her heart. She heard the boys rummaging about in the kitchen, and she called out to Oliver for help.

"I can't get up," she told him, and he ventured one step closer. "Get your father."

"He's gone over the ridge," Oliver said.

"Then get Aunt Harriet."

Harriet was not an early riser, and Ida knew it would be some time before they returned. She would have to rouse herself. She returned Mary to the cradle. Then she set her feet on the floor. She thought deliberately about how they met the floor at the pads of her toes, the balls of her feet, her heels. Surely she could stand. Surely she could walk across the room to the washbasin. And she did. Once she was up, she imagined it might be all right. She would feed the babies and dress and make it to the station on time. Then she looked in the mirror above the basin and saw that the skin on the upper mound of her breast was flaming red. Anabel gurgled in the cradle.

Ida knew it was mastitis. She'd had it once with Oliver. She remembered a story her physician father had told, of a woman in Schenectady who'd died after an abscess the size of a plum had burst inside her breast. The first thing she must do was let Anabel drain that breast.

Wrapping a shawl around herself, Ida stepped one foot after the other into the kitchen. The boys had stoked the fire, and she put the kettle on. Anabel began a staccato cry from the bedroom, but she would have to wait. When the water was boiling, Ida tempered it with cold water from the pump and poured it into the washbasin. She dipped a washcloth in the hot water and wrung it out, then sat in the rocker and pressed the warm cloth to her breast. Sweat trickled from her forehead, and she wiped her eyes on the shoulder of her nightgown. In a moment, milk began to drip from her nipple. Anabel was crying with some force, and when Ida settled the baby on her lap, she latched on with a vengeful suck that made Ida cry out. She thought of what she'd done in childbirth. By the time she'd had Alice, her third baby, she'd learned she must let go rather than fight the pain, for it would always win. She tried this tactic again, resting her head on the back of the rocker and breathing deeply. As she exhaled, she sat inside the pain itself, a great room with a cold floor and a light so bright it hurt to look. With each pull of the baby's tongue, that light stabbed at her. But it would be over soon, and then Harriet would be here to help.

By the time Oliver brought Harriet, Anabel had finished and was fussing in her cradle. Ida sat spent in the rocker, her nightgown loosened to release the heat from her chest, her eyes closed, too sick to care for any modesty in front of her boys.

"What can I get you, Ida?" Harriet said close to her, and Ida opened her eyes.

"Snow," Ida said. "Some snow in a towel."

"Oliver," Harriet said over her shoulder. "Get Dr. Van de Klerk."

"No," Ida said. "I want to see Mrs. Schreiber."

When Ida awoke, Mrs. Schreiber was standing at the bedside with her hands on her hips. "I hope they're paying you well," she said.

"Not well enough," Ida said, trying to smile.

Mrs. Schreiber gently lifted Ida's nightgown from her breast. "Oh, my dear," she said. The heat of the infection was rising; Ida's collarbone felt warm now, too. Mrs. Schreiber fingered Anabel's sling, which was hung over the bedpost. "Here's the culprit, I would imagine," she said. "It's put pressure on your breast and backed up the milk. I'm sorry, Ida. I shouldn't have suggested it."

"I couldn't have lived without it these last few months."

Mrs. Schreiber dropped the sling, and Ida wondered whether she was thinking she might not live at all.

"We'll start with a comfrey poultice. I'll make it up while you nurse them. But chew this first." She reached into her basket and held out a clove of garlic. "It'll get at the infection."

Ida chewed the garlic until her eyes and nose watered. Mrs. Schreiber followed the remedy with a large cup of water. Then Harriet brought the babies into the room.

At the sight of Mary's wide-open, wailing mouth, Ida faltered. "You'll want something for the pain," Mrs. Schreiber said. Ida nodded, and Mrs. Schreiber gave her a piece of bark to chew on. "The chewing will help distract you as well," she said, though Ida doubted it.

She took Mary first, latching her onto the fevered breast this time. She cried out, then allowed a low moan to rumble in her throat as she paddled through the pain, on and on as if across an endless lake. Finally Harriet threw a cloth over her shoulder and took Mary from Ida. Mrs. Schreiber lifted Anabel out of her cradle and settled her in Ida's lap to drain the healthy breast. Even the surge of milk through Ida's left breast seared in the right.

When the babies were done, Mrs. Schreiber sat at the edge of the bed and opened Ida's nightgown wide, then laid a warm poultice over both breasts. Ida breathed deeply, and the scent of comfrey breezed over her. "This will do for today," Mrs. Schreiber said, wiping her hands on her apron. "You make another tomorrow," she said to Harriet. "And Ida, I want you to drink half a cup of this tea every hour until there's some improvement." She pulled a pencil and a small notebook from her apron pocket and wrote down the recipe, then left two paper packets on the nightstand, labeled "mullein" and "lobelia."

"I'll get the first pot started before I go," Mrs. Schreiber said, and she touched Ida's shoulder as she stood.

Harriet lay Mary in the trundle bed and took Ida's hand, and Ida was swamped with gratitude and humility. The pain allowed her no words, so all she could do was squeeze Harriet's hand tight.

The next day Harriet returned with a young woman whom Ida recognized from Frances's Christmas party. "This is Cook's niece, Delia," Harriet told her. "She's come to care for you." Ida wanted to ask who would pay for her services, but couldn't in front of the young woman. Probably Frances and Harriet had agreed they'd rather pay for help than be up with Ida themselves.

So Delia moved in to cook and clean and care for the babies and sleep on a mattress behind the curtain in the front room. She was quiet and helpful, bringing the babies when they needed to nurse and leaving Ida to her thoughts and her sleep the rest of the time. Later, Ida would have no memory of that first week, slipping in and out of fever, her consciousness a series of disjointed sounds until she surfaced to nurse again. At one point she wondered whether the babies were being fed by someone else, for she felt she wasn't nursing them as often as she should, but she was too tired to ask or to care.

Mrs. Schreiber had apparently instructed Delia, for twice a day she prepared the poultice and offered Ida tea every waking hour until she was near sick of it. Preoccupied with his own worries, Frank didn't ask where the medicine and the advice had come from. He seemed not to understand how gravely ill Ida was, though it was a relief somehow not to have his attention. He slept upstairs again and came and went with hardly a word. Ida thought of the day the cow had calved and how protective Frank had been with her. He never sat at Ida's bedside to stroke her arm or whisper encouragement in her ear. Only Reuben surprised her by sitting with her often, saying little as he read his lessons or whittled a soft piece of wood. He had taken on the task of keeping watch, perhaps imagining his vigil would ensure that she would stay with him.

One afternoon Ida heard the anxious scrape and stall of ice plates shifting on the roof, until in brief succession they slid heavily to the ground in the late-winter rain. The sound called her back into time. The fever broke, and the redness receded from high on her breast. After a few days, she began to regain her strength. Delia continued to make the poultices, and Mrs. Schreiber came to call again and changed the recipe. "You'll be just fine," she said. "Another week and you'll be up and about. But take your time. It isn't often they let us stay in bed."

In her thinking time, Ida imagined all the places Alice might be: a roaring factory, a poorhouse, the bottom of the East River. Sick with worry, she mentally planned her trip to the city all over again. Easter was coming, the final rush before the growing season ended. Likely Harriet wouldn't agree to take Mary and Jasper again until after the holiday, and Ida would have to call on Jennie Morton once more. She hoped her unused ticket would be honored. Some days she thought of just getting up and leaving, for Delia was there. Then she would attempt the long walk to the outhouse, her shawl poor protection against the damp March air, and stumble to her bed too exhausted to take another step. How long would it be before she'd have the strength to travel? How long could Alice wait, or was it already too late?

When she wasn't thinking of Alice, Ida imagined how her life could be if Anabel were gone when she recovered. Mary was such an easy baby. She was nearly sitting up on her own. She could amuse herself with a jingling rattle or some other little toy. She needed to nurse just five times a day and usually slept all night. What a joy it would be to have only her to care for. Dr. Van de Klerk had been to call while Ida was fevered. She would tell Frank that the doctor had said to send the baby away. He would listen to the doctor.

By the end of the third week of her illness, Ida's right breast still felt sore to the touch, but it was no longer agony to nurse. After nursing Mary one evening and then Anabel, Ida fell asleep without any supper. Anabel woke in the night to nurse, then Ida slept hard again until morning, when Delia brought the baby to her along with a breakfast tray. Anabel finished quickly, and Ida shouldered her to pat her back and bring up the air. She called to Delia to bring Mary but received no response.

"Delia?" she called again, and the girl appeared in the doorway. "I'm ready for Mary. Is she in the kitchen with you?"

Delia stood still and spoke not a word. Ida felt a rushing throb in her breast and knew before she spoke what had happened.

"Would you bring me the other baby, please?" she asked again.

Delia took a step into the bedroom and folded her hands at her waist, and her voice quavered as she spoke. "Mr. Fletcher took her away early this morning."

Ida worked hard to resign herself to Mary's leaving. She didn't want Frank to see she was disturbed. In truth, she often awoke at night with a start, thinking she'd heard Mary's cry. Then she couldn't get to sleep for thinking where that baby was. Though she had written faithfully to Mary's father, she'd received just the one suspicious reply, and she had no confidence that the baby was with him, if he even existed. So where had she gone?

Ida feared Frank had done something terrible. She dreamed that Alice and the baby were together in a dark, formless cave, starving while they waited for help. Alice's face was bony and sharp, and she put Mary to her breast, though she had no milk.

14

The *Poughkeepsie Daily Eagle News* reported that nearly a million violets were shipped by the Underwood growers for Easter, and Ida reckoned the figure was about right. Easter had become a frivolous holiday, especially in the cities, with elaborate greeting cards and showy fashion parades. On the farm, the weeks leading up to Easter were among the most harried of the season. It was the final push to pick and ship as much of the harvest as possible before the beds were turned over and the growing season ended. Housework was set aside for the week leading up to Easter Sunday in order to ship the violets. In the last few days of the rush, Ida finally dressed and walked up to the packing room to contribute her share of the work. She wasn't able to stand as long as the others, but she did what she could.

Even Frances was in the packing room with Ida and Harriet and her two older girls one evening that week after the regular help had gone home. Though the greenhouse glass on the sides of the packing room let in some evening light, eventually they had to light a lantern, and the shadowed work became harder on the eyes and a great deal more tedious. Ida was surprised to see that Frances was still adept at bundling the violets: gathering a nosegay in her left hand, arraying the shiny galax leaves around it, then wrap-

ping it with the long, loose end of string that the picker had left
and tucking the string between the stems. Another of them would
fasten on a boot to keep the nosegay moist and lay the flowers at
an angle in the packing boxes, wrapping them with white waxed
paper to protect them during shipping. Conversation among the
women from town was often lively around the packing table, but
in the evening everyone was eager to finish, so they worked in
rapid silence, racing the setting sun.

The Easter rush ran right up to Sunday morning. When Norris and Oliver climbed up in the wagon at five A.M. to make the
last delivery to the Coburg depot, several workers stood about and
applauded. Then everyone rushed to do morning chores and eat
breakfast and dress for church. Afterward there was another grand
meal at William and Frances's house, cooked on Frances's new
Sterling range, which she had shown off to every woman who entered the house, but which she would rarely use herself. Ida was
glad to see Delia there, helping Cook with the meal. She had been
sent home the week before, after spending the entire month of
March caring for Ida. After dinner, Ida slipped into the nearest
greenhouse to bunch up a few fragrant bouquets for Delia to take
home.

Another season had nearly ended. Ida had only one baby to
nurse, and that baby was finally calming. Her own health was recovered. The yellow buds of the daffodils were about to split, and
color was returning to the grass. Ida paid a call to Jennie Morton
and then Harriet. The first day they could agree upon for Ida's trip
to the city was a Friday two weeks hence.

On the Tuesday before Ida's trip, as she sat in the rocker after
lunch with Anabel at her breast, both of them suspended between
waking and sleep, there was a tentative knock at the door. Ida released the baby's suction and fumbled to fasten her corset and button her shirtwaist. Jasper got up from the floor, where he'd been
playing with his toy soldiers, and ran to the door. Ida lifted the

baby to her shoulder and shook the milk lethargy from her head as she followed Jasper to see who had come to call.

It was Joe Jacobs, glancing over his shoulder up the hill. "Mrs. Fletcher," he said, "may I come in?"

"Certainly," Ida said, stepping aside. Joe had never been in her home, and it was an odd time for him to come, while the others were up at the greenhouses, collecting the cuttings.

Joe pressed the door closed, and something in the way his jaw twitched frightened her. She bounced the baby, who let out a burp.

"Mr. Fletcher—Mr. Harold—said I could come down here for just a minute," Joe said, and she could hear him working to control his voice. "I told him you'd sent a message up to me." Ida nodded, trying to follow his words. "Mrs. Fletcher, Alice is in trouble."

The word "trouble" was spoken not as a fear but as a fact, and Ida was almost grateful to know she had not been crazy or suspicious. She had not merely imagined that something was wrong. But barreling over that relief was the sickening certainty that she had waited too long. What did Joe Jacobs know that she did not? And how did he know it?

The questions would wait. She took out the blue envelope and showed him the letter from the woman named Bridie Douglass.

"That's the same address I use to correspond with Alice," he said, pointing to the address at the end of the letter. "It's not where she's staying. But this Mrs. Gilhooley mails letters for her."

"So you've heard from her! Where is she?"

"She's written me a few times," Joe said.

Ida felt a flush of jealousy and then shame. She had failed Alice, and somehow Joe had not. "What kind of trouble is she in?"

Joe bowed his head and said quietly, "I'm not sure, Mrs. Fletcher, but I have my suspicions."

Ida's arms went weak, and she laid Anabel in her cradle, afraid she might drop her. When she stood again, her hands were quivering, and she hid them under her apron.

"I'm going to the city tomorrow," he said.

"Do you know where to find her?" Ida asked. "I was writing to her in care of a Miss Sligh, but the address was wrong."

"I don't know about Miss Sligh," Joe said. "And I don't know where Alice is, but I'm going to see Mrs. Gilhooley. I thought you'd want to come with me."

He issued this invitation uncertainly. Could he possibly imagine she wouldn't want to go? "Yes," she said firmly. "We should go together. But I've already made arrangements for the children for Friday. Can you wait just two more days?"

Joe took a breath as if to speak, then looked at her, his eyes dark. Ida felt she was facing the final judgment of her life's work. "All right," he said finally. "Two more days."

On Thursday evening Ida packed a bundle for Jasper and another for Anabel. It was possible she might not return in a single day. She said nothing of this to Jennie Morton when she dropped off the baby early in the morning. To Harriet, who took Jasper, she said little more. There would be time for apologies and explanations later. Let Frank worry if he came home for supper and she was gone. He and the boys would have to fend for themselves, and he would know exactly where Ida was.

15

When Alice and Claudie were twelve years old, they surprised Norris and Oliver once in the hayloft. The girls had been searching for Prissy's new kittens, and from the far dark corner of the loft, they heard the boys at the top of the ladder. Alice thought it was a game of hide-and-seek: she pushed Claudie into the hay, and they giggled into their hands as they heard the boys moving closer. Then Norris stumbled over Claudie's foot, and after recovering from the surprise and the girls' delighted shrieks, he cornered them, and Alice suddenly tasted the sour remains of her lunch in her throat.

"You girls want to see something?" Norris said, and before they could respond, he had unbuttoned his trousers and exposed his penis, sticking straight at them like a divining rod.

"Bully for you," Claudie said. "Every boy's got one of those."

Norris knelt and spat on his hand and began stroking himself, at first slowly, with his eyes on Claudie, who had quieted and was kneeling between the disheveled bales of hay. Alice knelt behind her, and she caught Oliver's eye before he turned his head away. Norris stroked faster and faster, and then, to the girls' amazement, a gush of creamy, white fluid spurted from the tip of his penis onto the hay-strewn floor. Norris fell to one hand, then studied Claudie through his dark bangs and smiled.

"Come on," Oliver said, tugging at his shoulder, but Norris took his time sitting back and buttoning his fly. Then he tossed some loose hay on the puddle he'd left.

"What do you think of that?" he said to Claudie.

"Come on," Oliver said again, and Alice noticed the tendons in his neck standing tight under his skin.

"Someday your husband will put his cock inside you and squirt you just like that," Norris said, locked in a stare with Claudie. "Don't you think you'd like that?"

Claudie stood swiftly and kicked a footful of hay into Norris's face. He reeled against Oliver, and the girls made a run for the ladder, reaching the ground and the safe range of the grown-ups before the boys could reach the top.

On her first night in the city, Alice sat up in her new bed and thought of that day in the hayloft. She wasn't sure at first why the memory had come to her, but as she listened to the footsteps above her head—the light click of women's heels and the heavier thump of men's—and the piano music and the loud voices, she began to suspect the worst of this place to which her father had brought her.

Claudie had told her about "white slavery," about innocent girls visiting the city who were stolen from the street when no one was looking and taken to women's boardinghouses, where they were courted by men for money. The two of them had had several conversations about what this courting could possibly entail—why would a man pay for it? Then they had remembered that afternoon in the hayloft. Putting together some things their mothers had said, and things they had seen in the barnyard, they'd worked it out themselves. Could it be that Alice's father had brought her to that kind of place?

After the horse show, there had been some sort of dispute between her father and his friend Mr. Sligh, a spindly man with a dirty gray mustache, who had met them there. The show itself had been thrilling. Alice had never seen so many people—thousands of them—in one place, and she could hardly believe they were indoors, under a ceiling so high and vast that its electric lights seemed like stars. The men wore frock coats and silky top hats, and the women were dressed as elegantly as those in the fashion plates in Aunt Frances's magazines. A brass band played under the din of voices, and a trumpet announced the entry of each horse, every one of them a beautiful creature. The horses pulled coaches or trotted or jumped, their oddly docked tails and braided manes making them seem as fashionable as the humans who watched them. It had been an overwhelming, enchanting day. But when it was time to go home, Mr. Sligh pulled her father aside. She saw him glance her way as they talked in low voices. Something about the man frightened her; she heard him say forcefully to her father, "What do you *want*, Fletcher?" as if aggravated by something her father couldn't decide. Then Mr. Sligh left, and her father took her on a horsecar separate from the others and brought her here, to this strange house in a crowded neighborhood. Her father spoke with a haughty, well-dressed woman while Alice waited in a dark parlor, and then he left, and Alice sat terrified, waiting and wondering what was to happen to her. No one came for a long while, and finally Alice went to the window and opened the drapes just a crack, and she saw her father standing in front of a lunchroom across the street, hat pulled low, hands in his pockets, watching the house.

Finally an old housemaid named Ivy took her to a dark bedroom the size of a large closet off the kitchen in the basement level of the building. The large, low-ceilinged kitchen featured three high windows near the dining table with a view at street level. Alice's cramped room had no window at all. The plaster was crumbling off the lath in some places, and the whitewash was dingy gray. The single iron bed stood beside a roughly constructed nightstand with one drawer and an oil lamp on top. Across from the bed were a small, empty wardrobe and a washstand holding a mismatched tin ewer and porcelain basin. A square of oilcloth protected the floor below. Perhaps because it was next to the kitchen, the room had no stove, and Alice imagined she would have to keep the door open if she wanted the room to take in any warmth.

In the morning Alice was awakened by the raining of coal into a hod, followed by the slamming of pots on a metal surface. She had no idea of the time, for the room was completely dark. She huddled farther under the covers, trying to collect the warmth of her body around her, wondering what she would be asked to do once she rose and whether she would see her father today.

There was singing in the kitchen in some language she didn't recognize. The song was slow and quiet, almost tuneless, and it broke off suddenly with the sound of footsteps on the stairs. Someone else had entered the kitchen, but no one spoke. In another moment, there was a rap on Alice's door, and Ivy opened it just wide enough to announce to her, "You're late. Chores to do," as if they had been following a routine for years. Then she shut the door.

Alice sat up. She had slept in her chemise, leaving her dress at the foot of the bed along with her stockings and shoes and wrap. She had kept her grandmother's locket around her neck, thinking it might protect her in this unknown place. Her father hadn't even warned her to pack, and she wondered what she would do when it was time to launder her clothing. She considered getting dressed and simply walking out onto the street and finding her way home, but she had no idea where she was, and she had no money. She should do as she was told and hope her father would return. Maybe the work would be all right; maybe she could make some money to send home and save some for herself.

The floor was cold and damp as stone on her bare feet, and she hurried to pull on her stockings and shoes. The water in the ewer was as cold as the pump water at home, and there was no mirror at which to brush her hair and pin it up. She did the best she could to dress neatly, then stepped into the kitchen and closed her door behind her. Later in the day, before bedtime, she would open it again to let in some heat.

The cook at the range had her back to Alice, and Ivy was nowhere to be seen. "Excuse me," Alice said, and the woman looked over her shoulder. She was a young black woman with a red kerchief tied around her head to cover her hair. She raised her eyebrows, then turned back to the range.

Alice stood for some time, debating what to do: sit down at the table? Go upstairs? Ask how she could help in the kitchen? Except for the occasional tap of the cook's spoon against the pot, the house was still. Finally Alice went back in her room and sat on the edge of the bed. Her hands were cold, and she tucked them under her skirts to warm them. She thought of a poem she and her classmates had memorized at school the year before, "Hiawatha's Childhood." It had a soothing, singsong rhythm, and she began to recite it under her breath, but when she got to the part about the things Nokomis taught the child Hiawatha, she was stuck. She tried again, but all she could think of was the joking way Claudie had said it—"Showed him Ishkadish, the comet, Ishkadish, kabish, ka-boodle"—and not the way it was really supposed to go.

"What are you doing, girl?" Ivy said at the door, and Alice jumped. "We've work to do." Alice stood. "Won't last long," Ivy muttered as Alice followed her through the kitchen and up the back stairs to the main level of the house, where she and her father had entered the night before through the heavy front door with the brass knob. This floor had higher ceilings and fancy wallpaper and carpeting like Aunt Frances's, which ran all the way up the wide front staircase. Alice followed Ivy up the stairs to the second floor, down an uncarpeted hallway with several closed doors, and up a bare stairway to a third floor. There was a small parlor on the third-floor landing with a Chinese rug, a coffee table, a couch, and two armchairs. An ashtray and some ladies' magazines and a half-full tumbler of water made a jumbled still life on the table. Someone's knitting had been left on the couch, and an embroidered pillow had been tossed on the floor. On this level, too, there were several closed doors. Alice followed Ivy around the upper landing to a slim door—a linen closet five shelves high, each stacked with clean white sheets. "Once the girls is up, you make all the beds. You know how to make a bed?"

"Yes," Alice said.

"There's six of them. It takes a while. Yours and mine gets changed once a week. I do Mrs. Hargrave's. You don't go into her suite."

Alice had no idea where Mrs. Hargrave's suite was, but she nodded.

"You change them at night, too," Ivy said. "About halfway through. Mrs. Hargrave likes to keep a clean establishment." Alice felt her chest tighten and took a furtive breath, the kind she sometimes took if she was crying and couldn't control it. Ivy looked skeptical. She seemed to think Alice might be gone tomorrow, and Alice herself hoped this was true. She hoped her father would come today.

"They won't be up for a while, but you can tidy up here," Ivy said, leading Alice down the hall to the open parlor. "Sweep the carpet and the floors. The men track in a lot of dirt. Both floors you do, and the stairs. The carpet on the first floor hall, the sitting room, the piano parlor. But stay out of Mrs. Hargrave's study. I do that." It was clearly a point of pride for Ivy that she cleaned Mrs. Hargrave's private spaces. Alice was just as happy to stay away from Mrs. Hargrave, the haughty woman who had been syrupy-sweet with her father but extremely curt with Alice, regarding her through thick spectacles that made her eyes look as big as a cat's.

"Broom closet is here," Ivy said, gesturing to another slim door on the other side of the third-floor parlor. "You can go have your breakfast first. I've eaten." She closed the closet door and looked directly at Alice for the first time. Alice was surprised to see that she wasn't as old as she had first appeared. Her hands were old, and she walked with a slow limp, but the skin on her face was hardly wrinkled. Alice wondered whether in the past she'd been one of the girls who slept late into the morning. They were behind those closed doors, all of them. Alice was afraid of them. She hoped she wouldn't have to talk to any of them. Perhaps if she worked quickly enough, she would miss them altogether.

"That all you have to wear?" Ivy asked, and Alice fingered her Sunday dress, which she'd worn to the horse show. Now her only nice clothing was going to be ruined by housework.

"Yes," Alice said. "I didn't know I was coming." This comment seemed to puzzle Ivy. It puzzled Alice, too, for as she said it, she thought again how strange it was that her father had deposited her here at the end of what was to have been a special day in the city. The desperation of this situation dizzied her.

"I'll get you an apron," Ivy said. "Maybe one of the girls has an old dress you can wear." Alice didn't want their old dresses. She wanted nothing to do with any of them, or their sheets, or this place, for her suspicions had been confirmed. But when she descended the back stairs to the kitchen, a warm bowl of oatmeal was waiting for her on the dining table with a cup of coffee, and she was grateful for something to eat. The cook even gave her seconds.

By supper that night, Alice had met most of the girls. There was no avoiding them, though she had tried. As she'd been cleaning the third-floor parlor and hallway, two of them had awakened, and she'd hurried down to the second floor, then to the first as more of them had come out. She'd stayed in the piano parlor as long as she could, though it was the most offensive part of the house, with a scuffed wood floor that reeked of beer, six sticky tables, many feet of mirrors to clean, a player piano, a narrow bar, and everywhere underfoot a gravel of nuts and dried mud and even broken glass. The sitting room in front, where she had waited the day before, looked more like the parlor of an upper-class home. A huge mirror in a gilded frame loomed over a fireplace, and pairs of easy chairs were arranged in the corners. Over a velvet-covered sofa hung a large chromolithograph with a plaque announcing its title: *The Abduction of Persephone*. Alice was alarmed to see spilled behind the goddess's figure a basket of violets. Heavy drapes on the room's two windows kept out the light and the gaze of onlookers from the street. Alice was disgusted by the thought of who had been in these rooms. She hated to touch anything.

And upstairs, the beds. Some of the girls had nice quilts or coverlets, which she folded and set aside. But many of the sheets had damp circles at the edges, as if someone had sat on the edge and wet them. The rooms smelled musty, and after the first two, Alice began cracking the windows to let in some fresh air. She tried to think of herself as a nurse, stripping hospital beds, which made the job bearable, and for a good part of the morning she managed almost to believe the masquerade, until on the third floor she was caught off guard by a girl who walked into the room while she was pulling off the top sheet.

"Hello, there," the girl said, stopping in the doorway with her hands on her hips. She was wearing a short nightgown with no robe, and she held a cigarette loosely between two fingers of her right hand. "I'm Jessie." She pressed the cigarette in her mouth so she could hold out her right hand, like a man, to shake Alice's. Alice held the sheets tight against her stomach and nodded.

"Shy? That's all right," Jessie said. "See you later," and she turned in a swirl of chiffon and left.

Soon after, when Alice had carried the dirty sheets to the laundry chute on the second floor and was coming up for clean sheets, she discovered too late that several girls were congregated in the hallway parlor, eating their breakfast—though it was noon or later—from trays the cook had sent up on the dumbwaiter.

"Oh, look here," said Jessie. "This is the new housemaid. What's your name?" and Alice, to be polite, was forced to respond.

"Alice, very pretty," Jessie said. "You know me, and this is Bridie, and Glory, and Rose. There's two other girls, too. Katerina is new, but she doesn't speak English. And Lena just sleeps late." The other girls laughed at this, all but the one named Glory, whose blank expression didn't change. The girl named Bridie sat with one ankle crossed over the other knee, making a hammock of her skirts in which a newborn baby slept.

"Pleased to meet you," Alice said, though she was not at all pleased.

"Are you from New York?" Jessie asked, but Alice lowered her eyes and rounded the corner toward the linen closet. No need for conversation. She must keep her own counsel and wait for her father to return.

Her father did not return. Nor was there word from anyone. It was as if Alice Fletcher had fallen down the rabbit hole, and the girl who picked violets and hung laundry and played with her baby brother had never existed. Now she was Alice the housemaid, who swept the floors and washed the mirrors and changed the sheets and tried to keep away from the men who pounded through the house in the dark, their clouds of cigar smoke hanging in the halls, their presence musky and close. There was something unleashed about them, and Alice never felt safe after dark, for she was there among them, wiping the tables, fetching a bottle, changing the sheets halfway through the night, as Ivy had instructed. Always she feared being mistaken for one of the girls. She wore a simple borrowed work dress—something Bella the cook had brought from home—and a white apron, and kept her hair in a girlish braid down her back, which she hoped made her appear unsophisticated.

Toward the end of that first month, as Alice began to resign herself to the work, a heavy snowfall gave the girls an unexpected holiday. The first airy flakes floated through with nonchalance in midafternoon as Alice shook the dust mop out the back door. Within the hour, the snow was weighted with ice, tapping like uncooked grains of rice against the windows, and by four o'clock the slick sidewalks were white. Alice watched a pack of children run from the corner and slide through the shallow snow in their thin-soled shoes. She thought of her brothers and wondered whether she would ever see them again.

When she heard the girls congregating upstairs, she felt her usual loneliness more keenly, for it was the kind of evening on which her family would sit close together at the stove and she or her mother might read aloud. She imagined some harm could come from fraternizing with the girls, but she also imagined she'd go mad if confined to her own stifling room with nothing to read, nothing to do but think and cry. She'd had her fill of that.

The conversation upstairs seemed inexplicably merry—were they drinking? "Alice!" someone called out, seeing the top of her head as she came up the stairs.

Jessie lay on the Turkish couch, wearing a silk kimono and blowing wobbly doughnuts of smoke toward the ceiling. Alice had never seen such a trick, and she gawked at the novelty of it before she realized what she was doing and feigned disinterest again.

"Look at that glorious snow!" Lena called out from her doorway, where she stood in a pink ruffled nightgown, stretching her arms overhead. She was just waking up from her daytime nap.

"Let's get a game of cards going," Jessie suggested. "If we're lucky, no one will get here tonight. What do you think, Lena? Is it piling up?"

"Not just piling up, but blowing dervishes! How about a game of euchre? Come on, Alice. Sit down."

"Do you reckon we could get Bella to make us some popcorn?" They laughed as if they were cousins on a summer visit. Rose and Lena brought the counterpanes from their beds, and Alice found herself seated on a pillow on the floor beside the silent Glory. Jessie passed around some cigarettes, courtesy of one of her regulars, and Bridie, her baby on a blanket on the floor beside her, shuffled the deck of cards. Alice was tutored throughout the game by Bridie, who shared her hand. When the baby began to fuss, Bridie handed the cards to Alice and bared her breast in front of them all to nurse it. The girls took no notice until the baby's whimpers became screams and Bridie left with it to pace the second-floor hallway, as she often did late in the day. Alice wondered what she did with the baby when the men were visiting.

After several hands, a bell mounted on the wall rang, signaling their dinner was ready, and the girls threw in their cards and stood and stretched their legs. When Jessie saw Alice hesitating, she motioned for her to follow. "You eat with us now," she said, taking charge.

In the kitchen, Bella was slopping pieces of mutton and globs of overcooked carrots onto whiteware dishes. Alice normally ate later, with Bella and Ivy, but Bella didn't seem to care when Alice sat with the others; she simply pulled another plate from the shelf. The girls sat around the mottled pine dining table on chairs with caned seats and ate their dinner and drank their mineral water or beer and laughed and argued like a rowdy family. Glory, who never spoke a word, retreated to a rocking chair in the corner as soon as she was finished to read the newspaper by gaslight, and Jessie lit another cigarette and tipped back on her chair. Alice looked out the shallow windows at the top of the wall and wondered again how she could get out of here.

"Mrs. Hargrave is out," Bella said when she came to collect their dishes. She handed Rose a letter, adding, "So I've brought you this now." The girls teased as Rose turned away to read her letter in private. Jessie raised her glass and toasted to a Mr. Wetherby, a regular of Rose's who was secretly courting her, and Rose looked up from her reading to shove Jessie's shoulder. Alice couldn't imagine why a man would consider marrying a woman whom he had paid for sexual relations, but through the course of the conversation, she learned that Rose's aspiration was to become his permanent mistress rather than his wife, an outcome the other girls seemed to think was desirable. A good hour was spent ruminating on Mr. Wetherby's intentions. The conversation would have been a waste to Alice but for one fact she learned: Mrs. Hargrave forbade anyone to receive mail, but a woman named Gert delivered and mailed letters for the girls.

"You can give out Gert's address," Rose explained. "She lives down in the Sixth Ward, and she comes up here to take the laundry." Alice had already met Gert, who came with her large gray sacks and collected the laundry three times weekly. Each time she came, she brought the clean sheets, wrapped in brown paper parcels, and collected the next load of dirty laundry. Alice had been grateful to discover she wouldn't have to do that tremendous laundry herself, but she'd felt a sorry guilt the first time she watched Gert hunch over and pull her cart up the sidewalk.

"She used to be one of the girls here," Lena said.

"She brings our mail to Bella, and next morning Bella sneaks it to us with our breakfast, while Mrs. Hargrave is still asleep. Do you have anybody to write to?" Jessie teased Alice.

"How do you send a letter out?" Alice asked.

"Same way, under your breakfast plate," Jessie said. "I can loan you some stationery and some stamps until you get your pay."

"Do you need a pen and ink?" Rose asked, and Alice thanked them both.

Later that evening, when it was clear no men would be visiting in the storm and Bella had gone home for the night, Alice sat alone at the dining table with the borrowed paper and pen and considered to whom she should write first. She wasn't sure about her mother—had she known of the plan to leave Alice here? She should write first to Joe. But had she any right to imagine he could love her still? Even by association, she would be guilty in the eyes of many. The gravity of her situation settled over her, and she turned down the light and watched the snow fall in the halo of the streetlamps. She fell asleep with her head in her arms on the table. In the morning when she awoke, the blank paper lay beside her, and some unrecalled dream of seconds earlier made her bold. She hurried through a simple note to Joe—what had she to lose?—and a similar note to her mother, and when she left the breakfast table, the two small envelopes were tucked beneath her dirty plate.

16

On a piece of brown paper wrapping, Alice had written a calendar. She had missed the first couple of weeks, but the days of the week were easy to tell here. Saturday nights were the busiest, and on Sunday morning she could hear the church bells in the neighborhood. Gert came on Saturdays, Mondays, and Thursdays. And from Mrs. Hargrave's newspaper, which made it to the dining table a day late, Alice could check the date. So she knew it was a Monday, December fifth, when her father came to call.

She heard his voice from the piano parlor, where she was dusting, but by the time she reached the front hall, Mrs. Hargrave's study door had clicked shut. Alice pressed her ear to the door. She could hear Mrs. Hargrave and her father speaking but couldn't make out the words. At one point her father laughed, and she stepped back with a start. She'd never heard him laugh as if he were actually amused. Or she had, but not since she was a little girl. For a moment she wondered whether the man in Mrs. Hargrave's study was not her father at all but a caller whose voice merely resembled his.

Footsteps approached the study door. Alice quickly applied her dusting cloth to the newel post and started up the stairs, dusting the banister. She was on the third step when she heard Mrs. Hargrave's voice behind her: "Alice, there you are. Please come in here."

Alice folded the dusting cloth in the pocket of her apron and followed Mrs. Hargrave into the study, a room she had never seen. She felt her heartbeat in her temples and worried that her knees might buckle under her. Yes, there he was, her father. Sitting on Mrs. Hargrave's sofa, legs crossed, hat in his lap. When he saw Alice, he hesitated as if he didn't recognize her. Then he hurried to stand, and she saw the confidence drain from him as he stiffened his arms and crossed them over his chest.

"Pa," she said, her voice catching, for she knew as she said it that all her hopes of being taken home were futile. He was not here to greet her or embrace her or rescue her. The girls had told her that Mrs. Hargrave settled up with them on a Monday twice a month, and that she and Bella and Ivy would be paid on one of those same Mondays. It was payday.

"Alice," he said. Her throat went lumpy and she knew she was about to cry. She knew, too, that doing so would only irritate him. "Mrs. Hargrave says you're doing a satisfactory job." He nodded toward Mrs. Hargrave, who stood behind her desk like a chess queen, draped in a purple dress with bishop sleeves and beaded trim, a gaudy watch pinned to her bosom.

"I'll leave you two alone," Mrs. Hargrave said, and she left through another door. Alice stood just inside the study doorway. She caught the first tear with the back of her hand.

"Your mother and I appreciate your hard work," her father continued. He held up an envelope then, and she was sure her money was inside it. It's money for Ma and Jasper and everyone, she told herself. I don't need anything. "You like it here all right, do you?"

The question was a surprise; her father had never asked what she thought of anything. Her response was of no consequence, but she saw no reason to lie to him.

"No," she said. "I want to go home."

"There's twenty dollars in here," her father said, stepping toward her and giving her a peek into the envelope before drawing it back and folding it into the inside pocket of his jacket. "Five dollars a week. We need you to stay awhile longer."

"How is Ma?" she asked. "And the boys?"

"They're all well." He glanced at the door through which Mrs. Hargrave had left. Then he looked at her, his lips a crack across a face of rock.

"Did Ma get my letter? She hasn't written."

"She sent you a package of clothing," her father said, nodding at a brown paper parcel on Mrs. Hargrave's sofa. He wouldn't meet her stare. "Twenty dollars is good for a month's work, Alice." He cast his eyes up at the ceiling. "We sure do appreciate it, all of us."

In the silence that followed, as her father watched the ceiling and she watched his face, Alice understood what he was thinking. She understood, too, that he was ashamed. But not ashamed enough to take her home. It was no accident that he had brought her to this place to work. His hand was still inside his jacket, holding on to the envelope. Alice's tears spilled out too quickly to be caught, and she smeared her face with her palms. She wanted to jump on him and take her money. With twenty dollars, she could figure out a way to get to the train station. She was smart. She would find a way home. But then he would be there. And her mother. Had her mother consented to this? The fact that she'd sent a package with him suggested she had.

Alice's father looked in her direction, though not precisely at her. Instead, he was eyeing her bosom, as the men often did. "Your mother asked me to bring home that locket," he said. Alice pressed her right hand over the warm heart-shaped necklace. She hadn't taken it off since she'd arrived. Sometimes she fell asleep with her fingers over it. "She thinks it would be safer at home," he said. "She wouldn't want anything to happen to it."

"Does she know where I am?" Alice could tell by the way he hesitated that he was considering a lie, though whether what he said was a lie or not, she couldn't tell.

"She knows," he said.

"I want to keep it with me."

He reached out both his hands, cupping them before her, waiting for her to put the locket in them. She stood resolute, palm at her chest.

He stepped closer to her, and she felt his anger like a wave of summer heat in her face. She squinted at his cupped hands, and she spat. A shocking clap hit her face, and the locket chain scratched as he pulled it from her neck, though his hands moved so fast, she never saw them. She ran for the door, and as she yanked it behind her, it banged more loudly than she could have hoped. She ran up two flights of stairs, past the empty third-floor parlor, and stepped into the broom closet, where she cried among the fusty mops and brooms until she was sure he was gone.

"Was that you who slammed the door this morning?" Rose asked her later as Alice swept the third-floor hallway and several of the girls sat lounging in their parlor.

"I'm sorry if I woke you," Alice said.

The girls were impressed at her gumption, and when they told her to take a rest, she obliged, sitting at the edge of one of the armchairs and resting her head in her hands. Jessie was there, and Rose and Lena. Katerina, who always kept to herself, and Glory, who often did, were both in their rooms. So was Bridie, and while the girls let Alice sit quietly with them, she thought she heard weeping from Bridie's room.

"Her baby is gone," Jessie said.

"Oh, no!" Alice cried. What a fool she was to be causing her own scene when Bridie's baby was dead.

"It's all right," Jessie said. "She'll be over it. It's all for the best."

"What happened to her?" Alice asked.

"Mr. Fletcher took her away," said Rose. Alice felt a tickle up her arms, as if bugs were crawling on her skin. It felt so real that she moved to brush them away. She studied the girls' faces, but no one seemed to realize who Mr. Fletcher was. Rose was watching her knitting; Lena was reading the *Vogue* society paper, occasionally laughing as she read; and Jessie was smoking and staring at some far-off point beyond the ceiling. Bridie's choking sobs were more audible now, and Alice glanced over her shoulder at the door. Then she asked the question she needed the girls to answer. "Who's Mr. Fletcher?"

"Oh, a friend of Mrs. Hargrave's," Rose said, looking up from her knitting.

"A friend of Mr. Sligh's," Lena corrected.

"On the Sligh." Jessie snorted, and the girls laughed.

"Mr. Sligh likes the girls to be on top," Rose said with a gentle wink, realizing their language was too coarse for Alice.

"Mr. Fletcher is my father," Alice said.

"Your father! I swear!"

"Mr. Fletcher is your father?"

Alice stood awkwardly and circled behind the armchair, distancing herself from them, but she didn't want to leave the conversation. Not yet. She must find out everything. She held on to the back of the chair and watched as Jessie sat up straight and stubbed out her cigarette in the ashtray.

"Well, that beats all," Jessie said. "I've heard of girls being driven to a house of ill fame for lots of reasons, but their father bringing them ain't one of 'em."

"He brought her here to be a housemaid," Rose reminded her.

"Sure he did," Jessie said.

Alice heard the squeak of a doorknob, and Bridie, dressing robe tied tightly at her waist, a large handkerchief in her hand, stepped from her room. They all waited as she approached the parlor and sat on the couch next to Jessie, who patted her on the leg. "Baby's better off, right?" she said, and Bridie nodded, though she did not seem convinced. "Mr. Fletcher is Alice's father," Jessie told her, and Bridie looked up at Alice with wide, gleaming eyes. Alice was afraid Bridie might lunge at her, and she prepared to run, but instead a few tears slipped over Bridie's cheeks and her mouth puckered.

"I'm sorry," Alice said, shaking her head.

"It's all right," Bridie said, sniffing into her handkerchief. "Jessie's right. Anastasia is better off. Mr. Fletcher said he knows a woman who can nurse her until he finds a good family to adopt her. She'll have a much better life than I could ever give her."

"Do you know anything about it?" Lena asked, but Alice found herself unable to speak. Her mother. Her mother was a part of this scheme. Alice's mind scurried from one possibility to another, searching for an escape from the news coming at her, trying to find the exit hole that would tell her things were not as they appeared.

"He took another baby, too, before mine," Bridie said. "A girl named Nancy got pregnant first. She wouldn't let the doctor come because she knew what he was up to, so Mrs. Hargrave tried to get rid of it by feeding her cod-liver oil."

Jessie leaned over the edge of the couch and pretended to gag.

"It didn't work," Bridie continued. "And then I knew to watch out when I found I was carrying a baby, too."

"If I got pregnant, I'd just get rid of it," Jessie said, shrugging.

"What do you mean?" Alice asked, then saw that she shouldn't have, for they gave her varying expressions of pity and contempt.

"Look out the window on a Saturday night," Jessie said. "You'll see them lined up around the corner to see the doctor. For five dollars, he takes care of them."

"One of the doctors is a woman," Bridie said, correcting her.

"Well, she does the same thing."

"But why . . ." Alice asked, her question trailing off because she wasn't certain she even understood what they were talking about.

"Too many mouths to feed," Lena said. "Or they've had intercourse with a man not their husband. By choice or not."

"We don't have to go stand out there. Mrs. Hargrave brings the doctor to us," Jessie said, as if this made their situation more desirable.

"I had it done twice," Bridie said sharply to Jessie. "I wasn't doing it again." Jessie waved her hand dismissively and picked up a new cigarette.

"We first met Mr. Fletcher when he came for Nancy's baby," Bridie told Alice. "Mr. Sligh brought him. They're friends from some flower warehouse. A few days after he took her baby, Nancy disappeared."

"Where did she go?" Alice asked. The fact that someone had left this house gave her a jolt of hope.

"Nobody knows," Jessie said grimly, and she struck a match on the sole of her shoe. "So, what are you going to do now, Alice Fletcher?"

"Don't be unkind," Bridie said.

Jessie sucked on her cigarette, then said directly to Alice, "I'm only joking."

"Did you get your pay today?" Rose asked.

"My father took it."

"All of it?"

Alice felt her throat tightening again.

"Come sit down," Bridie said, patting the couch next to her and scooting closer to Jessie, who gave her a quick hug around the shoulders. Alice sat beside them.

"I'm sorry about your baby," she whispered, and Bridie wiped Alice's teary face with her damp handkerchief.

"It's all right. It's for the best," she said. "But my tits are killing me!" Alice cringed, though the laughter of the girls seemed to cheer Bridie.

"You have to bind them," Rose said.

"Later," Bridie said. Then she reached her arm around Alice and said to her, "Listen. If you want some money of your own, there's just one way to do it."

Alice knew what they were about to say, but she was too tired to protest. Let them say it.

"If you start turning tricks, you'll be able to keep some of the money yourself," Bridie said. "It's not so awful as you might think."

"As long as you don't get the clap," Lena said.

"We can teach you what to do," Bridie said.

"Her father will just take that money, too," said Rose. "She's best off not getting started."

"He won't know about the extras," Jessie said, leaning forward.

"That's right," Bridie said. "He'll get your regular pay—well, Mrs. Hargrave gets half, and he'll get the other half. But any special services you do are behind the bedroom door. The men pay you directly. You find a good place to hide that extra cash, and it's all yours. You could make enough in a few weeks to buy yourself a ticket anywhere."

"At my last place it was easier," Lena said. "We just robbed them."

"Stop it, now," Rose said. "Don't pressure her." But the others were enthusiastic about the plan, and in order to extricate herself from the conversation, Alice had to promise she would think about it. She smiled weakly at them as she left the smoky parlor. She held the railing to steady herself all the way down the back stairs to the kitchen, where Bella sat with a huge kettle between her legs, peeling potatoes. Alice passed by without a word and closed the door of her room behind her. The bedcovers were cold, the pillow was cold, and when she touched the place where her locket usually lay, she felt instead the flaring scratch on her neck. She lay there in the cold, caring for nothing, until Ivy pounded on the door asking why she hadn't cleaned the piano parlor. The men would be here soon.

17

A letter came from Joe. As Alice sat at the edge of her bed, reading it over and over again, she despaired for her old life. There must be some way to reclaim it. She would write to Joe and tell him where she was, and he would come to get her, and she would go home. She pressed the letter against her face, searching for a familiar smell, and against her heart. Then she read it again and again and again, until the words were empty.

For over a week she avoided answering the letter, though she slept with it under her pillow, fingering it like a child's rag doll. Then one Friday afternoon when Bella had a cold and didn't want to venture out, Alice was sent to purchase some sausage and vegetables at the market up the street. Rarely did she leave the building, except to step out the alley door to empty the slop pots in the privy or shake the dust from a throw rug. Sometimes in the evening the other girls left the house in pairs and brought men back, but otherwise they mostly stayed in, too, while a little boy from the neighborhood served as their "lighthouse," handing out cards on the street. Katerina and Glory were forbidden to leave the house at all.

Heading out this brittle, sunny day on her errand gave Alice a slap of courage. The air was the same sharp winter air that had stung her cheeks on the farm, and the same sun warmed her back. She liked the click of her heels on the granite sidewalk; she felt important, walking somewhere with a purpose. A gentleman even tipped his hat to her as she passed him crossing the street. No one knew who she was or where she had come from. She could be an immigrant woman buying food for her family. She could be anyone—a shop clerk or a secretary or a teacher. She mustn't give up. If she were to find a position of her own, she could leave Mrs. Hargrave's and start her own life, and her father would never find her. If only she could come up with a bit of honest cash to get started, to pay for a room in a reputable boardinghouse, then Joe really could come to the city to visit her.

When she had delivered the groceries to Bella and finished her chores, Alice stole half an hour before supper to reply to Joe's letter. If he were to keep writing, he must think she was in a normal domestic situation, so she chose her words with care, trying to sound like the old Alice. She waited until morning to read the letter over before sealing it and leaving it for Bella under her plate.

That morning, a Saturday, Mrs. Hargrave wanted the sitting room and the piano parlor decorated for Christmas. Ivy unrolled a sheet full of greens on the sitting room floor, and she and Alice wired them in garlands across the mantel and around the large mirror, adding some old red ribbons and pinecones. Alice marveled at the incongruity of recognizing a Christian holiday in this house but said nothing to Ivy, who never spoke except to chastise or complain.

That night the house was full, with men waiting in the piano parlor over glasses of beer. One regular, a Mr. Johanssen, whom the girls called Johnny, sat playing the piano as if he didn't care whether he ever made it upstairs. Two other men stood near him, singing bawdy ballads and laughing and drinking while the girls in their low-necked, high-skirted costumes circulated among the other customers, teasing and laughing, sometimes dancing with them for a few turns, but all the while moving them along as quickly as possible. Jessie was an expert at this. She would disappear up the stairs with one man, and in the time it took Alice to collect a tray of dirty glasses, deliver it to the kitchen, fill another tray, and deliver drinks to the tables, Jessie could be downstairs again, picking up another john. She charged the most of all the girls and had told Alice she aspired to run her own sporting club someday. Not even Mrs. Hargrave owned her own establishment; she merely managed it for a man they'd never met. But Alice could see that if anyone was likely to succeed at this business, it was Jessie.

Because the piano parlor was so crowded and because the girls couldn't keep up with the demand, this evening the men were left to drink more than usual. Mrs. Hargrave had set a two-beer limit. If the men got drunk, there might be trouble, and it took them longer upstairs as well. But it was hard to keep track of who had drunk how much, and the room appeared smaller and noisier each time Alice reentered. Saturdays were sometimes this way; on the other nights Alice was often spared the ordeal of working in the piano parlor, for traffic was light. Tonight she felt hands on her bottom and her hips as she passed, and she kept her arms close to protect her breasts as she carried the trays. Men called out to her, but she paid them no mind. If the girls were there, they would correct the men: "She's only the housemaid," though sometimes they'd say her name and then the men would call out, "Alice! I love you! Come here, darlin'! She's the sweetest girl here!" and other comments that were hard to ignore, for they were insistent and the room was close. "Aw, leave her alone," Rose or Bridie or Lena would say if they were there.

This Saturday night at times none of them was there. Ivy was busy shuttling men up to Katerina and Glory, who weren't allowed downstairs when the men were present, while Mrs. Hargrave greeted customers at the door and collected cash in a velvet pouch at her belt. So no one noticed the nondescript man who often came on Saturday and kept to himself in the corner until one of the girls approached him. He was average in every way, of an ordinary height with a moderate mustache and professional but inexpensive clothing. He sat with his hat on the table and didn't make a ruckus, and whichever girl approached him first was the one he would go with. No one noticed him wander out of the sitting room and down the hall to the back of the house, where he surprised Alice as she came around the corner with an empty tray. She caught her breath as she saw him against the wall where he didn't belong, but she walked on past him, keeping her pace. Then a tug pulled her up short. The tug wasn't hard enough to cause her to fall or drop her tray, but it was enough to stop her, for he had her braid in his hand, and with it he reeled her in close.

"Put that tray right here on the floor, miss," he said in her ear, and she smelled the gin on his breath and knew he'd been drinking before he arrived, for no hard liquor was served in the piano parlor.

"Let me go, sir," Alice said, pressing the empty tray like armor against her chest. The man flipped his wrist and wrapped her braid tighter around his hand. "I must ask you again to let me go," Alice said, raising her voice to be clearly heard over the racket from the parlor on the other side of the wall. "I'm just the housemaid. You must wait for one of the girls."

"You look fine to me," he said.

Her hands were shaking, and as the man took the tray from her and dropped it on the floor, she breathed in to scream. His hand clapped over her mouth. After that, it happened quickly. She tried not to think about it later, to let it be just a thud, a rip, a cry without definition or detail, but snatches of it kept coming at her, so she lived them over and over and over—the pinch of his whole hand on the inside of her thigh, the sound her head made against the plaster wall, the slip of her boot heel on the waxed floor and the way her feet lost contact, the awful burning and pounding, the ease with which a clump of his hair gave way in her grip, the kick he left her with when she collapsed against the wall, more a nudge like her father might have given the cat to move her away from the stove.

Something warm seeped from inside her, and Alice wondered whether it was her own blood or whether it had come from him. She was hot and hollow, and she feared everything inside her would fall out. She crawled on hands and knees to the back landing and stumbled down the stairs to the kitchen, where Bella stood washing the dishes.

"What?" she said when she saw Alice, but she seemed to understand almost instantly what had happened. She took Alice to bed, and Alice allowed her to wash her private parts with a warm washcloth and help her into a chemise and cover her with an extra blanket. "Who did this?" Bella demanded, but Alice didn't know the man's name, and when she tried to describe him, he sounded just like all the others.

There was little reason to resist now. Alice could see no route but the one that led further into this life.

She took to singing aloud in her room, hymns and children's songs. Rose commented once how cheerful she seemed, but really, it was the only way to keep other thoughts from her head. It was worst at night, in the dark, for sleep no longer came easily, even at the end of a hard day of work. Bridie taught her to take a shot of gin and gave her a bottle. Alice didn't want to do it, but it helped. She imagined its searing heat was burning her clean inside, and afterward she slept heavily and remembered no dreams in the morning. The idea that she might become a drunk frightened her almost as much as the things that had already happened, so she took care never to drink except at bedtime. Later, Rose brought her a bottle of laudanum, and she found that a small quantity provided more soothing release than the gin. She steadfastly refused

Jessie's offers of morphine, however, not just because she'd heard terrible stories about it but because she couldn't bring herself to use the hypodermic needle.

January's payday passed; Alice saw neither her father nor her money. Only when she received letters from Joe did she momentarily become herself again. But then she watched the girls climb the front stairs and wondered if anything separated her from them any longer. She habitually averted her face from the mirrors, and she did one thing all the girls had done when they'd first taken to the life: she changed her name.

"Pick something sweet the johns will like," they told her at the dinner table. She didn't bother protesting that it wasn't about pleasing the men. "Marie Louise," she said, naming the double-petaled purple violet, the variety her family grew the most, and before long the girls had shortened it to the more modern-sounding Millie. From then on, she no longer heard her own name. She no longer had to think about what had become of Alice; she was hidden someplace where they couldn't touch her, the girls or Mrs. Hargrave or the men who pawed at her as she passed with their drinks. Only Joe used that name now. She loved the way he wrote it, the A like a huge, lopsided heart whose tail crossed the start of the looping L so she could see he had written the A separately and lifted the pen before continuing, as if the A were important and special.

Sometimes she imagined something could happen to crack her out of this situation. Sometimes, after Glory had finished the paper and left it neatly folded on a chair, Alice would pick it up and read the advertisements for clerks and secretaries and shopgirls. "Might as well stay here," Bella said to her once, but she didn't explain what she meant, and anyway, Alice had no means of answering the ads. She had no work experience, no money for carfare or rent, no hope of finding her way around the city.

Finally, one afternoon, she agreed to let the girls show her what to do. She imagined she could make her own money for a week or two, then go someplace where no one knew her. What if she stepped off the train in Philadelphia or Washington or Baltimore and said she was a farm girl looking for honest work? She broke her long silence with a brief reply to Joe's last letter: though she loved him still, he must stop thinking of her. She could never be with him now. It would be best for her to stop mooning over his letters and resign herself to her true circumstances.

In Bridie's darkened bedroom, with the brocade drapes pulled shut for privacy, the girls instructed Alice how to wash a man first with a washcloth and some soap, and while she was doing that, to check his wick for open sores or a rash and squeeze it to find whether it had any hard lumps or oozing that indicated the clap. If so, she was to send him away. They'd all had it. The treatment was unpleasant, and sometimes it kept them from working, so they lost income besides. There were worse things she could catch as well; they knew one girl who'd gotten dark purple sores on her palms and face, and she'd been ruined, so Millie mustn't be afraid to send a man away if he had the signs.

They taught her to wash the men again when they were finished, and herself, too. They showed her how to use a rubber syringe to douche with a baking soda solution over the chamber pot if she had time between tricks, and at the very least, at the end of the night. They gave her a sponge with a ribbon on it and showed her how to soak it in vinegar and position it deep inside her to protect herself from a pregnancy.

Lena demonstrated how to shave her legs because the johns liked that. They told her which johns to avoid if possible and how to secure those who were better for regular visits. They advised her to find a safe place to hide any cash she could collect for extra services. They were somewhat vague about these—let the men tell you what they want, they said—but one of them involved putting things in her mouth. She covered her mouth with her hands, and they laughed as if it were nothing, as if they had been teaching her a game, and teased her, "Millie, Millie, don't be silly." They gave her an old silk dress with a neckline that fell open and had to be pinned at the seams, and a sheer fichu to tie over it, which did nothing to increase the modesty of the costume.

That night, however, when Jessie called her over to meet a Mr. Gill, Alice told him she was "just the housemaid," then ran off with his lone empty glass on her tray. She stood at the top of the back stair landing, her spine pressed against the cold wall, her heart beating so hard it lifted her bodice. She couldn't do it. Not yet. She delivered Mr. Gill's glass to the sink and climbed the back stairs to change the linens.

In her second-floor room, Katerina was wailing. The door was ajar, and Katerina was alone, sitting on the floor against the bed, breasts uncovered, stockinged legs splayed wide, clawing at her most private parts, her ridged throat exposed as she lifted her chin and keened like a crow.

At the alarming sound, Rose came running. Her door banged against the wall where she'd flung it. Alice, who had stopped outside Katerina's door, had no idea what to do. Rose nudged her aside, and Alice saw Rose's last customer hopping on one foot toward the stairs as he struggled to replace his shoe. Rose knelt at Katerina's side and caught her hands and tried to get her to say what was wrong, though she knew not a word of Russian, and Katerina spoke only a few words of English she had learned from the girls. Wanting to be of use, Alice entered the room to strip the bed as she had planned, and as she threw back the top sheet, a putrid stench rose just after the sight of yellow pus streaked across the sheets.

"Dammit!" Rose cried, rising up on her knees to see the sheets for herself, and Alice knew without being told that it was the clap. "Change the sheets for her, Millie, would you?" Rose asked, and Alice hurried to oblige, wrapping the stained sheets in a tight ball that would warn Gert they were soiled and replacing them with fresh sheets from the closet while Rose helped Katerina to the basin, where she motioned she should bathe herself.

"No more tricks for you tonight," Rose said, helping Katerina into the bed with a pillow under her head and covers over her. The frightened look in Katerina's eyes softened a shade. Then Rose turned down the gas lamp, and Alice left the room behind her.

The following day, the doctor was called in, a handsome young man about Joe's age whom all the girls were sweet on. They were put out when Mrs. Hargrave ordered Alice to assist him, leaving them out in their parlor. Alice sat at Katerina's side and held up her knees, draped with a sheet, while the doctor painted her inside with what the girls later said was silver. Katerina's hand grabbed at Alice's arm, and Alice rubbed her knees and hummed a soothing tune, looking back and forth between the doctor and Katerina's twisted face.

The doctor returned twice the next day to see Katerina. He laid out a rubber pad on the bed and instructed Alice to roll a cotton sheet to elevate Katerina's hips over the chamber pot. Then he injected a hot solution into her, which spilled over her thighs and her bottom into the pot. He stanched the rest with gauze and left her lying there awhile, tears streaming into her ears, while Alice sang and rubbed her legs again. The smell was terrible, but Alice closed her eyes and tried to imagine she was singing Jasper to sleep. The doctor touched Katerina's arm kindly before he left the room, and Alice saw plainly: he pitied them all.

"What a doll," Lena said when he was barely out of earshot down the stairs. He had used the visit as an opportunity to perform exams on the rest of them.

"I wonder what it'd take to catch the interest of that one!" Rose agreed.

Alice wondered whether they were serious. If they had seen what he truly thought of them in that moment at Katerina's bedside, all their bravado would be shattered like so much china on the pantry floor.

And then: I'll never be one of them. The thought was followed by a cascade of relief. She would not be one of them.

The doctor had left a recipe the girls already knew—a mixture of some medicines in a half pint of table claret. Before supper they showed Katerina how to measure this concentrate into a pitcher of tepid water. She was to use a rubber syringe to treat herself twice every day, as the doctor had ordered. To be sure she understood their instructions, Bridie dropped her drawers and squatted over the chamber pot to demonstrate.

"Don't worry," Jessie said. "It usually works just great. In a few weeks, you'll be back to normal." Katerina attempted a smile, for she apparently understood Jessie's tone to be friendly, even if the words were lost on her. But she was allowed to rest for only a few nights. Then she was ordered to work again. Alice changed her sheets and the others' and washed beer glasses and swept and dusted and counseled herself: patience, patience. Something else would come to her if she could only be very patient. When she received Joe's reply to her letter, she boldly wrote to him. He wrote again, proposing marriage, but to a woman who no longer existed. Alice waited and considered her reply. When she was ready to risk what little she had left, as winter crawled from the city and the sun stretched high enough to clear the buildings across the street and hit the low dining room windows again, she told him as delicately as she could where she was. Then she waited.

18

Ida and Joe hardly spoke on the three-and-a-half-hour train trip down the river. Riding the train was almost like riding the river, for at many points the tracks hugged the river so closely, one could see only water below, and the foothills of the Catskill Mountains on the far shore. Ida watched the landscape bolt past her window through drifting smoke and soot. She felt as if she were sailing on an iceboat at breakneck speed, the hills billowing beside her. The morning sun stroked them orange and pink, every hummock and hollow drawn into focus by the light.

When they entered Manhattan, the train descended into a dark tunnel, and Ida and Joe collected their things. "Do you know how to get there?" she asked him.

"We'll hire a cab," he said. Ida had no money to spare and wondered how they would manage for the day, but Joe added, "I've been saving up to see her."

Outside Grand Central Depot, however, he changed his mind as he noted the superior dress of those stepping into the polished cabs parked on Vanderbilt Avenue. He left Ida to ask a policeman for directions, then led her on a long walk over to the Broadway cable car.

The farther they traveled downtown, the more crowded and

frightening the streets became. Horses and wagons competed with the cable car and pedestrians in a shouting, clopping, ringing maelstrom. Several times Ida feared that a horse or a man would be overrun by the car, which jerked on its cable like an unruly mule. As the conductor called out stops she couldn't tell apart, she stiffened her back and held her breath and resisted the compulsion to grab Joe, who stood before her. Finally he bent down and said, "This one."

They stepped off on the corner of Broadway and White, and Ida took Joe's arm and walked with him briskly away from the avenue. Here the street was narrower, crowded with vendors of food and dry goods, and men shouting their business, and women carrying baskets and babies and loads of firewood. Children darted across the traffic. Ida put her handkerchief to her face to cut the stench of rotting garbage. Joe scanned the addresses at each stoop. They passed a pack of boys who should have been in school but were throwing dice against a building instead. A fruit vendor shouted out his wares with a rising call at the end of every word: "Oran-*ges*! Bana-*nas*!" A gang of men, some of them smoking clay pipes, others chewing tobacco, paused their antagonistic conversation long enough to stare at the odd, well-dressed couple making their way so tentatively along the street.

Ida looked down at the sidewalk and waited until she and Joe had passed the men before mumbling, "It makes me appreciate the farm."

"Yes, ma'am, it makes one appreciate a lot," Joe agreed.

Number 157 was near the corner of Baxter Street. As they climbed the bluestone steps, Ida's milk let down; embarrassed, she dropped her hand from Joe's arm. Joe looked for a bell, and finding none, he straightened his collar as if straightening his courage and knocked.

"Y' let yourself in!" called a woman's voice from an open window above, and Joe recoiled from the door.

Ida took a deep breath. The street stank of horse urine. "Where may we find Mrs. Gilhooley?" she called out, ashamed at the volume of her own voice.

"Third floor, top o' the stairs," shouted the woman.

Joe shoved the door, and it opened onto a hallway so dark they had to stand for several seconds, letting their eyes adjust, before they could see the stairs. Even with her gloves on, Ida declined to touch either the wooden banister or the pocked plaster wall, staying to the center of the bowed stairs up one flight, rounding an airtight hallway, and up another flight to the third floor. There were two doors at the top of the stairs. Joe chose one and knocked. Then he took off his hat and held it before his chest.

"Mrs. Gilhooley?" he asked the woman who came to the door. She had opened it just wide enough to peek through.

"Yes," she said.

"My name is Joseph Jacobs, ma'am—"

"I'm not interested," she said, but before she could shut the door, Joe's hand flew out to hold it. Then he leaned aside, thinking, no doubt, that another woman might make a better impression.

"Mrs. Gilhooley," Ida said quickly. "My daughter's name is Alice Fletcher, and I'm hoping you can help me find her."

The woman's face relaxed into its wrinkles, but still she held the door nearly shut.

"I'm afraid for her safety," Ida said, her voice catching. "Please tell me if you know where she is."

The woman glanced again at Joe, and she said, "Joseph Jacobs . . . She writes to you, does she?"

"She does," Joe said.

Mrs. Gilhooley eased the door open and stepped aside. "Come in, then," she said.

The first room of the flat was a kitchen, though a child's bed was tucked between the wall and the cookstove. An open doorway led to a brighter room with a small fireplace and two windows overlooking a rear courtyard. A web of drab laundry hung from one building to the next and back. Pigeons roosted on an iron railing outside, and after she seated them at the parlor table, Mrs. Gilhooley tapped on the window to shoo them away. "Rats with wings," she said. "Can I brew you a cup of tea?"

Ida had no desire to drink the water from this home, but it would be impolite to decline, so she nodded. She removed her gloves and laid them in her lap while she waited.

"You want to know where Alice is," said Mrs. Gilhooley from the kitchen, which was separated from the parlor by a partial wall with a large window cut into it. "She's not far from here." Ida was struck by the informality with which she spoke of Alice. The woman reached behind a short clothesline of socks hung over the stove to get three teacups and saucers from a built-in shelf. Then she set a kettle to boil on the stove and joined them again in the parlor, wiping her hands on her apron before pulling out a chair. She studied Ida a good long while. Ida prepared herself for the news to come.

"I'm sorry to tell you, ma'am. It seems you don't know," said Mrs. Gilhooley. "Your daughter—" Here she broke off to look at Joe, as if assessing to whom the news should be delivered. "Your daughter's in a house of ill repute on Eldridge Street, north of Canal. Mrs. Hargrave's. It's not the worst establishment . . ." Ida held her breath, or rather it held her, for it was trapped in her ribs and choking her around the middle. She was afraid to release it— she might vomit. Mrs. Gilhooley leaned over with familiarity and patted her back. Joe sat still and calm and far away.

"It's not so bad as you'd imagine," said Mrs. Gilhooley, holding Ida's arm so she wished she'd let go. "So far as I'm aware, she's only the housemaid, though it's true that girls often cross over. You'll have to ask her about that yourself." She let go of Ida and sat back in her chair. There was something self-righteous in the way she regarded Ida, and Ida felt the fool.

"Mr. Fletcher took her there," Joe added.

"Frank set her up with factory work," Ida said, her resolve crumbling.

"No," Joe said. Ida bunched her skirts in her hands. If he had known all this, why hadn't he told her on the long ride to the city? How much else had Alice shared with him that she had withheld from her own mother?

"The money is good at Mrs. Hargrave's," said Mrs. Gilhooley, shaking her head as if she thought it were a shame. "I don't know what they pay her for cleaning, but the girls make a dollar a client, sometimes more." Joe looked away.

"God help us," Ida said. She stood and walked to the window and looked down at the courtyard. Several women mingled around a large washtub, while a pack of children chased one another in the dirt. The doors of four wooden outhouses mere steps from the water pump were all ajar to varying degrees. The voice of a child inside the flat startled Ida, and Mrs. Gilhooley excused herself to go into a dark bedroom off the kitchen, which Ida hadn't noticed earlier.

"The others will be home from school soon," Mrs. Gilhooley said when she returned to take the kettle off. "We insist they stay in school until they're twelve." She announced this fact with some degree of pride, and judging by the number of children she'd seen in the street, Ida imagined the pride was merited. "My oldest is out to work with his father."

Ida saw Joe check his pocket watch; they were both calculating to be out before the children came home. She thought of the letter she carried in her reticule, and seeing that time was short, she took it out and laid it on the table in front of Mrs. Gilhooley, who had set a teapot to steep on a trivet. "I received this letter some time ago," Ida said. "I'm sorry to say I never answered it. At the time, it made no sense. But I think you may know this young woman as well."

Mrs. Gilhooley picked up the letter and turned it over to see both sides, and Ida realized the woman couldn't read. "It's from a young lady named Bridie Douglass," Ida said.

"Oh, Bridie," said Mrs. Gilhooley. "She's at Mrs. Hargrave's, too. Are you the one who has her baby?" She smiled hopefully.

"I don't know," Ida faltered. "When was the baby born?"

Mrs. Gilhooley considered the question. "Early November, I'd say. A hale little girl."

"Anabel," Ida said faintly.

"Anastasia was what Bridie intended, I believe. But she never meant to keep the baby. Mr. Fletcher said he had a nursemaid for her, and he had an arrangement with another man, a Mr. Sligh, for adopting them out."

"Mr. Sligh, yes!" Ida said. Perhaps there had been a misunderstanding after all. "I was under the impression that Alice was staying with his sister."

"Oh, no, I don't think so," said Mrs. Gilhooley. "Not since November, anyway, when she came to Mrs. Hargrave's."

Alice had been in a brothel since November. Five months she had been there, and Ida had done nothing to help her.

"Excuse me, Mrs. Gilhooley," Joe said, "but were there other babies from Mrs. Hargrave's? You said adopting 'them.'"

"Yes, at least one other he took, a few months before that. Another baby girl."

Ida sat outside of herself. None of this could be happening.

"That one belonged to a girl who's no longer at Mrs. Hargrave's," Mrs. Gilhooley continued. "She managed to run off shortly after. No one knows what became of her." She lifted the lid off the teapot to check the color of the tea.

Ida squeezed her eyes shut and pressed her hands to her ears. She wanted to cry out to everyone to stop, stop!

What had become of Mary, then? And Frank—he had lied to her about everything. The depths of his deception astounded her, yet at the same time she had known. She'd known all along that something was wrong. She had known and done nothing.

"Mr. Sligh knew of a couple of wealthy families who wanted children and couldn't have them, so Mr. Fletcher offered to take the babies off Mrs. Hargrave's hands in exchange for earning a fee when the babies were placed with a family," Mrs. Gilhooley said. "I suppose Mr. Sligh and he split the money, I don't know. The girls didn't benefit, of course. But they knew their babies would be saved. That was plenty for them."

Ida looked around for a water closet, but it was just the three rooms, and there was no escape. Her stomach churned like the water in a laundry tub as she watched Mrs. Gilhooley pour the tea.

"Where can we find Mrs. Hargrave's?" Joe asked.

Mrs. Gilhooley set a teacup in front of Ida, who closed her eyes to avoid the sight of the steaming brown liquid. "If you're walking, go up Baxter to Canal. Then right on Canal and all the way 'cross the Bowery to Eldridge, where you make a left. It's number sixty-eight. Mind you, don't let on I sent you."

"I give you my word," Joe said. "If you don't mind, we'll take our leave. We're feeling urgent."

Ida was grateful not to touch the tea. She placed her hat on her head and stuck the hatpin through it. I must stand up now, she thought. I must stand and go out on that street.

"Good luck to you," Mrs. Gilhooley said. "I hope you'll find her well."

They walked as Mrs. Gilhooley had instructed, up the block and right onto Canal Street at an odd triangular intersection. Canal was wide and boisterous, teeming with people the likes of whom Ida had never seen: Hebrew men with long beards and diminutive round caps; Chinamen in odd, wide-sleeved jackets; dark-haired Italian men calling to one another in words she

couldn't understand; newsboys and rag pickers and unaccom-
panied children eyeing the fruit vendors and the bread vendors. They passed several gangs of indecently attired women,
showing their legs beneath shortened skirts and their breasts
through flimsy, low-cut bodices and calling out to every man
who passed. Ida averted her eyes, terrified that if she looked,
she might see Alice.

It was clear the alleys were being used not only as sleeping
quarters for filthy children but as outhouses, for the pungent
odor of urine stung Ida's eyes as she passed. Though she had
been to the city several times, she had never walked the streets
of the Lower East Side, and she had never, in her worst imagin-
ings, pictured Alice in such a place. No one should be in such
a place. As a furniture wagon passed them, the horse lifted its
tangled tail and dropped a mound of shit on the street. In the
country, with plenty of space, the piles of horse manure were a
mere nuisance. Here, with so many horses in such a crowded
place, it was nearly impossible to step in the street without
smearing one's shoe.

Joe pointed up Canal, and they walked some more, Ida's feet
swelling in her Sunday shoes, her skirts dusting up grime from
the sidewalks. Two young men pushed by, each with a load of
half-finished garments on his back. At the corner of Elizabeth Street, a woman sold flowers from two large baskets hung
around her neck. In the alleys, as they passed, Ida saw piles of
rags and paper trash, and on the streets ash cans, some of them
heaped full.

At the Bowery, they crossed through the speckled shade of the
elevated train tracks and waited for a pause in horsecar traffic to
scurry across the busy thoroughfare. The road sloped down from
the Bowery, and at the bottom of the hill, another row of fruit
stands drew Ida's hungry attention. Her stomach grumbled at the
sight of the polished apples, and though they were left over from

last fall's harvest and their provenance was questionable at best, she was too hungry to care. She had to eat something, for it was midafternoon and they'd gone without lunch. Joe bought an apple for her and an orange for himself, and up the street they purchased a stale loaf of bread from a woman carrying her wares in a sack sewn of old mattress ticking. Ida and Joe stood in the shade of a doorway, stepping aside twice for women entering the building, and ate their poor meal without speaking a word.

A large clock somewhere rang four. Joe took Ida's core and his orange peels and tossed them into the next alley, then held out the heel of bread to two boys running past, who snatched it without slowing their pace.

"Just a few blocks more," he said, and as he pushed down the street, Ida fell a step behind him. She knew she should be grateful to him, but at the same time, she hated him for being witness to their downfall. Even more, she hated herself.

They found Eldridge Street, and as they turned in to its narrow, shady confines, Ida felt she was walking to her own grave. Number 68 was a block up from Canal. The building was a five-story brick—an ordinary building like any other on the block, with a small gold plaque at the front door that said simply K. HARGRAVE. Joe pressed the bell.

"Oh, Joe," Ida whispered.

The door was opened by an elderly housemaid who stepped aside to let Joe in. Then, seeing a woman with him, her eyes widened. They all stood just inside with the door open to the street.

"We're here to see Mrs. Hargrave," Joe said. Ida stepped away from a tarnished, sour-smelling spittoon in the corner of the vestibule, so she was nearly touching Joe.

The old woman glanced from Joe to Ida several times before deciding to close the door. "May I tell her who's calling?"

"Mr. Joseph Jacobs and Mrs. Frank Fletcher," Joe said, and upon hearing Frank's name, the woman drew her head back and stared at Ida. Over the woman's shoulder, Ida could see a dark sitting room. The housemaid led them instead into a modest side parlor that seemed to serve as a study. "Wait here," she said, leaving the door ajar.

They sat together on a hard mohair sofa and waited. A coffee table before the sofa held a scattered copy of the *New York Journal*. Across from them was a large mahogany desk with a blotter, an inkpot, a gold cigarette lighter, and a lamp with a fancy silk shade. A telephone was mounted on another wall next to a large framed certificate that Ida couldn't read from this distance. The mantel over the fireplace to the left of the desk was bare, save a clock that ticked irregularly. The fireplace itself was covered with a convex tin plate and looked as if it hadn't been lit for some time.

"I'm afraid," Ida said.

"I am, too," said Joe.

A stereoscope sat on an end table next to the sofa, and Ida picked it up, thinking to distract herself with a scene of some faraway destination. Instead, when she placed the viewfinder to her eyes, she was assaulted by the three-dimensional image of a woman, naked to the waist, holding her own bare breasts in her hands to present them to the viewer and gazing directly in the camera with a sly smile. Ida hurriedly set down the stereoscope and said nothing to Joe.

The clock tottered, and they waited. Presently the front bell rang again, and the housemaid hobbled down the stairs to answer it. The man who entered appeared to be known to her. His extraordinarily long mustache was waxed into concentric curls that stood out stiffly from his cheeks, and he wore an ill-fitting tan suit. Ida shuddered at the sight of him, but the mention of the name Bridie caught her ear, and both she and Joe leaned forward to watch him jog up the staircase.

The housemaid stuck her head into the room and said, "Mrs. Hargrave will not see you and asks that you be on your way."

*   *   *

At the barbershop on the corner, Ida sat rigid in a cracked leather chair against the plate-glass window and watched the barber tie a limp smock at Joe's neck. He had been about to close shop when they'd arrived and had agreed to remain open only when Joe had offered him twenty-five cents, more than double the usual price, to have his mustache shaved. The barber had frowned at Ida following Joe in the door, and Joe had quickly introduced her as his mother. "Aaaa, let her stay," said a stooped man who was crouched beside one of the empty chairs with a whisk broom and dustpan, and the barber had nodded Ida to the chair against the window.

Joe lay tilted back as the barber set to work. The cloying perfume of the shave soap made Ida's stomach ache again. The place had seemed clean enough at first, but now that the barber was stropping a straight razor along a leather strap with a shhh-whip, shhh-whip, she feared it wasn't so clean after all. What if they cut Joe with a dirty razor? She was afraid, too, of the stooped man, who had winked at her as he passed with a dustpan full of gray hair. As she sat watching the barber, milk continued to soak through her corset pads, and she felt desperate for a place to relieve the pressure in her breasts.

The barber held the sharpened razor at the tender spot where Joe's underchin met his thin neck, and Ida closed her eyes. The two barbers had forgotten she was there, or they didn't care, for they began calling across the shop. "Smitty wasn't in." "No, the bastard!" "You stop an' have him pony up before you go home." "No, not tonight. I gotta catch the car." "Tonight!" and the barber stopped his short, labored strokes through Joe's thick mustache and shook the razor above his head. He was answered with the metallic clatter of the dustpan on the floor of the back room. The stooped man didn't come back, and the barber returned to his job with a grunt.

After he had removed Joe's mustache, he began again with a

fresh razor and a fresh lather of shaving soap. Joe lay patiently with his eyes closed as the barber pinched each section of skin tight and shucked the razor this way and that, with a quick flick between each stroke to wipe the razor on a cloth draped over his wrist. He moved swiftly—pinch, cut, wipe—from the left side of Joe's face and neck, around his chin, and to the right, finishing off the job with a few slaps of tonic and a shake of the smock as he pulled it away.

Joe stood uncertainly, and Ida watched him watch himself in the mirror as he wiped both his palms along the sides of his face. Then he placed two dimes and a nickel on the workstand. The barber had already stalked away.

Without his mustache, Joe looked a mere boy, white-faced and frightened. He looked so unlike himself that Ida had to fight to maintain her confidence in him. She stood and handed him his hat, and he cleared his throat.

"I think I'll put on my glasses, too," he said.

From a street vendor, Joe purchased a *New York Evening Post* for Ida to read while she waited. A lunchroom stood catercorner to Mrs. Hargrave's, and it was here that Joe seated Ida at a table in the window with her newspaper. She ordered a pot of tea and attempted to ignore the raucous Friday conversation of young ladies and men alike—factory workers, she guessed. She watched as, across the street, Joe removed his overcoat, draping it over his arm, and gained entrance from the housemaid. As soon as Ida was assured he would not be sent out, she left her table to visit the toilet room. She wrung out her soaking pads in the porcelain sink and attempted to express some milk, but her hands were trembling.

At her table, a china pot of tea awaited her with some sandwiches. This sign of civilization brought her to tears, and she picked up the napkin and covered her face, telling herself she must remain composed. There would be time for tears later. She laid the napkin across her lap and swallowed hard. Then she glanced out the window again at Mrs. Hargrave's.

There was no sign of Joe, nor of the business being conducted within. The building was four windows wide, each with a severe eyebrow of granite. Every window was covered by shades or drapes, so Ida could see no movement behind them. She wondered which window was Alice's, or whether she even had a window. Cloistered month after month—what would she do when she finally emerged?

Ida and Joe had agreed that he should not request her directly, so as not to arouse suspicion. He would ask for Bridie Douglass instead, and he would invite her to leave with them as well. Beyond that plan, they had no idea how things worked inside the house. Now that he was in, Joe would have to improvise, and Ida would have to wait.

19

On a warm April afternoon, after forcing their windows open to the spring air and playing a game of euchre, the girls went down to supper. Bella had cooked the usual Friday meal: smelly fish and overboiled potatoes with a cup of coffee or a mug of beer, depending on each girl's preference. But the girls were in good spirits, because there was to be chocolate cake for Jessie's birthday.

Alice had received no more letters from Joe in the two weeks since she'd told him what she could. This must be the end of their correspondence, and she would have to find another way out. Still, each time Gert came to pick up the laundry, Alice hoped against reason for some word from him. Sometimes the mail took a week to travel, though mostly it was quicker. She should have heard from him, if he planned to write at all.

When Alice arrived in the dining room for supper, Jessie was talking about the fat, dyspeptic businessman who came to see her every Tuesday night. How she could make a joke of the most awful situations was beyond Alice, but she had learned to join in the laughter. It did help to think of the men as funny—if you didn't, you would want to die. There were girls who had. Bridie had told her that was the reason Glory never spoke; at her last place of employment, a friend had overdosed on morphine.

The conversation moved on to the merits of this work over the jobs they'd had before. Rose and Bridie and Jessie and Lena had all chosen to come to Mrs. Hargrave's. All four had worked other jobs—at factories that made shoes and artificial flowers and cigars and buttons and boxes, and at laundries, which they agreed was the worst work of all. Lena described at length a box factory, where the noise of the machinery kept everyone from talking and the girls turned their skirts inside out so the glue stains wouldn't show later. They'd worked from eight in the morning until six at night and half a day on Saturday for four dollars a week. As one of the more experienced girls here, Lena could make that much in half a night, Alice calculated, with room and board besides. The worst thing about the factory, Lena said, was that she'd been fol-lowed everywhere by the manager, a pale-skinned man with rotten teeth who'd threatened her daily and at last had his way with her in his office, repeatedly, until she left without her last two weeks' pay. "Might as well get paid to do it," Lena said, and Alice's heart tightened. She had thought any one of the jobs they described could be a way out.

"What do you say, Millie?" Jessie said. "Things could be worse."

Alice tipped her head noncommittally and laid her fork on her empty plate.

Rose sipped her coffee and grimaced. "I'd like to know if Bella's using yesterday's grounds," she said.

"No, Tuesday's," Jessie said, and they all laughed. "I was out shopping today," she continued, and though Alice feigned disin-terest, she listened keenly. Jessie often left the house in the after-noon, sometimes in the company of one of her regular customers.

"You devil!" Bridie cried. "What did you get?"

"Mr. Dylan took me out," Jessie went on with a wicked smile, which prompted teasing from the others. Mr. Dylan was a stu-dent at Columbia College with a great deal of money. Every few weeks he would pay Jessie to dress up in some clothing he brought her and go out to dinner and the theater with him. This time he had taken her shopping for a new hat and three pairs of gloves and then bought her violets and some French creams and taken her driving to Brooklyn, where they had fornicated in his friend's parents' empty apartment. Jessie passed around the candies so each girl could try one, and Rose picked up the nosegay of violets and pressed it to her face. "Oh, I adore that smell!" she exclaimed. "Such sweet, innocent little flowers." She passed them to Alice, whose stomach soured at the smell of home. Swanley Whites. She wondered which Underwood farm they had come from.

"Look—they're mine to keep," Jessie said, and Alice saw she was wearing a pair of beautiful ivory-colored kid gloves with a row of four pearl buttons up the wrist.

"You're too lucky," Bridie said, and meant it. Even Alice felt envious, though it was humiliating to imagine a man treating her like a doll to be dressed and petted and then returned to the shelf.

"So, it's Friday," Jessie said, glancing up at the clock on the false mantel. "Will Farmer Boy be here? Let's take bets." Farmer Boy was a favorite butt of the girls' jokes, an inexperienced young man with a bowl haircut and sunburned cheeks who had tried each of them in turn. He tended to come early in the evening.

"He'd like you, Millie," Lena said.

"Yes, it's Millie's turn," Jessie agreed, and she and Lena laughed. They had made it their personal quest to bring her over to their side of the business. But since the doctor's visit, Alice had remained resolute.

"Miss Bridie, a gentleman to see you," said Ivy from the kitchen doorway.

"Dammit all," Bridie complained, hurrying to pick the slender bones out of her piece of fish. "Who is it?" she shouted after Ivy, but there was no response. "Probably that disgusting Froggie." Jessie wrinkled her nose as if Bridie had offended her. Bridie tipped down the rest of her beer. "Save me a piece of cake," she said, and hurried up the stairs to entertain her client.

As Alice climbed the back stairs to fetch the dustpan minutes later, she nearly met them in the hall—Bridie and an outrageously mustached man—and she ducked onto the rear landing so as not to be seen.

While she made a cursory pass through the second-floor hall-way with the broom and dustpan, she could hear the footsteps in Bridie's room above and the creak of the bedstead when Froggie was finished. She hid behind a door as he passed coming down, then stepped out to finish her work before any other men arrived. A few minutes later, she heard the girls congregating in the third-floor parlor, and she climbed the stairs to join them. For the first time, Katerina was there, sitting in one of the armchairs and sew-ing a button onto her spare nightgown, with Bridie's sewing kit on the ottoman in front of her. Alice watched her thread the needle the same way she did herself and wondered at the fact that they came from opposite ends of the earth yet accomplished this wom-an's task in exactly the same way.

Jessie's birthday cake sat on the coffee table, and she cut a gen-erous slice for each of them. When they finished, Lena traced her finger around the edge of everyone's plate, licking the leftover frosting. Bridie came out to join the others, and after she'd eaten her dessert, she shared a cigarette with Jessie, who sat sideways on a chair with her slippered feet dangling over the arm. Rose twirled her hair around one finger and stared at the ceiling. Alice pushed her broom dully up and down the hall. Once the evening had begun, the girls tucked themselves away.

The creak of footsteps warned them of Ivy's approach again. "Guess we'll have to head down there soon," Jessie said, not mov-ing. But it was Mrs. Hargrave's glossy, high-piled hair that came up the stairs, followed by her painted face and her heavy plum-colored dress.

"Alice Fletcher," Mrs. Hargrave said, and Alice's mind snagged on the sound of her old name. "Come with me."

Alice glanced at the girls, but they shook their heads, not knowing what was happening. Mrs. Hargrave led Alice down the stairs, and Alice expected she would be taken to the study. Was her father here again? Or had she done something wrong? She'd done everything Ivy asked of her, she hadn't broken a glass in weeks, she'd been polite and accommodating. Mrs. Hargrave opened the door to Katerina's second-floor room, and Alice stepped inside, thinking she was going to be shown some cleaning task she had overlooked or something that needed to be mended. But Mrs. Hargrave turned without a word and shut Alice in. Then a key rattled in the lock and the footsteps of the madam retreated.

"What?" Alice asked, her voice wobbling, though no one would hear it. She stood in the center of Katerina's room with nothing to hold on to except the thought that all her patience was about to end in defeat. It seemed Mrs. Hargrave had decided it was time for her to begin taking clients. Perhaps her father had ordered it. Alice ran to the door and banged on it, though the girls were already on the other side.

"Millie!" came Jessie's voice. "What's happened?"

"I don't know," Alice said, and she watched the doorknob jiggle.

"She's locked you in! What have you done?"

"I don't know," Alice said again. She couldn't speak aloud what she feared.

"Dammit!" cried Jessie, and she kicked the door.

"Don't," said Bridie. "You'll draw attention."

"I'd like to bloody draw attention! She has no right to lock her in!"

"She has a right to do whatever she wants," said Bridie. "What are you going to do, call the police?"

"Shut up," Jessie said. Three of the neighborhood police officers, including the chief, were her regular clients.

"I'm afraid," Alice said.

"Why would she lock her in Kat's room?" Bridie asked. Alice couldn't hear the rest of the conversation; they must be standing farther away. Alice checked the window to see if she could get out. It was only the second floor, but Katerina's window looked out on the air shaft rather than the street. Alice was trapped.

"We're going to find out what's happening," came Bridie's voice at the door. "Call up to me through the pipes if you need help. You can hear everything in my room from there." Alice found the pair of pipes running floor to ceiling at the far corner of the room.

"Miss Bridie," came Ivy's voice again. "Another gentleman to see you." It had struck Alice funny at first to hear these men referred to as gentlemen, but that was before she had realized how many conventional gentlemen visited Mrs. Hargrave's. She wondered who would be brought to Katerina's door. She would send him away, whoever he was. But she couldn't keep standing there in the middle of the room. She was tired of standing, tired of holding out. In the corner by the pipes, she sat against the wall and closed her eyes. If anything happened, she would be right there to call to Bridie.

She must have drifted off, because she thought she heard Joe's voice then. She couldn't hear the words, only the urgent tone. She strained to listen to what it was saying. Bridie was conversing with it. Then she knew she was awake. She shifted closer to the pipes, and finding them cool, she leaned her head against them. She could hear the conversation clearly.

"My God!" Bridie was saying. "Is she all right? What does she look like?" She sounded funny, as if she were crying.

The man's words were more difficult to make out, but the range of his voice sounded just like Joe's. Whoever he was, he was not carrying on the usual transaction.

"I can't," Bridie cried. "I want to so badly, but I can't."

Then, amid the words of the man, Alice heard her own name.

She rapped on the pipes and called out to Bridie, whose voice came back clearly: "Not so loud! The pipes go downstairs, too!"

Alice ran to the door and jiggled the knob, but it was locked tight. She had once seen her father pick the lock on the barn with a knife. She searched Katerina's nightstand drawer and found a pen, but the shaft was too wide. She had a few hairpins, but they bent and twisted and didn't budge the lock.

"Alice," came Joe's voice from the other side of the door, and she pressed her hands and face to it.

"I'm here," she said.

"I'm going to get you out. Collect your things."

Alice wondered where he was going to take her.

"Alice?" he said, and she heard the edge of desperation in his voice.

"Where will we go?"

"Home! I'm taking you home."

"I can't go home," she said, perhaps too quietly for him to hear, for he said again, more insistently, "Collect your things."

"I don't have anything," she said.

"All right. Then listen. Mrs. Hargrave has gone out. I'm going downstairs in a minute to distract the housemaid. You come down a minute behind me and go straight out the front door and across the street to the lunchroom."

"I can't go home," she said, her voice stronger, but there was no response, and she wondered if he had already left. She untied her apron, thinking to leave it behind, then noticed how worn the knees of her skirt were from kneeling on the floor to clean. She tied the apron again and touched her hair.

"Alice," came a whisper at the door. "It's Jessie. I've got some clothing for you. Courtesy of Mr. Dylan."

"How am I to get out of this room?" Alice asked.

"Are you ready?" came Joe's voice again. Alice wasn't sure she was ready for anything. "Remember," he said, "give me a minute with the housemaid, then walk straight out the door and cross the street to the lunchroom."

They worked on the lock first from the outside with several different implements. Then they slid something thin between the doorframe and the lock and tried to budge it that way, but again without success.

"This is going to make a racket," Joe said to the girls outside. "When I hit the door, you laugh as loudly as you can. Make it sound like nothing is wrong."

As he counted to three, Alice stepped clear. With a loud thud, the door bulged in place, and with his second hit, the bolt cracked through the frame and the door swung open. She didn't even recognize the man who stumbled into the room. He wore glasses and was clean-shaven, and she stood confused as he clasped her hands and kissed them quickly and said to her, "Hurry now." Then he was gone.

Jessie pulled at Alice's apron string. "Take that off!" she said, and Alice complied, then fumbled with Jessie to get her old work dress off and the new one on over her chemise. Bridie hastily pinned a hat on her head, and then Jessie slipped off her new kid gloves and handed them to Alice. They kissed her and pushed her out the bedroom door. Glory and Rose and Lena and Katerina stood together in the hallway and watched as she hurried down the stairs, holding the loosely pinned hat in place on her head, feeling odd and frightened.

As Joe had promised, neither he nor Ivy was in the front hall or sitting room, and Alice did as he had said. She turned the front doorknob and stepped out.

The setting sun blinded her, and she ducked her head to shield her eyes with the brim of the hat. She could see only the stone stoop at her feet and the base of the iron railing, which she fumbled to grasp. She was supposed to cross the street, but the glare and the movement and the noise paralyzed her. It was one thing to run a brief errand up the block and quite another to live out in the world. She considered turning back but knew she should not. Still, she couldn't move forward. She squinted from under the broad brim of Bridie's hat, down one step at a time to the sidewalk, then lifted her head to the street.

Her eyes were adjusting to the light, though she saw things in a blur: a vendor with a red push wagon; a scrawny, leafless tree; a policeman on horseback who didn't even notice the strange girl standing on Mrs. Hargrave's steps. A woman, waving her arms, dropped a blue cape behind her and ran into the street with no regard for the traffic. A harnessed horse veered sharply to the right to avoid her, and still the woman ran forward. Her striped shirt-waist had some kind of large wet stain across the front, and her hair was unpinned and falling lopsided off her head. She seemed to be waving at Alice. A second wagon coming the other way missed her by a wheel's width, and she stumbled up the curb as Alice realized: the woman was her mother.

NEW
CUTTINGS

Here's a photograph of my mother. This is probably the oldest photo I have of her. Oh, no—there's one other, it may be a tintype, from right before she married my father. It was taken in a portrait studio in Albany. I don't know where it is right now.

But in this snapshot here is my mother, holding my baby sister, and my brother Jasper is next to her. He was so cute, wasn't he? He grew up to be a handsome man, too. And this is me, on her other side, and my husband behind me. We weren't married yet. I think my aunt Grace must have taken this. She came to visit a few months after we arrived in Albany. We're on the footbridge at Washington Park Lake. This would have been autumn of 1899. It must have been a Sunday afternoon, since that was the only time my mother had off.

Where was your father?
He didn't come with us.

Oh! So, what made you move to Albany? Did your mother have family here?
Originally she did.

Were there better opportunities for work?
Better opportunities, yes.

It looks like you've saved some letters in here, too.
You can't read the letters.

—excerpt from an interview with Mrs. Alice Vreeland for
The Women of Albany County, July 6, 1972

20

In the dark of morning, Ida rang Mrs. Schreiber's bell. Alice stood one step below while Joe waited in the wagon. Alice had hardly spoken on their long journey by foot and horsecar and train and wagon to this doorstep, damp from an earlier rain that had missed the city. Droplets splashed soundlessly from a weak point in the gutter above, regular as Ida's heartbeat.

Mr. Schreiber opened the door a crack to see who was standing there at such an hour. "One moment," he said, and closed the door, leaving them on the porch. A minute later, Mrs. Schreiber opened the door wide and welcomed Ida as if she were making an afternoon call, though Mrs. Schreiber was dressed in her nightgown and robe. She led Ida and Alice into the parlor, stopping to light a lamp on her way, and they sat side by side on her sofa. Ida wanted to reach out and take Alice's hand, but she did not, mostly because she imagined that Alice might swat her hand away.

"How nice to see you, Alice," said Mrs. Schreiber, sitting across from them in a blue brocade armchair that was worn at the base where a cat had repeatedly sharpened its claws. Alice looked at her gloved hands and made no reply.

"And Ida. You're feeling better?"

"Much better than last you saw me," Ida said. "Thank you."

Mrs. Schreiber waited. What else should one say to visitors who came in the pit of the night?

"I have a large favor to ask of you," Ida said, and Mrs. Schreiber nodded. "I wonder if Alice could stay here for a few days, a week at most."

Mrs. Schreiber had surely been asked other favors relating to young ladies, and no doubt it was one of those she had anticipated.

"I'm afraid I can't pay you for her room and board, but I was hoping she might help you in the kitchen, or with the housekeeping or the laundry. It wouldn't be a long-term arrangement." Ida could see Mrs. Schreiber was trying to work out the reasoning behind this unusual request without being so bold as to ask.

"Alice has had quite a scare in New York," Ida said. "Involving something her father has done. I don't wish to say more than that. Except that it would be best if it weren't known that she's here."

"And then what?" Mrs. Schreiber asked.

Ida hesitated. To say it aloud would make it certain. "Then we shall go to my family home in Albany." There. That didn't sound so final. Merely an extended visit until things cleared up, though there was no family left in Albany, and no home.

Mrs. Schreiber regarded Alice not unkindly but with curiosity. "There is plenty of work here. I haven't taken down the drapes for a spring washing, and with some help, I could clean up the garden beds this week. I think we have an arrangement." She smiled and extended her hand, and Ida took it.

"Perhaps . . ." Ida said, floundering, and Mrs. Schreiber seemed suddenly uncomfortable. Ida let go of her hand. "I was just going to say that perhaps it would be best if Alice were to stay indoors. I wish I could say more."

"All right," Mrs. Schreiber said. "She'll help me in the house, then. Let me show you to your room, Alice. Have you any things with you?"

"I'll bring her things later," Ida said.

By the light of a single lamp, the three women climbed the stairs, two flights to the rooms in the garret. "It gets too hot up here midsummer, but the weather is still cool," Mrs. Schreiber said before she handed the lamp to Ida and turned the key in the lock. "I should think you'll get along well up here if it's only for a week."

The room had been shut up for some time, but Mrs. Schreiber wrested the single window open, and the cold night air hovered. "First we'll take care of these," she said, shaking dust off the curtains. Ida watched Alice's face, trying to meet her glance, but her daughter kept her eyes downcast. Finally she took both of Alice's hands and bent into her line of sight. She would have knelt before her if Mrs. Schreiber hadn't been there. She would have knelt in penance and bowed her head to the floor.

"I'll bring your things later," Ida said. "You'll be all right." Alice's nod was a better response than none. "I'll see myself out," Ida told their hostess.

On the street, Joe and his horse and wagon were waiting patiently. Ida gripped the brake handle and pulled herself up to the seat beside him. The night air stank of skunk.

"Thank you, Mr. Jacobs," she said, looking straight ahead. The village street was dark, save for the light glowing from a single house, where Ida knew an acquaintance to be up with her ailing mother. A raccoon rustled from under the quince in Mrs. Schreiber's yard and cast its luminous eyes up at them, then wobbled back under the shrub. Somewhere a cow lowed. Ida's job—the only job that mattered—had been to protect her children, and she had failed.

"I'll take you home," Joe said.

Ida was surprised all over again by his boyish appearance. In the absence of his mustache, his skin glowed white in the moonlight; his unfamiliar face must have bothered Alice as well. Ida shivered as a breeze spirited between them. She was thoroughly soaked and needed to collect Anabel as soon as possible.

"Would you take me to Mrs. Morton's? I need the baby."

Joe nodded and flicked the reins. As they pulled away, Ida looked up at Mrs. Schreiber's garret, but the window was dark.

After walking home from the Mortons' with the baby on her shoulder, Ida found Frank asleep. When she awoke in the morning, he was already out at the barn, and he didn't come in for breakfast. She stood in the yard, where a bank of daffodils buttered the grass, and she saw him up the hill, standing in the bed of a wagon, spreading old soil as other men shoveled it out a gap in the side of the greenhouse. Oliver and Reuben were up there with him. Late in the morning they moved over the ridge, and they didn't come to the house for lunch. Ida ignored the three burlap sacks of new cuttings Frank had left for her at the door.

When they came in for supper, Frank behaved as if Ida had never been gone, but she knew his fury was just beneath the surface. As she served his meat, he asked her, "How was your day in the city?"

Ida imagined he was trying to work out how much she knew. She wondered whether she was safe. Then she answered him, "Fine," and moved on to Reuben's plate.

"Did you see Alice?" Frank asked, picking up his knife and fork, and he smiled smugly. She felt she could slit his throat with the carving knife and never regret it. But his confidence meant he had decided she wasn't clever enough to have found Alice. Let him believe she was still at Mrs. Hargrave's.

"I wasn't able to see her. But I would like to try again sometime soon."

"Sometime," Frank said through a mouthful of food. "The chicken is delicious."

After supper, Ida washed the dishes and nursed Anabel, who was fussing in her old way. The day with Jennie Morton seemed to have set her off again. It took Ida a long time to calm her, but when she had and the baby and Jasper were both asleep, she made the excuse of going out to bring the new cuttings to Nora Hoskins's house, where they would trim them together. She hauled the sacks into the wagon, along with her paring knife knotted in a handkerchief, and left Oliver and Reuben in charge of the little ones. It was very unusual for her to go out in the evening, but she was no longer concerned about appearances. In a few days, she would be ready to go.

Mrs. Schreiber escorted Ida up to the garret, where Alice sat in a solitary captain's chair, wearing her nightgown and holding a book on her lap—the same book, Ida was surprised to note, that Anna Brinckerhoff had loaned her. Alice appeared more composed and peaceful than she'd been the day before. She had bathed and done her hair up in a neat topknot, and her clothing, which Oliver had delivered to the house earlier without knowing what was in the brown paper package, was hung from a hook on the wall. There were gray circles beneath her eyes that Ida was sure were not a trick of the lamplight, and as she held her place in the book with her thumb, Ida noted her wrists were as thin as saplings.

"I've read that as well," Ida said. "What do you think of Mrs. Stetson?"

"I've only just started it," Alice said, and set the book on the floor. "Mrs. Schreiber recommended it."

Ida sat on the edge of the bed. She took her time removing her wrap, which she folded in her lap.

"I'm not going with you, Mother," Alice said. She looked ridiculous in the nightgown she had worn as a girl when she was clearly a young woman now.

"What else can you do?" Ida asked.

Alice made no answer.

"You can't stay here."

"I know."

"Then you must come with me to Albany. We'll start again."

"Doing what?" It was not so much a question as an indictment of their inability as women to earn their own living. Ida felt her heart constrict just as her stomach did when it was hungry. She feared Alice was holding out hope of staying close to Joe.

"Alice," she said, but her throat tightened, too, and she was unable to speak another word. She stepped to her daughter and knelt before her, placing her hands on Alice's knees. Alice tucked her own hands under the folds of her nightgown.

"You can't stay here, my love," Ida whispered. "Don't you understand?" And she saw, looking into her daughter's cold eyes, that she understood too much. She knew things she would never tell Ida, and there was no protecting her any longer.

Ida let go of Alice's knees and rocked to rest on her heels. She lifted her face to the ceiling, where the light above the lamp faded to dark in the corners. She braced herself to look at Alice again. Something had changed in her for the worse, but possibly also for the better. No one would be permitted to tell her what to do ever again.

"I'm waiting for Joe to call," Alice said.

Ida shook her head. "Alice . . ." she began. "What other reasonable options do you have?"

"Maybe going back to the city."

"You've lost your senses!" She was sorry the moment she said it, though it was true. Alice turned her profile to Ida and gazed out the window with an expression that could have been mistaken for serenity. Her daughter seemed to be calculating her life as if it weren't her own but someone else's.

"Has he been in touch with you today?" Ida asked.

"He knows he has to keep it quiet that I'm here," Alice said. This was true enough. "He asked me to marry him."

"When?"

"In a letter, after he knew already what had become of me. Or at least he had an idea. He asked me to marry him." She stood and pushed past Ida to the bed, then scooted across it to lean against the wall, knees pulled up under the nightgown to her chin.

Ida sat on the edge of the bed near her. It hadn't been long at all since she had sat at her little girl's bedside to talk for a minute about her day at school and kiss her good night. The memory of that unspoiled child was too painful, and Ida pushed it aside.

"He doesn't know me anymore," Alice said, her face twisting around the ugly words. When she opened her mouth to cry, she made no sound.

Ida reached out to touch Alice's shoulder, but Alice pulled away and crouched against the plaster wall like a cornered rabbit. Ida drew back in shock, and for lack of a place to put her rejected hand, she gripped the brass knob of the bedpost.

"You may as well have killed me," Alice said in a low, measured voice. She spoke from that place where she'd tried to hide while she was Millie. Her mother's eyes were wide and frightened, and she shook her head. Alice fought the urge to reach out and scratch her face.

"Alice," her mother said, shaking her head slowly, never taking her eyes from her.

Alice pressed her palms against the wall behind her to steady herself and stood up, looming high over her mother. "You do whatever Pa tells you to. You let him send me off to the city, you never wrote to me or visited me, you profited from my situation. Why did you even come to get me? Did you think after all that time, there would be anything left of me?"

"But I did write to you!" Ida cried. "Alice, I didn't know where you were! He told me you were working in a factory, living with a lady he knew. I tried and tried to find you, but he stopped me at every turn, and then I got sick!"

"You were nursing the babies of *whores*," Alice said, and it felt good to say that word, for if she could say it, it might have less power when others said it, as eventually they were bound to do. Now that she'd left the brothel, she could see plainly enough that any distinction between her and the girls would not exist outside. She had served them and their clients. She had been broken by a man whose name she didn't even know. She had lived for five months among them. Anyone here who knew that would see her as one of them.

Her mother was still gripping the bedpost, still shaking her head, and Alice watched her for a sign of dishonesty, a tic or an action belying her words.

"That's what I am now, Mother," Alice continued. "I—am—a— whore. And it's because of you."

"No," Ida choked. "I've been sick over you since you left. I had no way of knowing what was happening!"

"Then you must have been *blind.*"

Ida knew this accusation held some truth. She had not seen, and what she had seen, she had not understood.

Alice saw that her words had cut as she'd intended. But Millie must be exposed for who she was. Alice dropped to her knees on the mattress. Her mother took another step away and watched, transfixed, as Alice crawled to the edge of the bed and swung her legs over it. As she fell backward into the position she had seen the girls in, hips just over the lip of the mattress, she spread her legs and pulled her nightgown high over her face. Ida saw the flash of white and turned away, but Alice did not move, so Ida did what her daughter wanted. She looked.

She saw the reddish wool of curly hair and the vulnerable pink nestled within, saw her daughter not as she had seen other women, in childbirth, the mouths of their birth canals bulging and resistant. Instead she saw the hidden furrow, the precious cleft of flesh that had become her daughter's heart, the site of her brokenness.

Ida saw the white surface of Alice's belly, the hollow of her navel, where once they had been joined, the undulations of her upper ribs, and above them the shroud of her nightgown over the contours of her breasts, her chin, and her face, covered like the face of the dead. She felt their two lives shatter like a block of ice dropped on the frozen surface of the river, fragments sliding in every direction, impossible to retrieve, melting even as they skimmed away. Ida lifted the nightgown off Alice's face and shook it out over her bare lap. Then she took her daughter's hand and helped her sit up. They sat together on the stiff mattress and spoke no more.

On her way home from Mrs. Schreiber's, Ida stopped the wagon at the edge of Mr. Aiken's farm. Working by moonlight, she hauled the three bags of new cuttings across his field and pushed them into the pond.

21

At Mrs. Schreiber's, Alice worked hard to avoid conversation, ate her supper silently with her hostess and the boarding guests, then retired to her room with Mrs. Schreiber's copy of *Women and Economics*. She sat up reading most of the night, even knowing that she would have to rise early. Though the book placed Alice outside its argument—she saw herself now as what Mrs. Stetson called "the other kind of woman"—she couldn't put it down, for it also claimed Alice was not so unlike young married women; Mrs. Stetson saw marriage itself as a form of prostitution in which women married men because it was their sole means of financial support. In fact, much of what the book had to say about marriage took Alice by surprise, and wishing above all never to be taken advantage of again, she read it with great care. This writer, whoever she was, did seem to understand the behavior of those young unmarried men whom Alice had met in New York. The author understood, too, the desire of women to do meaningful work, and the desire of young people in love to be together. But her optimistic view that marriage could change—that things were already changing—was beyond Alice. In the end, the book left her despairing even more deeply, for if she were to have a choice, it would be between prostituting herself as a married woman or living her life alone as a working woman.

She read the entire book in her week at Mrs. Schreiber's, for it was difficult to fall asleep. Between about nine o'clock and midnight, there were steady footsteps, and the indoor plumbing whistled intermittently, until finally the house settled and hushed. An hour or two after that, Alice would set aside the book and try to sleep. She got up frequently to watch out the window for unwelcome visitors in the yard below. Wouldn't her father have the sense to figure out she was staying here? If not here, she would have to be at the Shepherd's Crossing or the Post Road Hotel or at Mrs. Bryant's boardinghouse on the other side of town. But her father did not come.

Nor did Joe. All day long, Alice heard the doors of the house opening and closing and watched the boarders and visitors pass through the front gate. Each time the doorbell rang, it struck at the center of her chest. Could it be that after risking so much to find her and bring her home, he was walking away from all he had promised? She had believed him to be different. But was it possible that any man, even a man who'd once loved her—she knew he had—could overlook all that had happened to her? As the days at Mrs. Schreiber's passed, Alice began to feel she had learned the answer.

These thoughts made it difficult to sleep. She noticed, as she lay in the dark, how different were the night sounds of the village. In the city, traffic passing under the windows and the rumble of the elevated trains never ceased. Here, close to the Schreibers' barn, she heard the occasional snorting of the horses. The spring insects quivered. A foraging raccoon or skunk tipped over a bucket in the garden. Downstairs, a bedstead creaked. Alice thought of all the quiet nights in Underwood, when her mother had slept soundly beside her father while Alice had endured strangers touching her skirts and her hair, leering at her, and that one man . . . The men often hadn't stopped coming until two or even three o'clock in the morning. That was the time, before the sky began to lighten, when Alice had sat at the dining table and drunk a shot or two of liquor or taken her dose of laudanum. There would be no more laudanum and no more drink to help her sleep—not here, nor in her mother's house. She would have to learn to calm her mind herself. She would have to learn how to sleep again. Until that time, if it ever came, she imagined her nights would be this way, she lying prostrate, waiting for daylight.

Aside from her mother, Alice had only one visitor that week, an accidental one. Claudie came to the back door one evening after supper to pick up some tea for Avery and spied Alice through the kitchen window. Alice was washing the dishes—boardinghouse whiteware, just like the dishes at Mrs. Hargrave's—and when she heard Claudie's voice, her first instinct was not to duck out of sight but to look up.

"Alice?" Claudie called out in surprise, and Mrs. Schreiber stepped between them in a futile effort to hide her. "May I come in? Please?" Claudie asked Mrs. Schreiber, and Alice nodded her assent.

"What are you doing here?" Claudie asked, her arms stretched out for a hug, but Alice leaned away. She twisted the dishrag around her hand and sorted through all the possible lies she might tell her friend.

"You mustn't tell anyone I'm here," she finally managed to say.

"What? Why not?"

Alice shook her head and returned to the dishes. Claudie touched her shoulder, but when Alice refused to look at her, Claudie stepped back and dropped her hands.

"You can dry for me," Alice said, handing her a plate.

Claudie retrieved a towel from a drawer pull, and Mrs. Schreiber disappeared through the swinging door.

After a minute, seeing that Alice was not going to speak, Claudie began to talk herself, filling Alice in on all that had happened since she'd been gone.

Avery wasn't much better, she said. He had been out to church once or twice and sometimes sat on the sun porch if the weather was warm. He had tried walking with a cane down the drive and up to the house a couple of times, but it was too much for him, and a headache would crack through his skull afterward, sending him to bed for hours or even an entire day. Everyone else's lives had moved forward, and as Claudie chatted on about the girls they had known at school and some of the folks from church, Alice dwelt on that picture of Avery, left behind, dragging his way down and up the drive. She wished she could visit him and sit at the foot of his bed and read to him again. It wasn't that his company was so pleasant, but Alice felt she would understand him now. His suffering, the product of a supposedly heroic war, had become part of his everyday life, and as such, it was lived mostly in the privacy of his bedroom. If spoken of, it would be preceded or followed by the cheerful news of others with no regard for the fact that Avery must continue to live with it every moment of every day, for it appeared he would not make a full recovery. Alice's suffering was more private still, for no one outside her mother and Joe could ever know of it, though she, too, would carry the load throughout her life.

Eventually Claudie gave up on getting a response from Alice, and she bustled around the kitchen, opening drawers and cabinets to find where the clean dishes belonged. Frustrated in her search for the proper place to store a large ceramic mixing bowl, she stood at the center of the linoleum floor, clutching the bowl to her small bosom, and tears streamed down her cheeks.

"Where were you?" she asked Alice. "I wrote to you five times before Christmas, with no reply. And then your mother said the address was wrong, but she never gave me a new one."

"I didn't know you wrote me," Alice said.

"I was so worried about you!"

Alice dried her hands on her apron and took the bowl from Claudie, afraid that her friend would drop it. She reached to the shelf above the sink and set it there. Then she turned and folded her arms and shook her head. "I never got your letters."

"Then didn't you wonder that something was wrong? Did you think I wouldn't write to you?"

"No. I thought you would."

"You had my address, so why didn't you write to me?"

Alice couldn't answer this. Why was it that she had written only to Joe and to her mother, once, after she found out Gert would deliver her letters? She had foolishly imagined that everyone else had abandoned her. She supposed her fear of being discovered had also kept her from writing, though Claudie had been her closest, most trusted friend.

"You aren't the same, Alice," Claudie said. "What happened to you?" Alice didn't move. She felt impenetrable. "You can tell me," Claudie continued. "Maybe I can help."

"I don't think so," Alice said.

"Why aren't you at home?"

Evading this question, Alice told her, "My mother and I are moving to Albany," though she hadn't yet made up her mind whether she would go.

"When?"

"Later this week."

"Oh, no! Alice." Claudie stepped forward and put her arms around Alice, but Alice did not embrace her. She allowed Claudie to hold her, to rub her back and kiss her cheek, but when Claudie stepped away, Alice still held her arms folded over her chest.

"I don't understand," Claudie said. "I wish you would tell me."

"I can't." Alice turned to the steel sink, where soap bubbles were popping their way toward the gritty bottom. "There's nothing to tell," she added.

"There is," Claudie said. "I'm not a fool. But I can't make you tell . . . I'm engaged to be married."

This news was a surprise. For an instant Alice felt her old self lurch out, a girl who wanted to leap forward and hug her friend and dance around the room. "Congratulations," she said, and she held out her hands. As Claudie took them, Alice noticed for the first time the flat gold engagement band on Claudie's right hand. She feared Claudie would say it was Norris she was marrying, but she told Alice about the young man, a Poughkeepsie accountant named Richard Adams, whom she'd met at a Sunday school picnic. He was the second cousin of a girl they knew, a handsome young man except for his ears, which stuck out like headlamps. At this description, Claudie laughed in such a way that Alice could tell she loved even his silly ears.

"We're waiting a few years to be married," Claudie said. "He wants to be better established. And my parents want me to be twenty." She blushed at this last remark, and Alice missed the Claudie who, before, might have rolled her eyes and made a wry comment about becoming a woman. "I want to be married in the winter, so we can have violets everywhere," Claudie said, spreading her arms, as if this proclamation would impress Alice. "You probably stopped noticing them long ago, but they smell so beautiful, and I like that they stand for love and devotion. That's what I want from my husband. Can you believe I'm going to have a husband?"

Alice could not believe. As she listened to Claudie twitter on about her wedding plans, she tried to think of something she could believe. The violets as symbols of love and devotion? Alice nearly laughed aloud. Claudie was wrong; she hadn't stopped noticing the violets. They were at the root of all her father's troubles and, by extension, her own.

"You'll come back from Albany to visit, won't you? And you

must come back for the wedding when the time comes. You must," Claudie said. Then, more shyly, "I was hoping you would stand up with me."

"Oh, no, I can't do that," Alice said. Claudie seemed hurt, and Alice added, "But I'll try to visit, if I can." Unless everyone learned what had become of her.

"You must try very hard," Claudie said. She gave Alice the firm sort of look a mother gives her headstrong child, and Alice imagined Claudie as the mother of a pack of tumbling children. She and her husband would have a lovely home in Poughkeepsie and raise a beautiful family and live their whole happy lives together. Alice allowed herself the daydream of being the beloved spinster auntie who comes to visit and stays in the guest room all summer, playing with the children and drinking lemonade with the mother on the porch when all the children are in bed. But she couldn't imagine a time would ever come when she would be able to tell Claudie what had happened during her months in New York.

Claudie seemed to understand that their conversation was over. She took up the dish towel and finished drying the soapy dishes Alice set on the drainboard. They worked in tandem without speaking until the job was complete and they could see from the window the last light shuttling around the trunks of Mrs. Schreiber's fruit trees and sinking into the earth. Then Claudie kissed Alice and saw herself out.

22

It took Ida a full week to make her preparations. She baked extra bread and collected provisions in two boxes taken unnoticed from the packing room. She gathered household goods she imagined they would need: her best pots and pans, utensils and knives, a set of four dishes and cups, a pitcher and washbasin, her sewing kit, a lantern, an axe, the Bible and some other favorite books, extra linens, and blankets. In one of the washtubs she stowed an iron, a washboard, clothespins and some line, her smallest broom, and some rags. She took a few cuttings from the rosebush that had been a wedding gift from her father, and a few canes from the raspberries, her favorites, bundled in a scrap of burlap. She might not have a place to plant them on the other end, but she could try. Hopeful of a garden, she added a shovel and a hoe. All these supplies she stashed in the root cellar, where Frank was unlikely to see them.

She removed from her bedroom chest all those things they wouldn't need—fancy linens, clothing the children had outgrown, scraps of fabric she had hoped to use one day—and packed in it all the clothing for herself, Jasper, Reuben, Alice, and the baby. She would have to bring Anabel—or Ana, as she had begun calling her, since it served as a nickname for Anastasia, the name Bridie Douglass had intended.

Ida checked the envelope behind the woodbox where Frank had always kept his savings, but it contained only the usual amount of his pay. There was no extra money, either from what Alice presumably had made over the past several months or from Ida's nursing. Whatever they had earned, Frank apparently had saved elsewhere or spent outright. Perhaps he had paid some of it to his brothers, as Harriet had suggested. Ida would take what she needed at the last moment, so as not to arouse Frank's suspicion.

Their method of travel was tricky as well. The wagon that belonged to Frank was large enough for them all, but taking both the wagon and the horses was inviting trouble. Ida thought of leaving in the middle of the night. As long as no one heard them, they might get far enough to escape pursuit. She could dose Frank's evening beer with laudanum to help him sleep more heavily. But she didn't want to spend the rest of her life afraid that he would catch up with them. She would tell him when it was time, and she would go in the light of day.

It had occurred to her, of course, that they didn't have to go at all. They could stay as if nothing had happened, all except Alice, who would marry quickly, whoever would have her, and move away, as some girls did. If they lost their house to Norris, they would find another, and Frank would continue to work on this farm or the next. She had married him for better, for worse. Staying was not only possible, it was the quietest, least risky choice. But in confronting Ida, Alice had made clear what must be done.

During the day, Ida's attention to these plans kept her busy and sane, but at night she was haunted by the body lying next to her, softly raising the blanket with each even breath. She alternately wished to heal him and to take the axe from the woodbox and slice him through. Over and over, Ida combed through the past, trying to find those nits that had been hiding, waiting to hatch. When had he turned against her and against his own daughter?

She began with their meeting and worked her way forward. In the beginning, she had mistaken his quiet nature as being like her father's—thoughtful, distracted, but genuinely kind. It had taken her a long time, over a year after their marriage, to realize Frank's quiet came more from holding back, from suppressing his anger and resentment. Still, she had imagined herself to be on his side. She had thought he'd seen her as his ally, that the meanness about him was directed only at others, and justifiably. At what point had the difficulties they'd faced together become solvable in his mind by turning against her and against Alice?

And then she wondered: did he even see it that way? Did he love her enough to think of her as a person with her own feelings, capable of being betrayed? Or had he seen her all along as a mere object in his life, a tool to be used for an express purpose: a hoe for weeding, a shovel for digging, a wife for cooking and cleaning and bearing children. If that were true, he was capable of doing anything to her.

On the sixth evening after her return from the city, when Frank went out to check the greenhouses before bed, Ida gathered Oliver and Reuben at the kitchen table to tell them she was leaving and taking Reuben with her. She had spent many of her sleepless hours thinking through this conversation as well, wondering how she could impress upon her boys the seriousness of what their father had done without telling them what it was.

Oliver surprised her, as he often had this past year, by taking the news like his own man. "I know something's not right, Ma," he said. "But what will happen to him?"

She told him the truth: "I don't know."

"I want to stay with Pa!" Reuben protested.

"Your father may not be staying here," Ida said. "Uncle William and Uncle Harold have called in his debt. It's likely he'll lose this house, maybe even his job."

"This is our farm, too," Reuben said. Oliver cracked his knuckles one by one as he thought. Ida cringed at the sound but did not criticize. She watched Reuben watching Oliver and was exhausted by the prospect of having to convince him, too.

"Reuben can come with me," Oliver said finally. "I'm of age."

Ida moved to take Reuben's hand, but he pulled away from her. "I'm not going with you," he said. She felt so fragile that she feared another word from either of them would crack her open. She wanted desperately to take Reuben in her arms, but he wouldn't have it. What if he were to stay with Frank? It was an option she couldn't abide. She had already made one terrible mistake. She could not afford to make another.

"I'll help him find work for the summer," Oliver said. "And he'll finish school."

"No," Ida said firmly. How could she compel Reuben to come with her? He was fourteen, taller and stronger than she, and of all her children, the most stubborn. "I won't allow it, and you must back me up on that, Oliver."

Though he leaned toward her to object, he must have seen something in her face, for he stood tall again and took Reuben's shoulders. "You go with Ma," he said.

"No! I won't. I want to come with you."

"You'll be in the way," Oliver said. "I'll have a business to run, and I can't have a little kid underfoot."

"I can work, too!"

"You must finish school," Ida said, and Oliver nodded. She felt so grateful to him, her young man, that she feared she might cry.

Reuben wrenched from Oliver's grip and ran out the door, slamming it so hard that the latch failed to catch and the door bounced open to the night.

Oliver opened his arms. He was taller than Ida by a foot now, and her head fit under his chin. He held her as if he were the father and she the child. "He'll be all right," he said. "I'll go talk to him."

*   *   *

Ida lay sleepless beside Frank that night, waiting for him to be still. Ana awoke demanding to be fed, though at times she had slept through the night, and Frank stirred and muttered at the interruption. In half an hour the baby slumbered again, but Ida waited longer still to be certain Frank was asleep. Well past midnight, she pulled on her shoes and shawl over her nightdress and began hauling her goods out of the cellar, stacking them first in the garden and then in the wagon, which was parked in the barn. The task took her a long hour, during which she feared Frank or the baby would awaken, but when she finally slipped into bed, they were still asleep.

She lay alert, awaiting the hour when she would have to tell him she was leaving, wondering how she would ever manage to harness the horses and gather the children and drive into town to get Alice once he knew. Again she considered sneaking away. As the room's nighttime shadows shifted with the light of the traveling moon, Ida feared that these might be her last living hours, for she could imagine the worst in his response.

Frank slept fitfully himself and rose well before dawn, dressing quietly to avoid waking her. She heard him cut a slice of bread at the counter before the front door latch clicked. Then she leaned over to check on the baby and Jasper before dressing.

The dark spring morning was frosty, and Ida saw no sign of the lantern Frank would be carrying. No doubt he had headed over the ridge to check on the greenhouses again. He often went out to check them as if to keep them safe from some imagined disaster. She relied on the gibbous moon to guide her up to the ridge, and on the other side, she spotted his light, floating ghostlike down the center of greenhouse 24. It stopped and swung in place like a pendulum with no clock. She made out the shadow of his figure ducking to check something, then standing slowly with his hand pressed hard on his back, which must be paining him again. There was nothing in the houses to check, for the cuttings were all taking root in their raised beds outside, and the old soil had been shoveled from the beds. She saw he was wandering in search of a purpose. The gesture filled her with sadness, and she allowed it to sit with her a moment before she approached him.

The door to the greenhouse was ajar. Ida stepped through the packing room and down three steps to the dirt floor and said, "Frank."

His shoulders jumped, then he lowered his head to study something he held in his cupped hands—a dead starling, she saw as she moved closer. Or perhaps not quite dead, for Frank was alternately blowing gently at its yellow beak and whistling at it, a starling whistle, attempting to rouse the bird from its stupor. One of its shiny green wings ticked, but Ida couldn't tell whether it was Frank's breath or the starling making the movement. Sometimes they flew in through the open roof panels or crashed against the glass in confusion. Ida wasn't sorry to see a starling meet its end—they were a curse to her garden, always stealing her berries and fighting with the other birds. Ignoring her, Frank carried the dying bird all the way out the far end of the house, where he stooped to lay it in the grass. She waited for him as he ambled up the long center aisle toward her in the dark. No one else was there to witness—not another human, nor a bird, nor even a sweet-faced flower. Clods of dirt and cobwebs clung to the empty wooden beds, as if the entire crop had been stolen.

When he got close enough to be heard without raising his voice, Frank said, "What are you doing up here?"

"It's the only place I can speak to you privately," she said. A draft of night air brushed her back, and she shivered.

"You should be down in the house with the boys."

"They're all asleep."

"What do you want, Ida?" he said, his tone brittle, and she saw that he feared she knew everything. She didn't want to corner him like a possum in the dark. She didn't want to force him to lash out.

"Will you walk with me?"

"I'm checking the cuttings."

"They're fine, Frank."

"Don't you speak to me that way. Don't you patronize me." Spittle fell in the light as he spat out the P.

"All right," she said, using the calmest voice she could muster, and she walked slowly toward the door, watching his reflection in the glass, her heart pounding for fear he would jump on her and kill her. She reached the door and stepped up into the packing room, losing the benefit of his reflection, then through the room and out onto the grass, where she took deliberately slow steps toward the ridge. The shadows swung dizzily around her as he carried the lantern, and she stood looking over the farm and waited for him to catch up.

"I'm leaving this morning," she said when he was beside her. "I'm taking Alice and Reuben and the little ones with me. Oliver will stay."

Frank swung the lantern like a scythe and took five or six long steps down the hill. Then he stopped and shouted, "My sons have a right to this farm!" He might as well have whispered, for all the response the night gave him. She knew he was speaking not to her, not even to his brothers, but to an unjust world. From here, below the ridge, they could see the pointed turrets of William's Queen Anne house poking into the black sky as if to punch holes of brightness through it. A light was on in the kitchen. Ida searched for the lights of Harold's farmhouse down the hill and across the lane, a house of three daughters.

"It's not just," Ida said quietly. She tried to think how to get Frank to move on down the hill without touching him. She didn't want to be standing with him up here in the dark.

"I don't care what they do to me," Frank said. "But my sons deserve what's due them."

"And your daughter," Ida said. She felt tall as a late-day shadow thrown on the sky, stretching earth to heaven above it all. She felt the heft of justice behind her. Then she feared she would lose her footing and fall, for she remembered her own stupidity, the terrible error she had made in believing, without thinking, that Frank had equal concern for the welfare of all his children. A man who had that could be trusted to do what was right. But a man who cared only for the future of his sons was a danger to his daughters.

"I know what you did to Alice," Ida said. Let him kill her right here where she stood. If he was so righteous, let him kill her right here in the sight of God's stars. "I know where the babies came from, too," she continued. "I never believed you were capable of such a thing."

Frank snorted and kicked the earth.

"Factory work would have been bad enough," she said. "I'm not sure I could have forgiven you even that. But the devil must be in you to have done such a thing to your daughter."

"Factory work!" Frank shouted, then made a huffing sound like a laugh. A steely desire for vengeance flashed in Ida's hands, and she pulled her shawl tight to keep them close. "Multiply that by five, Ida. Twenty-five dollars a week or more! That's what she could have made if she'd tried. She could have saved us. But I *never* forced her to do a thing." He jabbed his finger at her, emphasizing his innocence.

"And what about her mail?" Ida asked. "You gave me a false address."

"I didn't want anyone interfering."

"Anyone? I'm not just anyone! And by God, you're right. I would have interfered if only I had been wise enough to see what was happening." Unable to contain her hands any longer, she grabbed at his shirtsleeve and shook his arm, but he didn't flinch. "What happened to Mary?" she demanded, for she must have it all, though she was terrified of the answer.

"A family on Madison Avenue paid me two hundred dollars for her," Frank said. "Two hundred dollars, Ida!" He was almost gleeful, and she could see that something in him had slipped. Of course. It had slipped long ago, but only now could she see it on the surface, in the jagged way he spun and tromped down the hill. As he neared the yard, he snuffed the lantern.

She stood halfway up the hill and watched him set the hot lantern on the stoop and then, without entering the house, veer toward the barn. A suggestion of daylight lay in the east, and birds had begun to chatter. The white blossoms of the abandoned pear trees shone in the moonlight. Ida stood for a time watching her house, waiting for something to happen. Frank was still in the barn when she reached the house and took the lantern in. She sat in her rocker, awaiting sunup before waking the children. She was too fearful to sleep, but as the time passed in quiet, she began to trust the stillness. Frank didn't come in the house, and when she went to harness the horses before waking Jasper and the baby, she found that Trip was gone, and so was the money behind the woodbox.

23

Frank's departure delayed Ida's plans, for now she had only one horse, not strong enough to pull the wagonload alone. The situation brought her the following evening to William's door. Standing in his front hallway, both of them unsure of how to proceed in these circumstances, Ida and William negotiated to exchange the heifer and her calf, eight of the hens and the rooster, and the chaise for one of the old work teams to drive Ida's wagon. Oliver could keep four of the hens, the old milk cow, and Trip's mate, Trudy, as well as whatever was left in the house. Then Ida told Oliver where Alice was staying and sent him into town to collect her.

While he was gone and Ida was putting the children to bed, there was a knock at the door. "Ma, it's Aunt Frances," Reuben called from the kitchen.

Frances had not been to the tenant house since Ida's bout with mastitis. Before that, Ida couldn't recall what would have brought her down here. Jasper's birth? As she tucked the covers around Jasper and sang him to sleep, Ida imagined the additional demands that might be made. What accounts did the women have to settle among themselves? Whatever they were, they would have to wait.

With Jasper drifting off and Ana asleep, Ida stood to face her next trial. She found Frances sitting at the kitchen table across from Reuben, who was reading with more industry than Ida had ever seen. Frances faced him, hands folded on the table, rubbing her thumbs together nervously.

"Evening, Frances," Ida said, and Frances stood to greet her. "Reuben, go upstairs to read, please," Ida said. "You may take the lantern with you."

The removal of the light made it difficult for Ida to read the expression on Frances's face.

"I came to say good-bye," Frances said after a time.

"Thank you," Ida said. A good-bye didn't require this formal audience at the kitchen table.

"I've always known about the debt. You know I keep the books. And I want my boy to have a good start. We all do, don't we." Ida made no move to acknowledge this. "But I don't see the need to drive a man past his limits for the sake of money," Frances continued. "Or really, for the sake of revenge. It isn't right, and I understand that. Even if my husband doesn't."

Ida gave her the kind of slight nod she might give a distant acquaintance on the street. Frances seemed to be waiting for Ida to say something in response, but Ida had nothing to say.

"You may think I'm more powerful than you," Frances said when the silence between them became uncomfortable. "But I'm a woman, too. I couldn't have grown a business with my own money this way without a husband—my husband," she corrected herself. "But it *is* my money that started all this. William cannot abide being reminded of that." Ida was surprised to hear her voice crack, and Frances looked away, the only sign Ida had in the darkness that she might be crying.

"He's a good man, William," Ida said. She had never imagined saying so. He hadn't been good to Frank, but he was good to his employees. He was devoted to his wife and his son. He was generous with the community. He wasn't the demon she and Frank had always agreed him to be.

"You needn't say so, Ida," Frances said. "He hasn't been good to you."

"No, but he thinks he has his reasons."

"It would be nice to feel . . ." Frances said very quietly. "It would be nice to believe that he chose me for something other than a fortune."

"Oh," Ida sighed, and she felt her own fortune, for she knew that in the beginning, she and Frank had chosen each other out of what had seemed to be love. "He was lucky to marry you," she said. "And not just because of your inheritance. You are accomplished and intelligent. I'm sure he saw those things in you when he chose you."

"It would be nice to be told so, that's all," Frances said. She reached into her cloak and drew out a business-sized envelope, which she slid on the table to Ida. "Best as I can figure, this is what you're owed. The amount Frank has paid them over all these years. It comes from my own family, not through William, and now it's yours again."

Ida didn't touch the envelope. She wished she could see Frances's face better. Was there some catch? Would she later be asked to repay this as a loan?

"There's four hundred sixty-four dollars," Frances said. "Enough to help you get started."

Ida was still afraid to touch the envelope.

"It's your money, Ida," Frances said, standing. "I hope you'll forgive me."

Seeing that she intended to go, Ida followed her to the door. As she opened it, she managed to say "Thank you," and Frances briefly held her, the first time she had embraced her since Ida had met her as a bride.

In the next instant, Frances set her hand on the doorframe. "Good night," she said.

On the seventh evening after her return, Alice went home with Oliver. He didn't ask questions, just gave her a quick kiss on the cheek and picked up her satchel containing the few things he had delivered earlier in the week. Outside, as he was helping her into the wagon, she spotted Mrs. Pruitt pushing Avery down the sidewalk in a wheelchair. It was dusk, and she had hoped to escape the village unseen. But Mrs. Pruitt slowly raised her hand in greeting, as if confused by Alice's presence, then touched Avery's shoulder, and he turned to see her. Alice stepped down from the wagon and crossed the street.

Avery looked better than he had the last time she'd seen him, with even a flush in his cheeks—was that on account of seeing her? She allowed Mrs. Pruitt to hug and kiss her, and then she gave Avery her hand. Mrs. Pruitt prattled on, asking questions about the move to Albany that Alice had to ignore. She directed her attention to Avery himself. They were compatriots now, left behind by the other young men and women, who would go off and marry and live their lives in the new century. Alice squeezed his hand, harder than she had intended, trying to somehow telegraph that she understood something of his life and he of hers. His pale eyes met hers, searching for her meaning. "Good luck to you, Alice," he said.

"Good luck to you, too," she said. "Be well." Then she pulled her hand from his and ran across the street, where Oliver, from his seat in the wagon, raised his hat to Mrs. Pruitt.

The sun rose before five-thirty on the morning of their departure, giving Ida plenty of time to prepare before the workers turned up for the day. She wanted to be gone before they and the rest of Underwood saw her. She heard Prissy mewling at the door and let her in. She tried to pick up the cat and rub her soft chest with affection, for she would have to live out her life here, mousing in the barn. Unaware of how things were about to change, the cat wrestled out of Ida's grasp and went poking her nose at the base of the sink, searching for something to eat. Ida poured her a splash of yesterday's milk and went in to see to Ana, who had begun to fuss in her old way.

Sitting in bed, Ida held the baby to her breast while opening a book so she could read a morning story to Jasper. The baby suckled for a few seconds, then whimpered. Ida put down the book and tried again, but again after a few sucks, Ana opened her mouth and howled. The other breast was no better. Ida laid the baby in the trundle bed and stood by the washbasin. A gentle touch, and she felt the prickling in her breasts, the release of her milk, and she leaned over the basin and massaged the base of her nipples between thumb and finger as she had done so many times. A slow trickle dribbled from her left breast, then stopped. From her right breast, she coaxed a few drops.

"Not to worry," she told herself. She put the kettle on and, fastening a few buttons to cover herself, took Jasper and his story-book out to the kitchen. The baby cried hungrily in the bedroom, but Ida let her go on, hoping she would cry herself out and fall asleep. By the time she had finished reading to Jasper, the water was hot. She poured some into the basin, tempering it with cold so it wouldn't scald her skin. Then she wet a washcloth and, after opening her shirtwaist again, pressed the hot compress on her breasts and waited. She imagined she could feel the weight of the milk. Her breasts were firm, as if they had something to yield. But when she tried again to massage the milk down, just a few drops fell into the basin of water, blue-gray clouds that spread and disappeared. Her milk was gone.

In the morning, Alice heard her mother fussing in the kitchen and washing at the basin. Jasper began to stomp about and speak in his midday voice, and Alice gave up on the little sleep she'd hoarded and rose to get breakfast. Reuben, looking so much taller than she had remembered, hitched Uncle William's old team to the wagon and brought it around front, and together she and Oliver and her mother packed the last few things. Aunt Harriet came across the lane in her apron with her girls following behind, and the four of them stood in the barnyard, viewing the preparations like mourners at a burial. Alice watched as Aunt Harriet embraced her mother for a long time, so long that she and her cousins grew embarrassed and turned their heads away. She'd had no idea that her mother even cared for Aunt Harriet. Then her aunt walked over to Alice, tears running unchecked down her face. She gripped Alice's arms and said to her, "Take good care of your mother now," as if it were Alice's mother who needed taking care of and not Alice herself. She had to remind herself that her mother had kept her word, and no one, including Aunt Harriet, knew what had happened in the city.

It was time to go. "Where is Reuben?" Ida asked, and her heart accelerated and jumped. She suddenly felt panicked to leave at once.

"I'll find him," Oliver said.

Ida kept busy straightening things in the back of the wagon while Alice walked Jasper to see the chickens one last time. Harriet's girls wandered away. Fifteen minutes later, Oliver jogged down the hill with Reuben by the arm. Behind them, Norris stood outside greenhouse 3, his hands in his pockets. There was no sign of William or Harold or Frances.

"I'm not going," Reuben announced as they neared the wagon.

"You are," Ida said. "Climb up there now. We're ready to leave."

Reuben yanked his arm, but Oliver stood firm. "You want me to lift him up there, Ma?" he asked.

"Come, Reuben," Ida said sternly. "You're keeping us waiting."

"I'm not *going*," he said, yanking again, and his face twisted as he strained against his brother's grip.

What was she to do? Tie him to the wagon? Nothing else would keep him from jumping out at the corner and running away. Or worse, running once they reached Albany.

"Oliver," Ida said, but the rest of her intended words dammed in her throat.

Oliver beheld her trembling face, and she saw the recognition pass over him. He let go of his brother's arm, and Reuben staggered and fell on the drive.

"I'll take good care of him, Ma," he said. "I promise." Reuben looked up at them, confused. "Get up and say a proper good-bye," Oliver commanded.

Ida could no longer hold her own broken pieces together, and she sobbed aloud as Reuben stood and walked to her, then allowed her to embrace him. She hated for the children to see her this way. Only Jasper remained innocent of their circumstances, and when he reached out to her from Alice's arms, his trust tore Ida's heart. She squeezed Reuben tightly and breathed him in, his earthy hair and his sweaty skin, then stepped back and regarded his bewildered face, but still she couldn't speak. She kissed his forehead and nudged him toward Oliver. Then her young man, her firstborn, enfolded her in his sturdy arms and whispered in her ear, "Don't worry, Ma." Then, to her surprise, "I love you." Unable to look at his face for fear she would lose her courage, Ida kissed him quickly and turned her head, then climbed up to the wagon seat.

Harriet handed up the baby in her basket, and Alice handed up Jasper, but before she could climb up herself, she was distracted by a movement on the driveway. The workers were starting to arrive; among them was Joe, riding up to the barn on his bicycle. He dismounted and leaned the bike against the north wall, where a few others were already parked. He stood there beside the barn, looking foolish with a ribbon tied around one leg of his trousers to keep it from catching in the gears. He hadn't the sense to walk up to her and take her in his arms and ask her again to be his wife. Instead he raised his cap and said directly to Alice, "Godspeed." She pulled herself up to the wagon seat; her mother clicked her tongue, and the old team lurched into motion.

24

Within an hour, they had driven north past the range of Alice's experience. She had never seen these roads just a few miles beyond her own town, and she recognized the obvious: there were other directions in which to go.

They stopped south of Germantown to eat lunch beside a fallow field and let Jasper run his legs tired. Ida tried to nurse the baby one last time, but Ana fussed and slapped her little hands on Ida's chest. Finally, Ida passed the baby to Alice and poured some cow's milk into a feeding bottle. Ana squirmed in Alice's arms, then settled and drank for a minute or two. Ida cried again, private tears that she wiped on her sleeve as she walked away from the wagon so as not to distract the baby by her presence. When she returned, Ana had pushed the bottle away and was sitting up in Alice's lap. Ida placed a scrap of bread in the baby's hand and said to Alice, "We'll try some pap tonight."

At twilight they engaged a room at a tavern in Hudson, where a bar fight awoke them at three A.M. After that Ana refused to sleep. The second day of travel was harder, exhausted as they were, and they passed the miles mostly in silence, save Jasper's singing. Long stretches of the road were overgrown and deserted. Everyone, it seemed, was traveling by steamship or train.

They reached the rumbling city of Albany midway through the third day. Ida had expected to cross the Hudson on the old ferry, but when they passed through the last tollhouse and inquired directions of the toll keeper, they learned there was now a bridge at South Ferry Street. The river was much narrower here than at Underwood, yet busier, with steamships and barges and tugboats and schooners passing one another like wagons on the streets of New York. They paid the fifteen-cent toll and began the short crossing. It felt otherworldly and frightening to be traveling over the river traffic, over the river itself, like angels gazing down on earth. Ida had never imagined anything like it. To steady herself, she shifted her gaze to the far waterfront, crammed with warehouses and ferry slips, factories and grain elevators and large hotels. SAILS AWNINGS TENTS, read one boldly painted building. PAINTS OILS STEAM ENGINE & BOAT SUPPLIES. Beer barrels lay stacked on their sides, waiting for shipment at the dock, and the air smelled of baking day.

And the capitol! When Ida had left with Frank in the summer of 1875, it had been under construction. Now it was a fantastical castle in the middle of the humble city, its red roof punctuating the otherwise drab landscape like a carnation on a gentleman's lapel. Things had changed even since Theodore Roosevelt had led his Rough Riders into battle under a year ago. Now he slept in Albany's executive mansion.

They were over the bridge, and Ida had to get her bearings. Here was Broadway, and a few blocks up, Steamboat Square, where the road took a bend to the west. She guided the team to the left up State Street, the widest avenue, with two sets of electric trolley tracks veining its center and the palatial capitol building at its head, where the street veered left to accommodate it.

Alice held the edge of her seat. People were staring at them, two women with two children in a wagon piled full of household goods. They looked pitiful. Above them, loops of trolley and telegraph wire seemed a net designed to trap them, and everywhere she turned, something reminded her of New York: the paper scraps blown up against the curb, the striped awnings pulled out over painted plate-glass windows, the clatter of hooves and wheels on the paving bricks, and the shouts of men and boys. Alice bowed her head and shut her eyes tight.

Past the brick and brownstone State Street Presbyterian Church and Emmanuel Baptist, with a grand new bell tower. Ida could feel her own pulse in her ears. Here it was. Dove Street. She guided the team to the left and entered her old neighborhood.

Alice's mother had spoken often of her girlhood in Albany, and Alice had pictured a spacious neighborhood of stately homes set back from the street, with green lawns and front porches where many of the scenes of her mother's young life had played out. Instead she found a narrow city street, with brownstone town homes standing shoulder to shoulder, their front stoops like tongues stuck out on the sidewalk. Her mother was thrilled by it all.

As they passed each building, she exclaimed at the changes or the things that were the same. "That beautiful ash tree has been there forever . . . Here's Mrs. Potter's place, but she's gone now . . . My best friend, Liza, lived here. I wonder what became of her . . . Dr. Maria Hull? A lady doctor. Imagine that . . . Oh, here's Mr. K.'s grocery. He has a long Dutch name. We could never pronounce it, so we called him Mr. K. . . . And Mrs. Van de Bogart still offers piano lessons. She needs to repaint her sign . . ."

They stopped in front of her girlhood home, and Alice leaned on the edge of the seat to study it. After Alice's grandfather's death, it had been sold, and now it looked unkempt. Chunks of mortar had fallen from between the bricks, and the window frames sorely needed painting. Mismatched curtains that might have been old sheets were hung inside the windows, protecting the inhabitants from the prying eyes of passersby on the sidewalk just outside. The driver of a carriage behind them called out to them to move along, for they were blocking traffic. Alice's mother commanded the horses, and they picked up their hooves and trotted forward, away from the sad old house. After that, her mother was silent for some time.

"Where shall we stop, then?" she asked finally. They pulled up beside a grocery, and she went in to purchase some bread and to ask directions. When she returned, she told Alice, "The grocer's cousin owns an inn up Broadway toward the canal. It's not as fine a neighborhood." She smiled as if this were cheerful news. A boardinghouse, a poor neighborhood. Alice drew her wrap more tightly over her chest.

Jasper banged his heels against the wagon seat and uttered a low whine. "We're almost home, my boy," Ida said, turning to touch his cheek.

"No!"

"Our new home. You'll see." To Alice, the absence of Joe and of Claudie, of Oliver and Reuben and even Norris and her other cousins, made the idea of "home" seem impossible in this place. The wagon lurched forward, and she feared for the future.

The Goldenrod Inn was not so terrible. Though there was a great deal of noisy traffic just outside its door, inside was a large dining room where Alice was relieved to see respectable women eating with men who appeared to be their husbands, and some children playing marbles in the corner. The innkeeper, Mr. Vreeland, greeted them politely. Before the week was out, Ida had been hired to assist the cook in the kitchen. While she worked, Alice tended the children and ran errands on occasion for the guests.

Mr. Vreeland was a widower with one son, a gregarious young man named Pieter who entertained the children by carrying the supper trays on his head and doing circus jumps over the banister. Mr. Vreeland was quieter, but kind and always on time with Ida's pay. Alice was never bothered by the rougher guests coming through—the canal workers and the peddlers and the single traveling men—for they weren't her responsibility, and anyway, she had learned that they were no worse than the men whose public good manners belied their private transgressions.

Though she and her mother shared tasks during the day and a bed at night, Alice kept her own counsel. They never spoke again of what had happened, or how it had happened, and both were left to quietly draw their own conclusions. It was impossible for Alice to fully absolve her mother of responsibility for her months in New York; what was possible was to simply live one day following another in a chain leading away from that time.

Alice kept their shared room tidy, and she kept the children busy. She helped her mother in the kitchen when there was a rush, and listened to Pieter sing silly, made-up lyrics to the tune of sea chanteys while he washed the bar glasses, a job that had been Alice's in another life. Eventually those lyrics began to address her: "I know a brown-eyed lass named Alice, / 'n' if I could, I'd build her a palace."

In the evenings, Alice sat in the rocker in the corner of the kitchen or, if the inn was quiet, at a table in a front window, doing the mending or reading the newspaper or a book borrowed from the library, and in time, she began to feel she was living a life.

A few nights after their arrival in Albany, Ida first had the dream that would return relentlessly throughout her life in one form or another.

She was walking up the farm hill, and it was windy. She was having trouble holding on to her hat, an old-fashioned bonnet. At first the dream was only about the bonnet—one of those dreams in which she must do something that in waking life would be straightforward but that in sleep was impossible for reasons she couldn't quite obtain. Ida knew that she was dreaming; she was wickedly plagued by that bonnet and wished only to wake up.

Then she saw Frank on the ridge. As she thought about it from her bed minutes later, with Alice asleep beside her and the unfamiliar shadows of furniture in odd places around her, it seemed that when she saw Frank, she lost track of the fact that she was dreaming.

At the sight of her, he waved a wave the whole length of his arm that arced across the sky. It was a wave unlike one he had ever given her, even as a young man, for its enthusiasm. Then he ran down the hill and embraced her. He was crying and begging her to understand that a terrible mistake had been made, another trick of his brothers. He would never do such a thing to Alice. He pressed a huge bouquet of wildflowers at her and swore he loved her so much. Wouldn't they all please come home? But Ida had tied her bonnet so tightly under her chin that it choked her.

She woke, confused, and sat up in the strange bed, which moaned and wobbled under her. She sat there for a long while, not knowing what time it was, hoping the sky would lighten, but it did not. She worried what they would do without him.

She missed him.

Not the man himself, made of bones and flesh, who was sleeping or walking somewhere on this earth, perhaps dreaming his own tortured dream. Not him.

But she missed desperately the idea of him, the man she'd thought he was. That man was more real to her than the one who had betrayed them all. She had been married to him for twenty-three years. All that time she had worked and slept beside him, washed the dirt from his clothing and cooked food for his sustenance, talked with him and held his hand, rubbed his sore back and cried into his chest, and given birth to five children who variously had his eyes, his hair, his gait, his reticence, his temper, his charm. All that time, had she actually been married to an idea and not understood the real man, not known one true scrap of him?

Yet that idea had such a hold on her that she *missed* it. When she lay down again, she turned away from Alice, her face to the plaster wall, hoping to guard her from the terrible secret of this longing.

Later, there would be rumors of Frank's whereabouts. Harriet would report that en route to New York on the train, Harold had met a man who knew Frank and claimed to have bought a horse from him in the city the week before. Ida would keep an intermittent correspondence with Bridie Douglass, sending notes about Ana's growth and health, and once Bridie would write that she thought she'd seen Mr. Fletcher across the street, standing in front of the lunchroom and watching Mrs. Hargrave's building, though she couldn't be certain. Oliver would write that Aunt Frances had forwarded to him in Boston an envelope with a New York City postmark. The envelope contained ten dollars, and Oliver believed the money had come from his father. Nevertheless, Ida would not hear from Frank herself, and with the passage of time, she would be able to release some of the fear she carried always in the stiffness of her shoulders, a fear that one day he would turn up. The rest of that fear would alter itself into worry and eventually, after a great while, into simple regret. She would never again have the luxury of relaxing into her chair and feeling the clean relief of a good day's work done, for always there would be Frank, though work and rest she would, and Frank be damned.

It looks like there's a diary in there, too.

Yes, it's my first diary, from 1900. In fact, I think I started it on New Year's Eve. My husband had just started courting me, and he gave it to me as a Christmas gift. We were married for sixty-two years.

Would you read something to me? I'm curious what you were thinking about the turn of the century.

Oh, I'd rather not.

Would you like some lemonade? I'll see if my granddaughter will bring us a glass.

No, thank you. What does the inscription say?

All right. I'll read just that. "To dearest Alice on the eve of the twentieth century. With each turn of the earth, my heart turns more to you."

I had forgotten that. How sweet . . . Oh, I do miss my Pieter.

—excerpt from an interview with Mrs. Alice Vreeland for
The Women of Albany County, July 6, 1972

14 May 1932
Rensselaer, New York
Dear Alice,

I write this letter directly to you, though you should share as much of it as you would like with Pieter. I have a few personal explanations to make that aren't appropriate to a formal document such as my will, and I want them to be in writing.

First, I want to be clear that I do wish you to be my executor. I am well aware that it is usually a man's job, but I don't intend it to be Pieter's, I intend it to be yours. Don't let him or Oliver or Jasper talk you out of it. They are all too busy with their own work. Show them this letter if you must. Also, the will is clear that your share of the money is to be yours, not Pieter's. This is not to say that I don't trust Pieter—you know I love him dearly—but I must treat everyone the same, and I do hope you'll keep an eye on Ana and Jerry. That is, the money is *hers* and hers alone. If there is any question of her legal standing as my heir, you will find the notarized letter from her mother in my safe deposit box. Of course, I've left some money for Aunt Grace, too, as well as my phonograph records and some old photographs.

I've listed in the will the few items that I have special attachments to and that should go to particular family members. Other than that, I don't care in the least who takes what, but do sell the rental property at once. I would do it myself if I had the energy, but it's already too late for that. I'm sorry to leave you with those details.

Also, don't be surprised that I've left quite a bit—as much as each of your shares—to the League of Women Voters. The church may be put off by this, not to mention your brothers. My attorney assures me it's all airtight, but if there should be any grumbling, I hope you will reinforce to everyone that it is exactly as I intended.

As you know, I wish to be buried beside Reuben. It is one of my greatest regrets that I allowed him to go off so young, and that I gave Oliver the burden of keeping him out of trouble, though I realize I had little choice. Oliver still blames himself for what happened leading up to the fight, though Reuben was his own man by then and couldn't have been stopped. You must keep reminding Oliver of that when I am no longer here to do so. It is my one consolation that when I die, I shall be beside Reuben again, and he will have his mama with him as she should have been all along.

This leads me to another thing I feel compelled to write down for you. I have been thinking a great deal about forgiveness these last months. I imagine it is something that many people think about as their lives come to an end, but of course you and I have more to forgive than some others. I need forgiveness, too, not only for allowing Reuben to go off, but of course for what happened to you. As our Lord says, "Forgive, and ye shall be forgiven." Much as I wish I could say I have found forgiveness for your father, I cannot, and I understand you don't even wish that, but I do think I have found more compassion for him, or my memory of him, as the years have passed, and that brings me some peace. I pray that you will find some peace as well, in your own time and your own way.

As for all the other things I would like to say to you, I shall save them to say in person, my darling girl. I know you hate for me to talk that way to you, but you are a mother, too (and soon a grandmother!), so you understand how deeply I love you. I don't expect any sort of deathbed reconciliation or drama. You and Pieter have been very good to me, especially this last year, and I am extremely grateful for that. You are on my heart always.

I look forward to seeing you again on Tuesday. I have been feeling good this week, except for the morning after I took those sleeping pills you gave me. I don't see how you can use them, and I wish you wouldn't. They made me foggy and lethargic all the next day, and if there is one thing I don't want, it's to miss the short remainder of life I have coming to me. Don't forget to return my glasses if you can find them in the car. I am still well enough to read mornings, but the old ones I have here are terrible, the wrong prescription entirely.

Love,
Mother

June 22, 1932

BUSINESS CAPSULE

UNDERWOOD—The Hudson Valley's last major violet grower will close its doors this week. Chas. Tenney & Sons, an Underwood grower for nearly forty years, has shipped its last bouquet and this week is auctioning off its greenhouses and other farming equipment. The land has been purchased by developer Creighton Roth of New York City. The auction will be held on the Tenney property, 22 Hickok Lane, at 10 a.m. Saturday. In the past decade, major growers James DuMont and Norris Fletcher have also left the business as the once-popular bloom has given way to carnations, roses, and orchids. DuMont now owns Riverside Orchards, where he farms apples. Fletcher is the owner and president of Fletcher & Sons, a commercial development and construction company. At the turn of the century, the valley's 400 violet houses produced six million blooms in a single growing season.

Are there any violet growers left today?

I doubt it. As far as I know, the violets went out with my mother in the early thirties.

That's interesting. Did you see them as being connected in some way?

Of course not; it's just an observation. Though my mother certainly worked hard for the violets, and they never did a thing for her. They were tough little flowers. They liked the cold, and they would ship halfway across the country and arrive intact. But my mother was even tougher than that.

My. I haven't looked through this box in a very long time.

That's a beautiful locket.

Yes. It belonged to my grandmother. There used to be a lock of my grandfather's hair in it.

It looks like this newspaper clipping is the most recent thing in here.

That might be so.

After your mother died, you stopped saving things?

My mother and I had a very difficult relationship.

Just the usual mother–daughter things?

Forgive me. I'm getting too personal.

You're making me think, that's all.

About what?

A lot of things.

Reading her last letter again . . . She really was a remarkable woman. I wish I had told her that. I always knew it.

That's exactly what this project is all about. Remembering remarkable women from this area who might otherwise go unnoticed into history.

I'd like my granddaughter, Susan, to come in here and sit with us. I have a few more things to say, and she'll need to leave to pick up her children soon.

Do you have the time? Gracious, we've been talking for two hours? Maybe you need to go.

No, no. I can stay as long as you want.

Susan?

You don't need to tape-record this part, do you?

It would be helpful.

I don't want this recorded. And you'll need to promise me that none of this will be published until I'm gone.

All right.

Susan. Sit right here, with us. When we're done, I'm going to give this box to you. It has all my old letters and newspaper clippings and a couple of journals and your great-great-grandmother's locket. But first I want to tell you something.

I want to tell you what happened to me in the winter of 1899, when I was just sixteen . . .

—End of tape. Excerpted from an interview with Mrs. Alice Vreeland for *The Women of Albany County*, July 6, 1972

AUTHOR'S NOTE

The area around Rhinebeck, New York, was known in the late nineteenth and early twentieth centuries as the "Violet Capital of the World." Remarkably, there is little evidence of that booming trade today, beyond the names of several local streets (including Garden Street in Red Hook, Violet Hill Road and Violet Place in Rhinebeck, and Violet Avenue in Poughkeepsie); a few remaining greenhouses growing other crops or standing in ruin; and the existence of one bed of Frey's Fragrant violets in a greenhouse on the Battenfeld farm in Red Hook. The Battenfelds now grow anemones and Christmas trees. While the details of violet growing are as accurate as I could render them, I took authorial license with one particular aspect of the business: although the industry had declined by 1932, when it is purported in my fictional newspaper account to have ended, in reality, violets later experienced a short-lived resurgence in popularity, and the last Hudson Valley violet farm was in business until the 1980s.

I have retained the names of many Hudson Valley locales, including Poughkeepsie, Hyde Park, Kingston and Rondout Creek, Tivoli, Germantown, Hudson, Kinderhook, and Albany. However, the town of Underwood—its people, its geography, its businesses, and its streets—is entirely fictitious. The only true-to-life character in the novel is Captain Eltinge Anderson of the steamship *Mary Powell,* whose brindle bull terrier Buster really did perform the trick of praying for the passengers. Donald C. Ringwald's thorough book *The Mary Powell* provided that anecdote and many details of steamship travel on the Hudson.

The sermon preached by Dominie Jacobs on the Spanish-American War (now often referred to as the War of 1898) is excerpted directly from a sermon that was delivered by the Reverend Dr. Henry Van Dyke, pastor of the Brick Presbyterian Church, New York City, on May 1, 1898. I am grateful to the Beinecke Rare Book and Manuscript Library at Yale University for access to that document.

Author Charlotte Perkins Stetson, whose book *Women and Economics* was widely read and discussed upon its publication in 1898, later became Charlotte Perkins Gilman and is perhaps best remembered today as the author of the oft-anthologized short story "The Yellow Wallpaper." *Women and Economics* is still available in several different editions and provides an interesting picture of the women's movement at the turn of the century and, by extension, of where that movement stands today.

The history of yellow fever during the Spanish-American War is also an interesting one. Most of its victims either died or made a full recovery. Avery's unusual outcome is based on the story of John R. Kissinger, an army private who was one of several volunteers in an experiment to test the theory that yellow fever was transmitted by mosquitoes. Unlike some of his peers, Kissinger survived the experiment, but he was left with permanent neurological damage. His story and the story of the Yellow Fever Commission, headed by Walter Reed, can be found on the University of Virginia website at http://yellowfever.lib.virginia.edu/reed/commission.html.

It was surprisingly difficult to obtain detailed information about the lives of prostitutes in late-nineteenth-century New York. While public health statistics are available, details of what day-to-day life was like inside the brothels are much more difficult to come by. Ruth Rosen's *The Lost Sisterhood: Prostitution in America, 1900–1918* and Karen Abbott's *Sin in the Second City* were most helpful. Other details of life in the city for women of that time came from Dorothy Richardson's fictionalized autobiography, *The Long Day: The Story of a New York Working Girl* (1905), reprinted in *Women at Work* (ed. William L. O'Neill) and from visits to the excellent New York Tenement Museum on the Lower East Side of Manhattan.

Other sources that were especially valuable to the research of this novel include Valerie Fildes's *Wet Nursing: A History from Antiquity to the Present* and Jacqueline H. Wolf's *Don't Kill Your Baby: Public Health and the Decline of Breastfeeding in the 19th and 20th Centuries;* Harvey Green's *The Light of the Home: An Intimate View of the Lives of Women in Victorian America;* the *1897 Sears, Roebuck Catalogue,* edited by Fred L. Israel; H. Wayne Morgan's *William McKinley and His America;* the classic *How the Other Half Lives* by Jacob A. Riis; Thomas J. Schlereth's *Victorian America: Transformations in Everyday Life;* David Traxel's *1898;* and the New York Transit Museum in Brooklyn Heights. Many other sources contributed in small ways to the historical flavor of this work.

ACKNOWLEDGMENTS

The first readers of this novel, in its many incarnations, helped to shape it from the beginning. For that work and for their faith that it would be more widely read someday, I am grateful to Mary Becelia, Tricia Dowcett-Bettencourt, Heather Jessen, Sharyn Nelson, Tracy Roberts, Mark Seidl, Alison Weems, and Robert Olmstead, whose generosity extended across a gap of more than twenty years.

A deep and heartfelt thank-you to Lisa Bankoff for opening this door and leading me through with her savvy and sage guidance, and to Trish Todd for her skilled readings and her enthusiasm for all things violet. Thanks also to all those who worked behind the scenes at ICM and Simon & Schuster to bring this novel to its readers.

Writing historical fiction requires the research assistance of many people. Rebecca Edwards lent her Gilded Age expertise to many passages in this novel. Kim Brinton told me what it's like to deliver a calf, Anne Kusilek described the feel of sewing on an antique machine, Roger Leonard offered numerous details about the nineteenth-century church, and Rick Cohn checked my music history. I am especially grateful to Fred Battenfeld for showing me around his greenhouses and teaching me about growing violets. I wish that Clare O'Neill Carr were here to celebrate with me the sharing of local history; she first told me about the violet past of my own hometown. My gratitude also extends to the staff and volunteers of the Museum of Rhinebeck History; the Egbert Benson Historical Society of Red Hook; the Albany Institute of History & Art Library; the LuEsther T. Mertz Library of the New York Botanical Garden; the Library of Congress; the Yale University Divinity School Library; Miller Memorial Library in Hamden, Connecticut; Wallingford Public Library; and most especially, my colleagues at the Arnold Bernhard Library at Quinnipiac University. Any errors I have made in the depiction of the Hudson Valley in the nineteenth century are mine alone.

Monica Bauer, Roxanne Hawn, and Bailey Walsh offered well-timed advice, for which I am especially grateful. Kim Herzog, a true friend, understood more than anyone what publishing this novel meant. Heartfelt thanks go also to the Czepiels—Anne, Bob, Susan, Jane, and Phil—for their enthusiasm and for making me their own. My colleagues in the First-Year Writing Program at Quinnipiac University constantly fuel my brain and have helped me more than they know. The encouragement of so many other friends and family members has kept me afloat.

The greatest thanks of all belongs to my family: to my parents, Bernice and Roger Leonard, who fostered the writer in me from the beginning; to my brothers, Doug and Greg Leonard, who tell the best stories ever; to Ellie and Meggie, with thanks for all the quiet Saturday mornings and for the joy of seeing their own writing blossom; and to Brad, always my first reader, my best friend, the one who in so many ways makes writing possible.

The violet industry is booming in 1898, and a Hudson Valley farm owned by the Fletcher family is turning a generous profit for its two oldest brothers. But Ida Fletcher, married to the black sheep youngest brother, has taken up wet-nursing in order to help her family, and her daughter, Alice, has been ordered by her father to leave school and find work or marry. As their family is about to lose their share of the farm, Ida and Alice make increasingly great sacrifices that set them against each other in a lifelong struggle for honesty and forgiveness.

The story is framed by an amateur historian's 1972 interview with Alice, whose redemption will come only with her willingness to break a silence of more than seventy years and recognize her mother's courage in the face of a changing world.

Topics & Questions for Discussion

1. *A Violet Season* is divided into four parts: "Whitewash," "Harvest," "The Stokehouse," and "New Cuttings." Discuss the significance of the book's title and the part titles. What is the significance of the violet itself in relation to both Ida's and Alice's journeys?

2. Discuss the relationships between the various female characters. Do you feel that they could have done more to support one another? Consider the three sisters-in-law, Harriet, Frances, and Ida; the girlhood friends Claudie and Alice; and the women who work in Mrs. Hargrave's house. Were you surprised that Alice never tried to write to Claudie? Do you think Ida might have had a better relationship with her sisters-in-law if she had tried opening up to them—and vice versa?

3. Compare and contrast Oliver, Avery, Norris, and Joe. How is each an illustration of the environment and societal expecta-

tions that shaped young men during this time? How have expectations changed—or remained the same—today?

4. As demonstrated by the character Anna Brinckerhoff and the inclusion of *Women and Economics,* this was a time when women were beginning to question traditional gender roles and exploring what their place was in marriage and in the wider world. Discuss the various examples of relationships between men and women throughout the novel. Consider Dr. Van de Klerk's reaction when he finds that Ida has "decided" to take on two babies or Frances's confession that she believes William married her solely for her fortune.

5. There is a moment, right after Frank announces he's left Alice in the city, when Ida storms out of the house, thinking to secure Alice's return by turning to William and Frances. But then she stops: "William and Frances had been there, too. . . . They must've questioned his judgment. But what was there to demand, to say, to do now? No one would do anything. . . . She could rely on no one." Do you think this is true, and that she did the best she could? Or do you feel Ida should have tried harder? How much of the blame do you feel lies with Ida? Do you agree with Alice's angry accusation that Ida was "blind"?

6. In justifying what he did to Alice, Frank says, "She could've saved us," even though he clearly cares only for the future of his sons. Discuss this irony in the context of the period and the way women were viewed and valued.

7. *A Violet Season* is told from both Alice's and Ida's perspectives. Why do you think the author chose to construct the novel this way? What does this add to the narrative? If you could have read more from one character's perspective in this novel, whose would it be? Is there another character's perspective you wish the author had included? What did you think of the interview sections of the novel, where Alice recalls her mother and everything that happened to them?

8. Do you think if Ida had mentioned the encounter she witnessed between Alice and Joe Jacobs to Frank, things could have turned out differently for Alice? What about if Alice had confided in her mother that she loved Joe right from the start? Why or why not?

9. Joe goes through an immense amount of trouble to save Alice from Mrs. Hargrave's. Were you surprised by his decision to abandon their relationship once he and Ida brought her home, his only words to her being a final "Godspeed"?

10. At the only point of confrontation between Frank and Alice, in Mrs. Hargrave's study, Frank forcibly takes Alice's locket. What is the significance of this action? Why do you think he did it?

11. Discuss the evolution of Frank's character. Did you find him as terrible and cold in the beginning as he becomes by the end? Or did you find him somewhat sympathetic at first, blighted by his circumstances and the grudges he and his brothers have been carrying for so long?

12. Alice and Ida both read *Women and Economics* by Charlotte Perkins Stetson, as follows:

> *In the passage Ida read that afternoon, Mrs. Stetson chastised the economic system for pressuring mothers to withhold from their daughters the truths about marriage and motherhood.*
>
> *Though the book placed Alice outside its argument . . . she couldn't put it down, for it also claimed Alice was not so unlike young married women; Mrs. Stetson saw marriage itself as a form of prostitution in which women married men because it was their sole means of financial support. . . . In the end, the book left her despairing even more deeply, for if she were to have a choice, it would be between prostituting herself as a married woman or living her life alone as a working woman.*

What do you think about the conclusions each woman draws from the passages that speak most to her? Discuss these ideas in the context of the time in which they were written, and in the context of our contemporary world. Do you still feel there's relevance in Mrs. Stetson's words?

13. At the end of the novel Ida reflects, "She missed him. Not the man himself. . . . But she missed desperately the idea of him, the man she'd thought he was. That man was more real to her than the one who had betrayed them all." Have you ever fallen in love with an idea, only to be confronted with a less appealing reality?

Enhance Your Book Club

1. Check out author Kathy Leonard Czepiel's website, www.KathyLeonardCzepiel.com, and learn more about her.

2. Divide parts of *Women and Economics: A Study of the Economic Relation Between Men and Women as a Factor in Social Evolution* by Charlotte Perkins Stetson (later, Charlotte Perkins Gilman) to read and discuss with your book club. What do you make of the author's opinions on marriage and family values? Does she have any ideas that still seem relevant today? Does she have any ideas that are unacceptable today? Did reading and discussing this book change any of your thoughts about or reactions to *A Violet Season*?

3. The poem in which Keats refers to the violet as "that queen of secrecy" is "Blue! 'Tis the life of heaven, the domain." Read the poem, below, aloud with your group and discuss its significance to the novel.

ANSWER TO A SONNET ENDING THUS:
Dark eyes are dearer far
Than those that mock the hyacinthine bell—
J. H. Reynolds.

Blue! 'Tis the life of heaven, the domain
Of Cynthia, the wide palace of the sun,
The tent of Hesperus, and all his train,
The bosomer of clouds, gold, grey, and dun.
Blue! 'Tis the life of waters—Ocean
And all its vassal streams, pools numberless,
May rage, and foam, and fret, but never can
Subside, if not to dark blue nativeness.
Blue! gentle cousin of the forest-green,
Married to green in all the sweetest flowers—
Forget-me-not, the blue-bell, and, that queen
Of secrecy, the violet. What strange powers
Hast thou, as a mere shadow! But how great,
When in an eye thou art, alive with fate!

At the turn of the century, the violet was thought to stand for constancy and devotion. Use a language of flowers dictionary (online or printed) and have each member look up the meaning of his or her favorite flower and share it with the group.

A Conversation with Kathy Leonard Czepiel

Congratulations on your first novel! What has been the most exciting part of the process so far?

The most exciting moment occurred on the November afternoon in 2010 when my agent first called, saying she was interested in representing my novel. The whole process of pitching and selling, revising, proofreading, publicizing, and marketing has been interesting to learn. There's a steep learning curve the first time around, but that makes it exciting.

How did you come to be a writer? Who are some of your favorite writers?

I've always loved writing. Even before I could write, I told my mother my stories, and she wrote them down in little stapled booklets for me to illustrate. I grew up in a family that valued reading and writing. I was probably the only kid in my school who had a typewriter in her bedroom.

That question about favorite writers opens the floodgates, but I'll try to keep it simple. A page called "Books I Love" is included on my website. In general, I tend toward American literature, and most of the contemporary fiction writers I read are women, though not by design. I'm just more drawn to their stories. If I had to choose just a few writers to read for the rest of my life, I'd probably pick Emily Dickinson, Henry David Thoreau, Marilynne Robinson, Alice Munro, and of course Shakespeare, who covers all the emotional ground of human experience. That's a crazy list with huge gaps. Ask me tomorrow, and it will be different.

You are a native of New York's mid-Hudson valley. What was it like growing up there? Did your familiarity with the area influence the setting of the novel?

Like many people, I didn't really appreciate the beauty of my hometown until I left. Now I know that the Hudson Valley is among the most beautiful places in the country, and, though I don't live there today, it still feels like home when I return. I grew up in a small town where we thought life was pretty boring when we were teenagers, and we really only paid attention to the river when we crossed it to go shopping at the mall. The Hudson River is cleaner now than it was when I was a kid, thanks to a number of wonderful environmental organizations, including Hudson River Sloop Clearwater. I once sailed on their historic sloop for a week as a volunteer and really got to be *on* the river—a thrill! I think it's pretty common for first novels to be set in a place that has deeply imprinted itself on the writer's life. The Hudson Valley is that place for me.

What inspired you to write A Violet Season?

I returned home a year or so after college to work for the local weekly newspaper, and that's when I learned that the area where I'd grown up had once been known as "the Violet Capital of the World." How was it possible that I never knew this before? In fact, most evidence of that once-booming industry has disappeared.

That was the seed for the novel, but I didn't know it right away. I had to do a lot more writing and living before I was ready to tackle a novel, and then the violets came back to me. I knew I would be working on the novel for a long time, so the subject had to be something really compelling to me. I thought the violets would be intriguing to readers as well.

What kind of research did you do for the novel? Did you know a lot about violet farming and wet-nursing before you started writing?

I knew nothing about violet farming. Almost all the research on the violets came from a single, fat file at the Museum of Rhinebeck History. I found other sources, but all of them led back to Rhinebeck. Then I visited a farmer named Fred Battenfeld in nearby Red Hook. His family once grew violets, and his father had been interviewed by someone at the museum. That interview became my most valuable written source. Fred has one bed of violets left, but his primary crops today are anemones and Christmas trees. He showed me around his greenhouses, which gave me the visuals, the smells, the feel of things. Then he answered a bunch of later e-mails as I ran into more questions, and he read pages and fact-checked the violet passages for me. The novel couldn't have been written without his help.

The wet-nursing was easier to research. There are lots of good books out there on the history of wet-nursing, and I had nursed both my own babies. That experience hasn't changed much, so it was easy for me to write about Ida nursing, even though the babies weren't her own.

The contrasts between how women are treated in contemporary society and how they were treated at the turn of the century are striking. Was highlighting the differences, the struggles women faced then, a vital component of the story you wanted to tell? Is there anything surprising you discovered?

I didn't set out to write a novel about women's work or the struggles they faced at the turn of the twentieth century, but it was inevitable that that theme would surface. I did have some surprises. I knew that women's work was physical and unrelenting, but I was struck by how backbreaking the weekly job of laundering was, which is why I took the time to tell about the process of doing laundry in detail. I was also surprised by some of the things I learned about life in the brothels, particularly that there was often real camaraderie among the girls—a sort of sisterhood—and that many of them had actually chosen that life. What this really tells us is how horribly limited their other options were. But for some women—those working in the more expensive brothels who made enough money to live quite comfortably—prostitution did seem to be, in their minds, an acceptable choice. I tried to demonstrate that in my portrayal of the day-to-day life at Mrs. Hargrave's without minimizing the very real perils of their existence, including disease, drug and alcohol addiction, and of course rape. It was a very fine line to walk, and I hope I did that part of the novel justice.

We understand that the love letters between Alice and Joe were inspired by actual love letters written by your own family members. Did you discover them while you were writing the novel?

In 1890 to 1891, during their engagement, my great-grandparents wrote a series of letters to each other. She was living in Nyack, New York, and he was in Newark, New Jersey. My father had transcribed the letters, since their handwriting was difficult to read, and I asked him for a copy of that transcription. Though its subject matter was entirely different, my great-grandparents' correspondence helped me get the voices right in the letters between Alice and Joe. I borrowed directly from my great-grandfather—whose name was also Joe—the closing to some of his letters, which I found quite touching: "I remain yours, Joe." Unlike Alice and Joe, my great-grandparents were married for forty years, until my great-grandfather's death, and had five children, the fourth of whom was my grandfather.

Are there still violet farms in existence today? What about wet nurses?

As far as I know, the only violet farm in the Northeast is the Battenfeld's Anemone Farm, but there may be others. These violets (sweet violets, Parma violets) are different from African violets, which you can find at many garden shops, but don't ask me to explain the taxonomy of the plants—that is not something I've learned! In the Northeast, we find a relative of the sweet violets growing wild in our lawns, but people often eradicate them as weeds in favor of keeping their grass pristine. Why not let the violets grow and enjoy them?

You can still find wet nurses, if you know whom to ask and where to look, though they work very quietly, partly because our society finds it taboo for one woman to nurse another's baby. We can only afford to have that attitude today because we have other alternatives for feeding our infants. Fortunately, that taboo doesn't extend to the milk itself. There are milk banks across the country to which women who have an abundant supply of breast milk can donate it for infants who need it. The FDA advocates the use of milk banks that have screened their donors and ensured the safety of their milk over the use of a wet nurse.

Many authors find that their characters are extensions of themselves, in one way or another. Do you identify with any of the characters in A Violet Season?

I would like to think of myself as a Mrs. Schreiber or a Mrs. Brinckerhoff, strong women able to see beyond their own time, working for change and helping other women. Truthfully, there's probably a lot of me in Ida. One character trait of hers that I recognize in myself is her no-nonsense practicality. But I didn't intentionally write myself into any of my characters. If anything, I usually work against that notion. Otherwise things tend to get boring pretty quickly, both for me and probably for the reader.

What are you currently reading?

I'm always reading more than one thing at a time—probably a bad habit. I'm currently in the middle of Nicole Krauss's novel *Great House* (her novel *The History of Love* is one of my all-time favorites), and I'm about to start *Half the Sky* by Nicholas D. Kristof and Sheryl WuDunn. I try to stick close to the classics, as well.

Next on deck will be some American writers of the 1920s and 1940s, since that's the period I'm writing about now. There's also a teetering pile of literary journals on the floor next to my bed. My current favorites are *Tin House, The Missouri Review,* and *One Story.* This makes it sound as if I read a lot, but really I spend much less time reading than I would like. I spend more time reading my students' papers than anything else.

What are you working on now?

I'm working on another historical novel, this one set in the early twentieth century just before the Depression and just after the First World War. Instead of violets, it is centered on a photography studio. I also have to learn how to build a house.

I'm also working on a collection of linked stories. And I have a nonfiction project that I'm beginning to toy with as well. I'm lucky that I've never experienced writer's block. I always have more ideas than I have time!

One last question (we have to ask): How do you pronounce your last name?

First of all, the *Z* is silent. There are lots of tricks my family uses to help people pronounce it. One of them is that it's what you do with an orange: see it, peel it. *See-peel.* Some people think I was crazy to take my husband's name and give up "Leonard," but I like having a quirky name. And I don't mind if you pronounce it wrong. You couldn't possibly come up with a pronunciation I haven't heard before!